SUPERBIA

SHADES OF SIN

COLETTE RHODES

COPYRIGHT © 2023 COLETTE RHODES
ALL RIGHTS RESERVED

THE CHARACTERS AND EVENTS PORTRAYED IN THIS BOOK ARE FICTITIOUS. ANY SIMILARITY TO REAL PERSONS, LIVING OR DEAD, IS COINCIDENTAL AND NOT INTENDED BY THE AUTHOR.

NO PART OF THIS BOOK MAY BE REPRODUCED, OR STORED IN A RETRIEVAL SYSTEM, OR TRANSMITTED IN ANY FORM OR BY ANY MEANS, ELECTRONIC, MECHANICAL, PHOTOCOPYING, RECORDING, OR OTHERWISE, WITHOUT EXPRESS WRITTEN PERMISSION OF THE PUBLISHER.

ILLUSTRATED PAPERBACK ISBN: 978-1-99-117325-6
DISCREET PAPERBACK ISBN: 978-1-99-117329-4
HARDCOVER ISBN: 978-1-99-117326-3

ILLUSTRATED CHARACTER COVER BY:
MYA SARACHO (@A.LOVEUNLACED)

DISCREET COVER BY: COLETTE

COLETTE RHODES

COPYRIGHT © 2023 COLETTE RHODES
ALL RIGHTS RESERVED

THE CHARACTERS AND EVENTS PORTRAYED IN THIS BOOK ARE FICTITIOUS. ANY SIMILARITY TO REAL PERSONS, LIVING OR DEAD, IS COINCIDENTAL AND NOT INTENDED BY THE AUTHOR.

NO PART OF THIS BOOK MAY BE REPRODUCED, OR STORED IN A RETRIEVAL SYSTEM, OR TRANSMITTED IN ANY FORM OR BY ANY MEANS, ELECTRONIC, MECHANICAL, PHOTOCOPYING, RECORDING, OR OTHERWISE, WITHOUT EXPRESS WRITTEN PERMISSION OF THE PUBLISHER.

ILLUSTRATED PAPERBACK ISBN: 978-1-99-117325-6
DISCREET PAPERBACK ISBN: 978-1-99-117329-4
HARDCOVER ISBN: 978-1-99-117326-3

ILLUSTRATED CHARACTER COVER BY:
MYA SARACHO (@A.LOVEUNLACED)

DISCREET COVER BY: COLETTE

SUPERBIA IS A MONSTER ROMANCE BETWEEN A HUMAN AND HER NOT-QUITE-HUMAN LOVER, SUITABLE FOR READERS OVER 18.

CW: MILD VIOLENCE, SEXUAL CONTENT, KNOTTING, LIGHT BREEDING KINK.

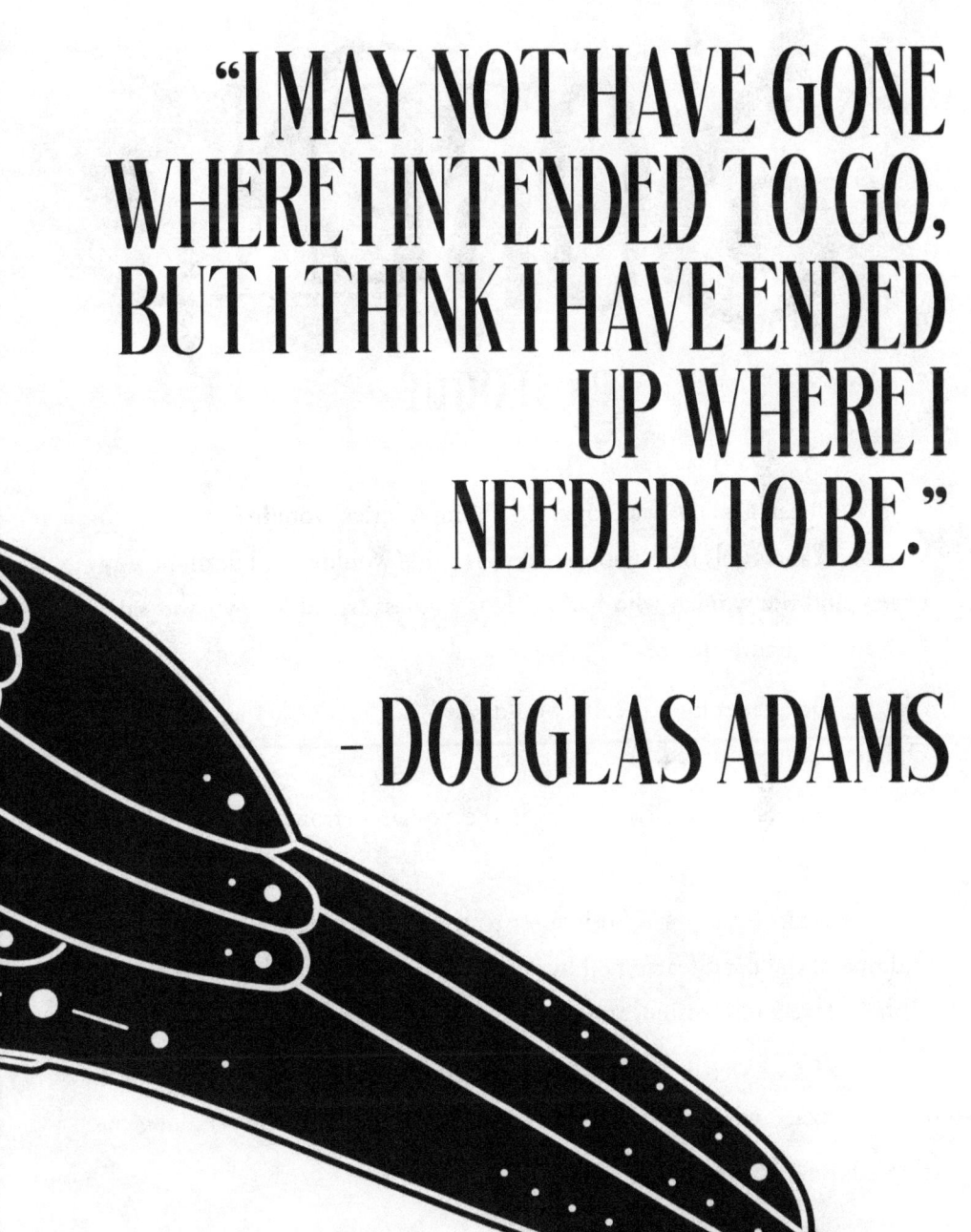

"I MAY NOT HAVE GONE WHERE I INTENDED TO GO, BUT I THINK I HAVE ENDED UP WHERE I NEEDED TO BE."

— DOUGLAS ADAMS

PROLOGUE

Queen Ophelia was gone. And King Allerick wouldn't rest until she was found and safely back in the shadow realm. *I* wouldn't rest until she—my queen, and the woman who had made my oldest friend happy—was safely back in the shadow realm.

The Shades in our realm would *revolt* if the miracle that was Queen Ophelia wasn't returned.

And the key to all of that lay in the woman in front of us. The *Hunter* in front of us.

Astrid Bishop was both sister to the beloved Queen of the Shades, and one of the most fearsome Hunters of her generation. She was someone Ophelia loved and trusted, and someone my entire realm hated.

And we were bringing her back there. Into our realm, our safe space, the only place where we *didn't* have to worry about Hunters stalking our every step in the night.

Coming to her home had been a long shot, but she'd been waiting for us, ready and willing to help. But we couldn't communicate here—in the human realm, Allerick and I were specters. Defenseless, silent specters. We had to bring her home with us so we could form a plan, find out where Ophelia was being held and how to get to her, but it wasn't without risk.

"I don't trust her," I told Allerick, speaking into his mind the way we could in this form. For all that Astrid *looked* like her sister, they were nothing alike in temperament. And I was the Captain of the Guard, responsible for Allerick's safety, even moreso when he was blinded by worry for his wife.

"How surprising. She's a bigger threat to us here than in our realm."

"We could do what Meridia probably did and stop in the in-between," I challenged, choking slightly on my traitorous sister's name. That she'd been conspiring with the Hunters as one of her many attempts at Allerick's throne was distressing, to say the least. *"We still have the visual advantage that way."*

"I won't put her at such a disadvantage. We can talk right next to the portal, then immediately return her here." Allerick was too honorable. Or perhaps just too in love with his wife. Speaking in the swirling, disorienting darkness of the in-between *would* be frightening for Astrid, but she'd killed who knows how many Shades in her hunting career, and I wasn't going to let the king be the next on that list.

"I want it noted that I don't like this idea."

I floated forward, putting myself between Allerick and Astrid, and gestured for her to turn the lamp off. The shadowy sleeve of my cloak drifted through the air with the movement, and Astrid swallowed loudly before flicking the lamp off.

But why didn't she *smell* more afraid?

Ophelia broadcast every emotion she felt through her scent, but Astrid's was almost non-existent in comparison. There was a faint whiff of sourness, of something negative, but considering the circumstances, she should be a lot more frightened.

I moved behind her, invisible to her in the darkness, and wrapped both arms around her shoulders, ready to restrain her the moment my form solidified. She shuddered in my grip, able to feel the sensation of me, albeit lightly. Allerick rested a hand on my shoulder, guiding us into the in-between and keeping us connected so we didn't lose each other in the darkness.

My solid form took hold, as did Allerick's behind me. In the human realm, Astrid was the threat, and we were floating targets to the Hunters who could see us where humans couldn't.

But here...

Astrid was stiff and uncomfortable against me, the top of her head barely brushing my shoulder. Small. Fragile, even.

With short, slow legs.

I sensed Allerick's curiosity as I scooped her up, carrying her in my arms with more gentleness than she deserved.

It was only because I could discreetly pat her down for weapons this way, I told myself. If she had silver daggers strapped to her thighs, I'd be able to feel them.

"I can walk," Astrid hissed.

"Aren't you clever?" I murmured, hoping my voice didn't carry. Hoping Allerick hadn't caught such a moment of undignified immaturity, though he was right behind me.

Get it together, I told myself. *She's dangerous, and awful, up to her eyeballs in dead Shades. And she's the best hope we have of finding Ophelia.*

Astrid grew even more rigid as we exited the portal into the shade realm. If she wasn't who she was, I might feel sorry for her. My grip tightened infinitesimally, the idea of letting her run rampant in this realm setting off every warning instinct I had.

"You can put me down now," Astrid gritted out, looking up at me with wide, alarmed eyes. Probably at how tightly I was holding onto her.

But she still didn't smell afraid, and if she wasn't afraid, it was because she didn't need to be. Because she was entirely confident in her own abilities, in her strength, in her cunning.

I lowered her slowly to the ground, not taking my eyes off her for a second as I stepped away.

Astrid Bishop was wildly dangerous, an unprecedented threat that this realm had never seen before, and I dearly hoped we'd never see again.

We'd get the information we needed, send her back to the human realm, and get the queen back.

And I'd ask Ophelia very politely to sever her relationship with her poisonous sister.

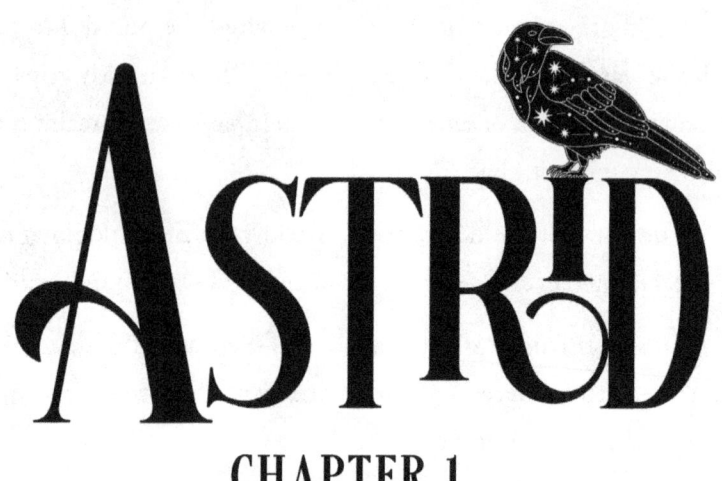

ASTRID

CHAPTER 1

If I was back in the human realm, I'd be sweating my tits off at the gym right now. Ideally wearing the most industrial pair of noise-canceling headphones I owned, blasting some quality angry-girl rock music, and letting everyone know with my resting bitch face that they shouldn't be fooled by the cute matching workout clothes because nothing about me was approachable.

Instead, I was sitting in some kind of Hunter friendship circle with four other women in the land of the Shades—the ones I'd been trained from birth to kill—trying to think of a single, non-depressing fact about myself to share as per my sister's instructions. Apparently "getting to know each other in a relaxed, comfortable setting" meant sitting on hard chairs in a circle in a damp stone room, taking turns at being interesting.

"I'll go first!" Ophelia clapped her hands with a peppy enthusiasm that seemed at odds with the grim living room of the stately home we'd been assigned. She looked around the three assembled Hunters—ex-Hunters—and me with a beaming smile on her face, smoothing down her emerald, very regal-looking dress. "My name is Ophelia Bishop, and technically I'm the queen here, but don't worry about that, just treat me like anyone else."

I raised an eyebrow at her from across the circle and she narrowed her eyes back at me. There was absolutely no way King Allerick would accept his wife being treated like everybody else and she knew it.

"Back in the human realm, I was kicked out of the Hunters when I was a teenager for drawing naughty monster pictures," she continued, grinning along with one of the others while I fought down my instinctual response to be horrified and/or scandalized at the very thought. "The Hunter Council basically offered me up as a sacrifice to secure the treaty with the Shades that they never intended on honoring, which is how I ended up here, married to the king. Fortunately, Allerick and I fell in love and now we're mated, so it all worked out in the end."

She shifted her long dark red hair to one side, exposing the silvery scar of the bite mark Allerick had left on her neck. The other women leaned in closer, asking questions while I tuned out, going to the happy introvert place in my head where I wasn't surrounded by strangers. I didn't need the debrief on mating bites, that shit was *not* in my future.

The only time any Shade would use their teeth on me would be to maul me to death.

"Anyway! Enough about me. I promise we can talk more about this stuff later," Ophelia deflected with a laugh, smoothing down her hair to cover the scar. She was probably worried that she'd scare them all off if she got into *too* much bitey detail. "I want to get to know all of you."

She turned to face the woman next to her—a beautiful, curvaceous woman with rich brown skin and wavy black hair.

"Oh, right. My turn." She tucked her hair behind her ear, looking immensely uncomfortable at all the attention. I immediately liked her. "Uh, well, my name is Meera."

I'd been the one to round up all these Hunters to come here to the shadow realm, and I vaguely knew their backstories from having high-level clearance at the Council. All of these women had been kicked out for one reason or another—though I was guessing whatever the Council had on record was an exaggerated version of what had actually happened, as it had been in Ophelia's case.

Meera didn't deserve what had happened to her. Maybe it had all worked out for the best and she'd find her happily ever after amongst the Shades, but she *really* shouldn't have been kicked out of the Hunters in the first place. She'd just been a scapegoat.

"I guess my interesting fact is that I'm a doula," Meera volunteered, though it sounded more like a question than a statement. "Or I was, I guess."

"You can totally be a doula here," Ophelia replied instantly, eyes lighting up. "Do you know how to remove an IUD? I really want to get pregnant. I mean, not right away, but you know. Sometime."

"Oh. Um—"

What?

"Are you fucking insane?" I asked, cutting off Meera's reply. I was pretty sure doulas didn't remove IUDs anyway. "How would that even work?"

Ophelia's smile turned catlike. "Well, when a mommy and a daddy love each other very much—"

"Hilarious," I deadpanned. "You know I was referring to your spawn. How would that work? You're different... *species*."

Even if they weren't, Ophelia had just gotten here; now she was thinking about Shade babies?

"First of all, my future children shall hereby never be referred to as 'spawn', by royal decree." Ophelia shot me a derisive look as one of the others snorted.

"I'm pretty sure that's not how decrees work."

"Of course it is." Ophelia flipped her hair back, her face transforming into a coy smile that promised trouble. "Second of all, no idea. But we used to be prime breeding stock around these parts, so I assume the combination of his batter and my oven will work just fine."

Right, apparently the Hunters had once been the Hunt*ed*, pursued relentlessly by horny Shades for mating purposes until our ancestors escaped to the human realm over a millennia ago. Instead of feeding off the lust of their Hunted lovers, the Shades had turned to feeding off the fear of oblivious humans, and my kind had gone from prey to predator in a realm that the Shades were hugely disadvantaged in.

And Ophelia had managed to distill all of that into *batter*.

"What a terrible day to have ears," I muttered.

"And between a Shade healer and a, er, *ex*-Hunter doula, I'll be in safe hands," Ophelia finished, shooting Meera a beaming smile which she *very* tentatively returned. I felt a sense of kinship with her already—she had a healthy sense of "is this for real?" about her.

"Babies grow nails in the womb, did you know that?" one of the Hunters asked. She was a burst of color that I was sure all the Shades would go wild about in this almost entirely gray realm, with long, curly, pale pink hair and freckly bronze skin, colorful tattoos covering every inch of her arms and legs. "I wonder if a Hunter-Shade baby grows claws in the womb."

She clicked her long, fake silver nails together, looking at them contemplatively. *Verity*. Oh, I remembered her banishment story well. She and Ophelia would probably be fast friends.

"I'm all about babies—I want, like, fifteen of them—but if they're scratching up my insides with super sharp Shade claws then, I dunno... Maybe I'll just have, like, five or six. You know?" Verity shrugged.

"Alright, I think I'm gonna just... go," I told Ophelia with a tight smile, slipping out of my seat and backing towards the door. "You guys can talk about babies and baby-making and stuff, and I'll see you around."

"Astrid!" Ophelia called after me. "Get back in here! We're bonding! This is bonding time! We can talk about other stuff!"

I shut the heavy wooden door behind me, hurrying down the stone hall towards the foyer.

Even if they talked about something else, that whole friendship circle situation wasn't *for* me. It was for that kind of Hunter—or *ex*-Hunters, as we were going by now.

I'd brought these women here. The Hunters Council had been wooing the Shades with a treaty, claiming that Shades could go to approved areas of the human realm to safely feed on human fear, but it was all a ruse. A small concession in order to gain greater control over the Shades in the long run.

What they hadn't accounted for was my sister. Ophelia had traveled here to marry the Shade king as part of the treaty agreement. She'd been mistreated and abandoned by the Hunters years ago, and when the Council had asked me to broach the idea of being the monster king's bride after so many others had turned it down, I should have told them to go fuck themselves.

Ultimately, it was a good thing. Ophelia and Allerick were the kind of in-love that gave the people around them a contact high. Describing their relationship and the depth of feeling between them had made it easy for me to convince other jilted Hunters to come here, to give the Shades an alternative to risking their lives to feed on human fear.

Risking their lives by encountering Hunters like me. Hunters who'd been trained since birth in the art of killing Shades. Who'd followed the rules to the letter and done everything right.

Except I'd never been in the right. I'd been very, very wrong.

The others weren't like me. They were good. They were going to stay here and fill the power stores by banging monsters—because apparently that was a viable alternative to sucking up human fear—and mating a Shade and having babies that may or may not shred uteruses with their vicious little infant claws.

Those things were not in the cards for me, and I was fine with that.

I absently rubbed the pad of my thumb over the smooth, rounded end of my nails. More fine about some things than others.

We were a small group at the moment—there had been more of us at the original confrontation, but it turned out that walking away from your entire life was actually not an overnight process for most people. Verity, Tallulah, Meera, and I had nothing to lose, but others had lives that were a little more complicated.

Soon. I'd go back for them soon, as agreed. They just needed some time to get their affairs in order.

Elverston House—a cold, damp, stone castle a couple miles from the main palace—was surrounded by a walled garden that acted as a boundary to keep Elverston House purely a Hunter-only space, so the others weren't overwhelmed by Shades wanting to get into their power-generating panties. Members of the Guard made sure no Shades bothered us here, and I felt their eyes on me the moment I pushed open the heavy wooden double doors and headed down the stone steps.

There was an itchy restlessness under my skin, and I wanted to release it somehow—to rage or scream or hit something—but I couldn't, not without drawing more negative attention to myself. Even just going for a *run* would be nice. Something. Some small level of freedom to keep me sane.

Maybe I could go for a walk. A super harmless, hands spread at all times to show I was unarmed kind of walk. Not even far from Elverston House, but just enough to put some space between me and the former Hunters who were actually happy to be here.

The cavernous stone entry hall opened out to a front garden made up of raised garden beds, arranged in shapes with no hard corners so pathways could wind their way between them to the boundary of the property. The boundary that the Shades couldn't cross, by order of the king.

While the Shades—more specifically, the Captain of the Guard—were careful not to make us feel as though we were imprisoned here, they were always watching us discreetly from a distance.

Watching *me*.

I supposed there was something to be said for the fact that I was so utterly terrifying that I was under constant surveillance. I had worked for this reputation after all, even though now that I was in this realm, it was more of a curse than a blessing.

The things I'd once won awards for now made up my rap sheet. It was a real head fuck.

Beyond the boundary line was a river that ran past both this house and the grand palace where my sister and her husband lived. I'd always wanted to kill an afternoon there, maybe go for a swim and find out if there were weird shadow fish that lived in the weird shadow realm, but part of being on my best behavior was spending most of my time in the house and never giving anyone cause for alarm.

I did attend dinners in the palace dining hall, and regularly ventured out to do supply runs back to the human realm—with Captain Soren quite literally shadowing my every move—because us ex-Hunters needed things like vegetables, and medication, and high-fructose corn syrup. Maybe I'd naively hoped that by volunteering for that role that I'd ingratiate myself a little with the Shades, but it only seemed to make them distrust me more.

Maybe a short solo outing to the river would help show them how peaceful and obliging I could be. I had to make nice, had to win them over in spite of my very unwinning personality because I'd thoroughly torched my bridges back in the human realm and I didn't want to be homeless.

Before I'd even made it halfway across the strip of tree-covered land between the boundary and the river, I felt the Shades converging. In the human realm, they were silent wraiths, who could only be detected by sight, and only by those with Hunter genes.

Not here.

In their own realm, they were flesh and blood. Well, definitely flesh. Maybe blood? I hadn't actually seen any of them bleed to know. They were also basically impervious to attack, as well as faster and stronger than I could ever hope to be, and equipped with vicious claws and horns in all shapes and sizes. While, like everything else in this world, their skin was some shade of gray, they had glowing eyes that came in every possible color. They didn't have eyeballs that moved around like a human's did, making it impossible to work out what exactly they were looking at. It all added to the unsettling, rather eerie picture they made.

In the human realm, the Shades feared me. Here, it was a wonder I hadn't been turned into Astrid-shaped confetti yet.

"Where are you going, Hunter?" someone growled. Probably a member of Captain Soren's Guard.

"To look at the river. Get some fresh air. Perhaps go for a swim. If you're all *very* lucky, I'll drown."

"I doubt it," Captain Soren drawled, seeming to materialize out of nowhere, stepping out from the trees. He'd probably been following me since the moment I left Elverston House, thinking I hadn't noticed. "If we were *lucky*, you wouldn't be in this realm in the first place."

"Captain." I inclined my head with a mocking smile. "*Again*. You just can't get enough of me, can you? If you want to spend some quality time together outside of the delightful supply runs that I enjoy so much, you only have to ask."

I *could* be peaceful and obliging. Honestly, I could. But Soren had a knack for dismantling my sense of self-preservation. He was just such a…

Such a…

Raging asshole.

Yes, that was it. He was just such a raging asshole, that he always managed to get under my skin despite my best efforts.

Soren inched closer as I spoke, the parts of his skin not concealed by the uniform-like shadow clothing he wore practically vibrating with rage.

It did really nice things to his arm muscles when he was all puffed up with annoyance at me. Not that I was into Shades the way the other ex-Hunters were, but I could appreciate the Captain's ropey forearms and hulking shoulders. And sure, there was something kind of majestic about those sharp, angular horns that reminded me of lightning bolts. The front of them formed the ridge above his eyes in place of moveable eyebrows, and what *eyes* they were. It was like looking into the sun staring into his bright, golden gaze. And just as dangerous.

"You are delusional. *Beyond* delusional," he spluttered, his outrage making him lose his usually articulate edge. *Success.* "I don't *want* to be around you. I'm here to make sure you don't kill anyone. Anyone *else.*"

Well, yes, I supposed I deserved that. There was no nuance in how they saw me here, no distinction between how I'd been acting in the interests of protecting humans in that realm, versus my respect for the rules here. But I couldn't expect them to see that, because they were the victims. I swallowed thickly at the reminder, the constant simmer of in my chest bubbling to the surface.

"You don't trust any of your Guard to do that?" I challenged, finding my footing on safer ground—aka, terrorizing Soren. "It doesn't speak to your strength or skill as captain if you can't delegate, you know."

Soren took another step closer. If I were a foot taller, we'd almost be nose-to-nose. As it was, I was lined up with his shadow-covered nipples.

Assuming Shades had nipples.

Did they have nipples?

I briefly contemplated asking Ophelia, but she was an oversharer and I didn't want to learn anything about my brother-in-law that I couldn't unlearn.

"Don't forget your place, *Hunter*," Soren warned, voice low and even. I smiled up at him, though there was nothing happy about it.

"You don't have to worry about that, Cap. Now, am I allowed to shadow bathe by the river in peace or not?"

"Verner, keep an eye on her," Soren barked, not taking his gaze off me for a second. I wasn't sure I'd ever met anyone whose attention was so potent that it made me want to wilt under their watch, but Soren's might be the exception. He just... *looked* so closely. As though the face I presented to the world wasn't enough, and he had to find more.

Except there wasn't more—this was all there was to me. Maybe he was trying to find similarities between me and my sister. Where she was all soft and sweet, I was hard edges and bitterness. I must have absorbed all of Mom's bitchiness in the womb, leaving none to infect Ophelia by the time she came along.

"See you on the next supply run, *Astra*."

"It's *Astrid*. And that's not until tomorrow. We both know you'll see me at dinner, Captain."

It wasn't quite mandatory to attend dinner in the palace, but it was highly encouraged. An opportunity for the ex-Hunters who'd moved here to get to know the Shades so they'd fall in love and power the realm and have little sharp-nailed hybrid babies.

I doubted anyone would care if *I* skipped dinner, but I liked to go.

I gave him a mock salute, backing away so I could keep my eye on my enemy.

SOREN

CHAPTER 2

"I don't like this."

Allerick gave me an exasperated look as we waited outside the portal in front of the palace for *her* to show up with her escort. "Are you going to tell me that every time?"

"Yes." I glared at my friend and king, frustrated at this entire situation. I understood, logically, that the Hunters who'd traveled to our realm needed supplies, but I didn't see why the least trustworthy out of all of them needed to be the one to get them.

I would happily escort any of the other Hunters back to the human realm to get clothes and vegetables and whatever else they needed. I just didn't want to escort *her*.

Remembering the impertinent smile she'd given me near the river the other day set my teeth on edge. Even if I hadn't known who she was—a murderous Hunter with an untold number of deaths to her name—there would still be something *about* her that made me...

Wary.

"Doesn't her history concern you at all?" I pressed. Allerick was a good king, sometimes bored by the day-to-day running of the realm, but overall dedicated to ensuring our people were happy and well cared for. I couldn't comprehend how he was okay with Astrid's presence here.

"Of course," Allerick replied easily. "I'm not an idiot. I hear your concerns, Soren. I do. And as much as I love my wife, I don't blindly trust her sister just because she does. But Astrid turned her back on everything she knew to help us. My wife wouldn't be here without her. None of the other ex-Hunters would be either. Her past is damning, but people can change."

"That doesn't mean they will. Allerick, every trip she takes back to the human realm opens us up to more risk. If she chooses to meet with other Hunters there to plot something against us, there's nothing I can do to stop her. Every time she goes into a brightly lit store while I blend into the darkness outside, there's no guarantee that she'll return. She knows too much."

"It hasn't happened yet, and we're not exactly disclosing the inner workings of the realm to her. Besides, I think of all the ex-Hunters who defected to this realm, the Hunters Council probably hate Astrid the most. The Hunters didn't turn their back on her like they did with Ophelia or the others. Astrid turned her back on *them*."

I hated when Allerick made sense.

He'd been doing more and more of that recently. His father was the last king, and there had been no doubt that Allerick would inherit the throne one day because he'd always wielded the most power. Perhaps because he'd always known this was his birthright, he'd taken his authority for granted. Since he'd married Ophelia, Allerick was a far more thoughtful ruler.

"She asked to return to her apartment today," I pointed out. Just a few miles from where the North American seat of the Hunters Council was.

"Because many of the ex-Hunters left the belongings they couldn't carry at her empty apartment. The intention to collect those things was always there," Allerick sighed, exasperated with my suspicions. Well, too bad. If he wanted a less diligent Captain of the Guard, he could choose someone else for the position. "Besides, who would you send in her place? All the ex-Hunters who have traveled to this realm are banished, and returning to the human realm puts them in very real danger. The only one even remotely equipped to handle themselves in a physical confrontation is Astrid."

"Oh, I don't know," a flat, feminine voice said from behind us. I whirled around, finding Astrid standing right behind me with her arms crossed, an impatient look on her face. Though that wasn't surprising—she always looked some combination of impatient or annoyed. Unfortunately, it didn't detract from her beauty in the slightest. Astrid was sharp lines and toned muscle, with haunting dark brown eyes and auburn hair that fell straight to her shoulders, though she usually tied it up.

I wished she didn't. It only drew attention to her smooth, unmarked neck. Ever since Allerick bit Ophelia and reintroduced the concept of mating marks—a tradition that had died when the Hunt*ed* had fled our realm over a thousand years ago—I'd been curious about the process, to say the least.

"Meera always did quite well in knife-throwing contests, from what I've heard," Astrid continued, drumming her fingers on her arm as she spoke. She favored red, but was wearing dark clothes today for our stealth supply run. "And Tallulah has been bragging about her impressive right hook. If nothing else, Verity's acrylics rival any Shade's claws I've ever seen. I'm sure she could hold off a Hunter until the Battery Protection Squad has a chance to sweep them back into the shadows."

"Battery?" Allerick asked wryly, not as disturbed as he should be at the way Astrid seemed to appear out of nowhere. I'd never seen a human move as sneakily as she did, and it made me nervous.

As it should. Allerick was being the naive one here, claiming we weren't disclosing anything sensitive in front of her. How would we know, when she was so good at creeping around?

"That's what we are, aren't we? Lust batteries to fill the power stores until a more permanent solution is found."

Allerick cleared his throat. "Only if that's something the ex-Hunters want to engage in, of course. After chaste, supervised courtships to make sure no one is under any pressure. No ex-Hunter will be made to do anything they don't want to do—"

"Oh, I'm pretty sure they *want*," Astrid interjected with a hollow laugh. I wasn't sure I'd ever heard her laugh in genuine amusement. Was that jealousy in her tone? Disapproval at the other former Hunters lusting after Shades? "They *want* just fine. But we're batteries nonetheless."

"Well, you aren't," I pointed out, a derisiveness in my voice that seemed to come out only for her. "No one wants to fuck you, for power or otherwise, even with the survival of the realm depending on it."

"Soren!" Allerick barked. Astrid and I both held our ground, staring each other down. On reflection, the words had come out harsher than I'd intended, but they were true. Unlike the other ex-Hunters who'd ventured to this realm, the *innocent* ex-Hunters, Astrid was deadly. She wasn't a failure of a Hunter like her sister. She was the pinnacle of Hunter society, their best of the best.

Fucking her would be like sticking my dick in a barrel of silver daggers and hoping not to be fatally injured.

"I spend a lot of time with those ex-Hunters and it's not like anyone's clamoring to get under your shadows either, *Captain*." Astrid gave me a syrupy sweet, entirely false smile. I snorted, not dignifying her lie with a response. I'd spent enough time monitoring Elverston House since Astrid had arrived to know that she had, in fact, spent very little time with the other ex-Hunters.

As much as I wanted to attribute that to her dreadful personality, I could admit that her solitude appeared Astrid's choice.

"Where is Andrus?" Allerick clipped, fed up with both of us. "He was meant to meet you at the border of Elverston House to escort you here."

"Was he?" Astrid asked absently. "I guess I forgot to wait for him."

Allerick huffed a quiet laugh. "It seems pointless to assign anyone to walk you around the place at this point."

"I'm so glad we're in agreement on that, big bro," Astrid said, almost cheerfully. "Shall we?" she asked me, gesturing at the portal. "Not that I have other places to be, but I know for a fact that one of those ladies is going to be annoyed with me if I don't promptly return with a menstrual cup."

"Wait, we need to discuss getting rid of her escort—"

"Yes, you should get going," Allerick said hastily, all but shoving me towards the portal, constantly aware of keeping that small group of women happy so they would temporarily power our entire kingdom. Not that they were currently—we'd been surviving off what was in the stores, with the king and queen's plentiful contributions keeping it reasonably stocked.

It would be ideal if the other ex-Hunters allowed Shades of their choosing to feed off their lust, so those Shades in turn could siphon the excess to the stores, but we were all being careful that no one was rushed or pressured into something they weren't comfortable with. For now, there was nothing more than the odd flirtation.

"Fine, but we're discussing it when I get back. First thing." I strode towards the portal, Astrid falling into step next to me.

Even *that* annoyed me. I watched her from a distance, I saw the graceful yet unassuming way she *normally* walked around the realm, popping up unexpectedly when she'd decided she'd had enough of Elverston House. Whenever she was next to me, she swaggered obnoxiously, and I was pretty sure it was because she knew how much it irritated me.

As much as I'd like to, I wasn't allowed to lose her in the in-between, so I wrapped my hand around her upper arm at the last minute like I always did, claws digging ever so slightly into her flesh.

Before we were entirely over the threshold that led to the in-between, Allerick spoke again, his voice faint. "By the way, I'd like Astrid to join the Guard, under your personal instruction, Captain Soren. We can discuss the details when you get back."

"What the fuck?" I barked, spinning on my heel to march back out into the shadow realm and give my king a piece of my mind.

"Don't," Astrid said in a bored voice, grabbing my wrist before I could move away. *Right, I wasn't meant to lose her.* Huffing in annoyance, I shook her off and resumed my impersonal hold on her arm. "Let him stew in his guilt for a little longer. That was a chicken shit move to drop that on us right before we left and he knows it."

Chicken... shit? The phrase was weird and obviously human, but I got the gist of it. "Don't speak badly of my king. And don't give me orders."

"Because I work for you now?" Astrid smirked. "*Under* your *personal* instruction?"

"Because you are a guest in my realm, and an unwelcome one at that," I shot back. "You don't work for me, you will never work for me."

"Is that so?" she hummed, gesturing into the swirling, encroaching darkness of the in-between for me to lead the way. "I maintain that you just can't get enough of me, Cap. We spend more time together by the day."

Insufferable, infuriating woman.

I wasn't going to engage. The more I spoke, the more she found ways to twist my words.

As much as I hated her, I could concede that the Hunter demonstrated a great deal of trust by going through the in-between with me. She could no longer find her way out on her own on the human realm end—whatever it was that made Hunters *Hunters* meant they could travel through the in-between via portals, but as far as we could tell, most of their portals had been closed. Probably to stop any other Hunters defecting to the shadow realm.

The portals on our side were open, so Astrid could get to the in-between but the only way through the shadow veil to the human realm was accompanied by a Shade to navigate.

I could walk Astrid into the deepest, darkest part of the ocean and leave her there, and she'd be helpless to stop me.

Fortunately for her, I wasn't the monster she'd been raised to believe all Shades were.

"I thought Shades were big on power and authority?" she said mildly, breaking the silence. "Be sure to let me know what the king says when you refuse his command to *personally* train me up as a guard."

Maybe I should leave her in the ocean after all.

SOREN

CHAPTER 3

In the past, I'd accompanied Astrid on supply runs to less populated areas. Fewer humans around to feed from meant fewer Shades visited those places, and the Hunters didn't bother monitoring them as closely.

Allerick was right that the plan had always been to pick up the things the other ex-Hunters had left at Astrid's home, and though I'd argued against it, I couldn't put it off any longer.

Denver was the belly of the beast, and we were entering it.

Her small house was pitch black, set up in preparation for this day, and my solid form vanished into nothingness as we stepped through the in-between, directly into her living room.

I floated near the door, feeling helpless and frustrated as I always did in this realm, while Astrid knocked against one of the boxes stacked in the center of the room, cursing loudly.

"Oh my god, this is going to take hours. There is so much shit in here. Okay, stand back, shadow man, I'm gonna turn the lamp on."

Of course she was. Her eyes were basically useless compared to mine. It was a wonder Hunters managed to find any of us in the darkness.

I just had to *trust* that she was only going to turn on one lamp rather than flooding the room with enough light to shove me forcibly back into the in-between.

If I could have made a sound, I would have laughed at the picture Astrid made, fumbling around in the darkness, running her fingertips over the edges of boxes and the back of the couch until she found the lamp. However, that amusement died the instant she clicked it on. A circle of soft light surrounded her, lighting up her features in a warm, golden color that didn't exist in the shadow realm yet. It did something interesting to her brown eyes, made them *glow* somehow.

Then the bedroom door opened.

Astrid jumped to attention, knocking a pile of books to the ground as she leaped over the couch, putting the furniture between her and the intruder.

"Astrid." The voice was soft, feminine, and non-confrontational, the name delivered with an air of familiarity. Astrid scrunched her eyes shut tightly, and it was odd to see her look anything less than poised, with a dash of murderous intent. "Astrid, darling, we're just here to talk. We just want to talk to you."

Oh great. We'd walked right into a trap.

The woman had to be Astrid and Ophelia's mother. She was taller than her daughters, with a haughty sort of face and graying hair. I wasn't overly familiar with human clothing, but I hazarded a guess that she was wearing sleepwear with a fluffy-looking robe over top that she was belting clumsily at the waist. She spared me a glance where I hovered by the door, and that split-second look was filled with more disdain than I'd ever seen from either of her daughters combined.

I could see where Astrid got it from.

"Mom? Why the hell are you here? Have you been *staying* here? This is *my* house," Astrid said, finally finding her voice and sounding suitably outraged.

"We stayed here so we could see you," a rough masculine voice replied. "I'd hoped you wouldn't have one of *them* with you, but I suppose that's the tragic reality we live in now." The woman stepped aside, making space for the man to stand next to her.

He was shorter, portly, with a face almost as red as his Astrid's hair.

"Dad," Astrid greeted flatly. "I can't imagine what you want to talk to me about," she added, all sarcasm and insincerity. I didn't mind it as much when it wasn't directed at me.

"Help us understand," her mother said softly. "You've always been such an intelligent girl, Astrid. Explain to us why you threw your beautiful life here away."

The thing about hearing Astrid's insincere voice every time she spoke was that it made it easy to identify that same hollow ring in her mother's voice. For a moment, I was baffled at Astrid's hesitation, at the fact that *she* didn't seem to be hearing it, but then again I knew what it felt like to give relatives more chances than they deserved.

I just hoped Astrid wasn't about to make the same idiotic mistake with her parents that I'd made with my sister. Some people couldn't be reasoned with and it wasn't worth trying.

"Perhaps we'll join you in the shadow realm," her mother cajoled. "Perhaps we truly have been wrong all this time."

Astrid glanced back at me, a flash of indecision on her face, one hand reaching vaguely in the direction of the lamp. All she had to do was turn it off, pitch us into darkness and I'd sweep her away before her parents said another word.

Just turn the lamp off.

"*Leave!*" I all but screamed, knowing she couldn't hear me. Only Ophelia could hear Shades in this realm, her mating bite tuning her into our conversations. "*They're lying to you! Turn the lamp off, Hunter. You're putting us both at risk.*"

"I can make them understand," Astrid whispered, only loud enough for my more sensitive ears to pick up. "I know you'll hate me for it, but I can make them *see* the truth. This is how we get more Hunters on our side, just give me a chance."

"*You'll kill me,*" I said frankly, speaking into nothingness because she couldn't fucking hear me. Every instinct in my body screamed at me to leave, but I couldn't. I'd promised to stick to Astrid's side on these supply runs, and I didn't want to disappoint my king by turning tail and running.

Why would she do this? Why would she put us in more danger than necessary?

Because she's wicked. You know this. You've always known.

"Astrid," her mother said, glancing at me. Fucking Hunters and their ability to see me. She took a step further into the room, then another, reaching for a switch on the wall.

Ah, for the *lights*.

It was unsurprising, of course. In fact, it was surprising they'd allowed themselves to be shrouded in darkness at all—they must have been desperate to catch Astrid off-guard.

Time seemed to stand still for a moment while Astrid's mother inched closer to the switch that would forcibly banish me back into the in-between while her daughter watched.

Of course she watched. I didn't know why I felt even remotely annoyed. Or was that sinking feeling disappointment?

She's seen enough of our world to make things difficult if she decided to share all that information with the Council.

Ophelia would be distressed.

It would create more work for me.

Yes, those were all valid, logical reasons to feel disappointment, it was nothing personal. It had nothing to do with Astrid meeting every low expectation I'd ever had of her.

This was exactly what I thought would happen. Exactly what I'd told Allerick would happen. Hopefully, Ophelia wasn't around when I laid out in excruciating detail just what a fucking traitor her sister was and reminded Allerick of all the reasons we should never have trusted her in the first place.

"Don't," Astrid clipped, her voice as monotone with her parents as it was when she spoke to Shades. "The lights stay off, or I leave."

I couldn't tell who was more surprised, her parents or me.

"Astrid," her father said in a low warning voice, taking a step towards her. "Don't be difficult."

She snorted indignantly. "I've spent my entire life not being difficult. Not rocking the boat. Look at where it's gotten me: Sneaking into my own fucking house in the middle of the night to pick up menstrual supplies and frozen vegetables."

Astrid tilted her chin up stubbornly, and I admired the haughty set of her jaw for a moment before remembering who she was and quashing the unwelcome feeling.

"You say that as though we should feel *sorry* for you." Her father laughed unkindly. "You're a traitor, Astrid. You only have yourself to blame for the fact that you're now a menial errand girl for monsters."

"But it's not too late, Astrid," her mother said hurriedly. "We can—"

"I thought this was about *you* learning the error of your ways," Astrid interrupted, but her mother forged on as though she hadn't heard her speak.

"We'll take you to the Council right now and you can apologize. Beg for their forgiveness. You don't have to live like this."

Trap, trap, fucking trap. Why were we here?

More importantly, why was *I* here?

Astrid was going to accept their offer. There was no way she wouldn't. I needed to get the fuck out.

Why would Astrid return to the shadow realm where she was universally despised when she could return to her comfortable life here? I hated the Hunters, but even I'd consider that offer if it meant getting out of the freezing, damp mausoleum that was Elverston House. I floated backwards, inching towards the wall that would lead me to what I hoped was the safety of outside where I could find a spot dark enough to disappear into. *If* this wasn't an ambush. *If* the entire house wasn't surrounded.

"I don't want their forgiveness."

I froze in place. Astrid gave nothing away, arms crossed over her chest, expression entirely blank. But there was no hesitation in her words, no shake in her voice.

There was a long pause before her father spoke. "What about ours?"

It struck me that I was actually witnessing an extremely personal moment between family members. A moment I wouldn't have liked witnessed if the roles were reversed.

But I wasn't going to leave.

"What about Ophelia's?" Astrid shot back fiercely. "You should be on *your* knees begging for *her* forgiveness. You threw her away when she was just a child."

A fact Astrid might be outraged about now, but she'd done *nothing* to rectify at the time. No, this was guilt talking. Perhaps not dissimilar to the guilt I felt when I thought of how my sister turned out—except my sister was a power-hungry maniac, and Astrid's was good and kind. Astrid deserved to feel guilty.

"Ophelia was old enough to understand what the consequences would be when she drew those revolting pictures. I hope your return isn't conditional on that," her mother snapped.

Astrid shook her head silently. "I'm not coming back. The Council knew all along that Shades and Hunters had an intertwined history and they hid it from us. They made the treaty in bad faith, never intending to honor it. Everything about the Hunters is rotten, from the roots up. Nothing could entice me back—"

Astrid's father laughed bitterly. "I always thought you were the smart one, but you might be even dumber than your sister." His wife shot him a reproachful look but said nothing. "You may as well kiss your mother goodbye now. Why would you go live in the home of your enemy? In their domain, where they are at their strongest and you are your most vulnerable? It's only a matter of time before you return from the shadow realm permanently—in a box."

I didn't understand the reference—some human custom no doubt—but if the intent had been to shock, then it had worked perfectly. Astrid was silent and still, the barest shake in her hands giving away just how much those words had rattled her.

"You're an excellent Hunter, Astrid. One of the best. You were designed for killing Shades. *Bred* for it, by two of the best Hunters of *our* generation."

The blunt, uncomfortable reminder of who Astrid was, of what exactly we'd let into our realm, caught me off-guard.

Just for a moment.

Which was just long enough.

A whistle. That was what every young Shade was trained to listen out for before they ventured to the human realm for the first time. What they were trained to fear.

A whistle of a blade meant it was probably too late.

Fucking Astrid.

I darted sideways to avoid the knife, willing this stupid, vulnerable form to go faster, knowing the blades always came in threes at least.

But the first one never found its mark.

Astrid let out a muffled scream, cutting it off so quickly that if she hadn't doubled over, I would have thought I'd imagined it.

"Astrid!" her mom screamed, staring at her daughter in horror. *Her hand*, I realized. Astrid had blocked the blade with her palm. I couldn't get any closer because of the lamp, but it seemed as though she was cradling the injured limb to her chest.

Astrid's father was frozen in position, arm still outstretched from loosing the blade intended for me. It would have found its mark, I had no doubt about that. There had only been a few feet between her and her father, and he'd thrown the blade *hard*. Hunters didn't heal the way Shades did. What would that mean for her?

"Is this your version of talking?" Astrid rasped, the hoarseness in her voice making me drift closer instinctively before the light repelled me again. "Telling me I'm stupid and throwing a knife at him—"

"It's not a '*him*', Astrid. It's an *it*. It's a monster. A *thing*. I thought we'd raised you better," her dad shouted, eyes wide with panic as he stared at his daughter's injured hand.

How much blood could humans lose before they perished? Astrid wasn't acting like it was a fatal wound, but I suspected that it hurt a lot more than she let on.

"A *he*," Astrid corrected, her voice barely above a whisper. "*He* has friends. A family. A job, a home, a life. They all do, and the Hunters treat them like moving dart boards at best, tools to be controlled at worst. What you're doing, what you raised me to do... It's sick. It's sick and it's wrong, and I hope that one day you'll figure out that you're on the wrong side, but I'm not confident you will."

Both of her parents were quiet, expressions unreadable. Another trait Astrid had gotten from them that Ophelia seemed to have missed.

"Which I guess means this is goodbye," Astrid whispered, her voice breaking on the last word.

"Wait! If you leave now, you can't come back," her mother gasped, eyes wild and desperate. Everything in Astrid's home was white, making the red of the blood pooling on the floor even more stark. "They're closing all the portals so no more Hunters follow you into the shadow realm. They only kept this one open because I begged them to let me see you, Astrid. Because I knew you'd come back to us, that you'd realize this is where you belonged."

Maybe the portals would all close, but that didn't matter, not really. So long as there was darkness in the human realm, there was a way for Astrid to return. She'd just need a Shade to accompany her.

"Come back to us, Astrid," her mother whispered.

Astrid swept the leg of the side table with her foot, sending the lamp crashing to the ground in one swift movement and plunging the room into darkness. I darted forward at the same time she stepped back, wrapping myself around her and all but diving into the in-between.

Astrid stumbled under my weight as my corporeal form took hold, and I scooped her into my arms, ignoring her slurred protests. It wasn't as though I wanted to carry her either.

"We really need to stop meeting like this, Captain," Astrid replied, attempting to hold herself rigid, though her head kept lolling against my shoulder before she corrected it again. "Do you like carrying me? Is that what it is? I think you like carrying me."

It was a weak attempt to downplay the gravity of the situation, delivered in an even weaker voice.

"You think wrong," I said gruffly. There was a slight tremble in my muscles as I walked back to the portal, one that I may have been able to attribute to shock.

Why had she blocked the knife?

What did it *mean*?

Did it even matter?

No matter what she'd done since, Astrid was a murderer. She'd killed who knew how many Shades over the years, and frankly, I thought Allerick was an idiot for letting her stay.

But she saved you, the traitorous voice in the back of my mind whispered. I'd been too focused on the argument between Astrid and her mother to notice her father readying the knife. It was an unacceptable lapse that would have gotten me killed, were it not for Astrid's impressively fast reflexes.

I owed her a life debt. It was an uncomfortable truth to accept.

Hopefully, she didn't realize yet what she'd done.

"Where are you taking me?" Astrid asked, her voice hoarse. I glanced down a moment, uneasily realizing that her brown eyes had that strange glossy look Ophelia's got when she was about to cry. Unlike her sister, no tears fell. Her scent barely changed either, so controlled was Astrid at all times. "Not to be dramatic or anything, I probably need some kind of medical attention and as far as I know, there aren't any doctors in the in-between."

How did she manage to sound so snarky and difficult even now?

"Then again, I'm guessing the Hunters canceled my insurance, so if you could just walk me on over to an emergency department in Canada or something, that'd be great. They have to help if you show up there, right? I think that's a rule."

"I will take you to see our healers. I cannot accompany you into a human medical facility, and the agreement was that you would be accompanied at all times."

"Right, right, right. Wouldn't want me doing anything crazy, like taking a fucking knife to save a Shade's life."

Oh good, she knew exactly what she'd done, and was going to hold this over my head forever.

"What do Shade healers do?" Astrid asked, over-correcting when her head rested against my shoulder for a moment and nearly rolling onto the ground in her haste to get away.

"Stay still," I grumbled, tightening my grip. "We're nearly there. They will care for you while your body heals. Bring you nutritious meals and keep you comfortable. For a Shade, they'd bring power from the stores as needed until the wound healed itself." The smell of her blood drowned out everything else, and I vaguely wondered if I'd ever forget the memory of it. "Your wound will heal itself, yes?"

Astrid paused for long enough that I wondered if she'd fallen asleep. "It'll heal."

"And will it—"

"It'll be fine," she interrupted. "I'll be fine."

That wasn't entirely reassuring.

"That's what I do," Astrid added wearily.

"What? What do you do?"

"Be *fine*," she muttered. "That's what I do. That's who I am. I'm the one who's always *fine*. You don't need to worry about me, Cap. Let's skip the healer, they won't be able to help anyway, and my presence would only make them uncomfortable."

The guards stationed at the portal immediately straightened when we emerged, their confusion clear as I replayed her words in my head.

"Great," Astrid mumbled. "Witnesses. Just what I need. Put me down. This is bad for my reputation."

"There's very little that could harm your reputation," I pointed out.

"Captain?" Verner said hesitantly.

I paused a few feet away from him, knowing Astrid wouldn't want to be crowded by hostile Shades. "There was an incident between the Hunter and her father. She needs a healer," I clipped.

"Yes, I see that," he agreed, his gaze fixed on her injured hand. "But shouldn't we disarm her first? The king was very clear that she shouldn't possess any silver..."

I stared at him in utter disbelief for a long moment. "It's embedded in her *flesh*."

Astrid took advantage of my momentary shock, barrel rolling out of my arms and landing on the ground using her good hand to brace her while she kept her injured one tucked to her chest. Her head was bowed, hair hiding her expression, but there was no hiding the tremble of her shoulders. Not just her shoulders—her entire body swayed, and I took a step towards her, intending to pick her up again.

Before I could, she began pushing up to stand. The guards were all on high alert, watching each slow, pained movement.

"Don't," I warned as Astrid's good hand wrapped around the handle of the blade.

She lifted her head, meeting my gaze. I'd never seen such fierceness, such determination, in anyone. It sent an alarming pang of recognition through me. Maybe I hated Astrid, but I couldn't deny that there was something about her that felt like I was looking in a mirror, one stubborn soul to another.

"Don't," I repeated, my voice barely above a growl. Her forehead creased in pain, jaw grinding together, but that was the only indication she gave that she was in pain.

She didn't listen to me. She never listened to me.

With the worst sound I'd ever heard in my life, the blade came free from her palm, a small waterfall of dark red blood with it. Astrid tossed the weapon at Verner's feet with a look venomous enough to wither a weaker Shade, but that wasn't what I was focused on. No, it was the steady flow of blood streaming freely down her hand and wrist that had my attention. That, and the fact that Astrid's face had turned an alarming shade of green.

Ophelia would have my head for this.

"There," she rasped. "I'm disarmed and totally harmless. Satisfied?"

"You've never been harmless a day in your life," I replied, meaning it as a compliment as I closed the gap between us, reaching for Astrid before she collapsed.

"I can walk," she hissed, swaying before catching herself with a small stumble. "I don't need you. I don't want you. I'm going back to Elverston House. Meera can help me. She's basically a doctor."

"You are delusional if you think you can walk that far unassisted," I snapped, ignoring her protests as I scooped her off the ground again, wincing slightly as the blood running down her arm hit my chest. "Come on."

Ignoring the stares of my fellow guards burning into my back, I made my way through the gardens toward Elverston House. How was Astrid so light? I'd built her up in my mind as a terrifying, murderous force of nature, and while I acknowledged that it would be stupid to underestimate her, she didn't feel quite so terrifying when I was carrying her like this.

She felt surprisingly fragile. I'd carried her before—for reasons I couldn't explain even in my own head—but this time felt different. Rather, *Astrid* felt different.

As if she could sense my thoughts, she began struggling again, forcing me to adjust my hold so I didn't drop her. "Don't be difficult."

She froze, and I realized a second too late that those were the exact three words her father had uttered. Her resounding silence was deafening.

The border of Elverston House loomed closer, and my skin itched with the need to get away, to wash Astrid's blood off my skin. It felt as though it was sinking into me, like it was a permanent stain on *my* soul.

"No one ever used to call me *difficult*. I was the least difficult. I did exactly as I was told," Astrid mumbled, so quietly that I wasn't sure if the words had been meant for my ears.

"We all know you were the consummate Hunter soldier, Astra," I replied quietly.

"You're such an asshole, Captain. All judgmental, sitting up there on your high horse. I wasn't sitting around in the human realm, plotting all the ways I could kill Shades for sport. I thought I was *helping*. That I was defending humanity. That I was doing the *right* thing."

I reminded myself that she'd called me an asshole and been brazenly disrespectful to my face from the moment we'd met to avoid the softer, more sympathetic feelings that were trying to surface.

"And what do you think now?" I challenged, my claws flexing where I was holding her. All of the lives that had been needlessly lost because of the Hunters' need to *defend humanity* were never far from my mind.

"And now, I know I was wrong."

The words were delivered quietly and evenly, with Astrid's signature lack of inflection, but I knew what they cost her. Perhaps it was that mirror at work again. There were few things I found more difficult than admitting I was wrong, even just in my own head.

"Astrid!" Meera shouted in alarm. She'd been sitting on a bench in the garden, but sprinted to the border to meet us the moment she saw our approach. "Oh my gosh, what happened?"

"Family reunion," Astrid deadpanned, her face growing paler by the second. "Do you think you can patch me up?"

"Me?" Meera replied in disbelief.

"Sure. You're good with blood, right? It's just a scratch. Put me down, Cap."

My grip tightened for a moment before I realized what I was doing. What the fuck was *wrong* with me? I couldn't carry her into the Shade-free zone that was Elverston House, nor did I want to. This wasn't my problem. She'd be fine with her own people.

"What are you doing?!" Meera shrieked as I lowered Astrid to her feet. "She can't *walk*."

"I'm fine," Astrid replied, though she sounded like she'd had too much to drink. "Lemme lean on you. I'm good. I'm going to walk it off."

"You can't walk off blood loss," Meera snapped, hauling Astrid's good arm over her shoulder and wrapping an arm around her waist, stumbling slightly at the extra weight. Verity and Tallulah must have spotted us from the window, both rushing down the path toward us.

See? She'd be fine. There were plenty of hands to help.

"Oh my god, what happened?" Verity asked, immediately coming to Astrid's other side and helping keep her upright. "You're just leaving her here, Captain?"

The accusing note in her voice took me by surprise. "I can't cross this border. There are rules—"

"And no exceptions, apparently," Verity interjected, shooting me a glare. "Come on, Astrid. Let's get you inside. Tallulah, can you—"

But Tallulah had already darted away, bending over a patch of garden and retching violently. "Sorry! I'm sorry!" she spluttered, waving her hand above her head. "Go ahead without me. I'm not good with, you know. Super gnarly, bloody wounds and stuff."

"Fuck's sake," Verity muttered, she and Meera already dragging a half-conscious Astrid away. All three of them stumbled, and I stopped breathing for a moment until they righted themselves.

"Where's Ophelia?" Tallulah asked, swiping her mouth with the back of her hand and peering past me. "Sorry, *Queen* Ophelia."

I blinked. "Back at the palace, I assume."

Tallulah frowned, and it was the first time I'd seen the usually beaming Hunter look anything less than happy. "She's not going to come and check on her sister?"

"Why would she?"

"Does she *know* that Astrid was hurt?"

I got the distinct impression that I was in trouble, which was a novel experience. "No, of course not."

"Okay..." Tallulah replied, drawing out the word. "Maybe we're experiencing some cultural differences here. Ophelia will very much want to know that Astrid is hurt."

"You're certain?" I confirmed, baffled by the concept. Nothing would distress a Shade more than having their weaknesses shared with anyone but a healer. Even if my sister hadn't been a scourge on society, even if we'd had a close sibling relationship, I'd have considered it a personal offense to have my injuries disclosed to her before I'd had adequate time to heal. Unless... "The injury is minor, is it not? Do humans die of hand wounds?"

Tallulah shifted uneasily, and there was a strange coiling tightness in my chest that I couldn't quite explain. "We're working one step above medieval medical care here, Captain. If it gets infected..."

Silence hung in the air for a long, painful moment. "I'll send for the queen."

"Thank you," Tallulah replied softly from behind me as I strode towards the palace.

Infection. The idea hadn't occurred to me. When Shades were injured, our power flooded the wound to heal it. We could starve to death, of course, if all of our power was drained and we weren't able to feed, but it was rare.

Tallulah hadn't made it sound rare.

I ignored the curious looks from the guards as I entered the palace, stopping in the entryway when I saw Calix, the half-feral palace chef who hated almost everyone and everything, carrying a crate of meat.

"Everything alright, Captain? You're looking a bit... well, shit, if I'm honest."

By the night, a blunter, ruder being didn't exist in this entire realm. "Fine. That broth you make when someone is recovering from a particularly difficult injury, could the Hunters drink it?"

Calix stared, somehow seeming to look down at me despite me being slightly taller. "Sure. They can eat whatever we eat, they just supplement it with other stuff. Except for one—Meera, is it?—who doesn't eat meat. Why? Is one of them injured?"

I wasn't sure of the rules. I *was* meant to tell Ophelia, but what about anyone else?

"Ah, you won't say." He tilted his head to the side. "Just tell me this, Captain. Are you asking me to make a curing broth for a murderer? Could you ask me in good conscience to do such a thing?"

I didn't have an answer and we both knew it.

Calix ran his tongue over his teeth, looking more serious than I'd ever seen him. "I'll see you around, Captain."

I made my way through the corridors to the royal wing, not speaking to anyone else.

ASTRID

CHAPTER 4

"Astrid! Where is she?!"

I shuffled further down the bed, hiding beneath the scratchy blanket. My hand throbbed beneath the bandages, and the blanket that was usually *slightly* itchy felt like sandpaper against my skin.

And Ophelia was so *loud*.

"She'll be here any moment," Meera said softly, cleaning up the supplies she'd used to stitch me back together.

Turns out, doulas *don't* really do stitches, as a general rule, but Meera had given it a good go. Tallulah might have done a neater job, considering she sewed for a living, but she would have passed out for sure.

"Astrid!" Ophelia yelled up the stairs.

Get it together.

I was hoping Soren wouldn't mention the whole incident between me and my parents, but it didn't look like I was going to get off that easily.

"It's a scratch," I told Meera firmly, propping myself up on my elbow and wriggling up the bed to sit back against the pillows. "She doesn't need to know how bad it was."

"Why?" Meera asked conversationally, making her way over to the bed. Without asking, she wiped away the sweat on my forehead with a cool, damp cloth and I cut her an irritable glare at the sudden physical contact. People weren't usually so *touchy* with me.

"We all need supplies from the human realm, and she'll never let me go back if she knows how bad it is. Tell the others not to say anything."

"I suppose it would be too obvious to point out that *not* going back might be the best course of action."

Ophelia's footsteps approached, the stone hall echoing with each clipped step. My room on the second floor was a plain space—gray stone walls, gray stone floor, black wooden ceiling, black wooden four-poster bed. There was a narrow wooden table across one wall where I'd stacked the clothes I'd brought here, a window with a low stone ledge wide enough to sit on, and that was it.

As pretty as Elverston House was, in a fortress kind of way, it was damp and cold, and unpleasant to live in.

"Did you not loudly lament our lack of antibiotics a few minutes ago?" I pointed out, raising an eyebrow at her. "The supply runs are essential. Let's not panic the queen unnecessarily."

Meera pursed her lips disapprovingly, giving me a curt nod before crossing the room to open the door for Ophelia. She slipped out behind her, and I hoped that she was warning the others to keep quiet.

I doubted it would be much of a hardship. I wasn't friends with the other ex-Hunters who lived here, and they would rightly prioritize having access to supplies over me as a person. As they should.

"Oh my god, are you okay?" Ophelia asked, rushing around the bed to my side. She looked wide-eyed and panicky, and I felt guilty for making her worry.

"Completely fine. Seriously. You didn't need to rush over here."

Ophelia ran her gaze critically over my face, down my arm to where my bandaged hand lay on top of the blanket.

"Astrid, you look *awful*. You don't need to be brave for my benefit, I'm not a little kid anymore. Let me *help* you."

"There's nothing to do," I assured her, attempting a weak smile that probably looked more like a grimace. "It's just a scratch. Meera fixed me up. I just need to sleep it off, that's all."

"There must be something here that can help," she muttered, perching on the edge of the bed, careful not to jostle me. "I'll ask Affra if there are any Shade medicines or something that might help."

She continued mumbling under her breath, and I knew she was trying to avoid the elephant in the room.

"He didn't mean for the blade to hit me," I told Ophelia quietly, interrupting her rambling.

"Did you know he was going to attack Soren?" she shot back, surprising me with the vehemence in her tone.

"Of course not."

"Right." Ophelia deflated slightly. "I mean, I didn't think so. I know you're not going back to their side, but I just had to make sure. You shouldn't have stayed to talk with them when they asked really, but you saved Soren's life."

"He must hate that," I snorted, ignoring the mild censure. Okay, maybe I shouldn't have hung around when I realized my parents were ambushing us. Soren had been flailing enough with his arms for me to realize that he'd wanted me to turn the lamp off and go.

"He's alive, so he can keep his complaining to himself," Ophelia replied with a sniff before giving me a slightly pitying look that made my skin feel too tight. Pity had always gone the opposite way between us, and this new dynamic made me feel unbalanced. "Soren said you wanted a chance to talk to them. That you thought you could make them understand."

"The Captain is a gossip," I grumbled, face burning with humiliation. *Of course*, he'd immediately relayed that to the king and queen and made me look like I was desperately seeking my parents out. "I did say that. I guess I thought I could. *Hoped* I could. It's hard to see them on the wrong side."

My parents had been my heroes. And now we were on opposite sides of a war, neither of us willing to budge.

Ophelia's smile was sympathetic. "I know. Your relationship with them is totally different to mine, and I get that it must be painful to not be able to get through to them. Sorry that Dad, you know, stabbed you."

I let out a surprised laugh, instantly regretting it as pain rocketed up my arm. Fortunately, Ophelia was too busy giggling to herself to notice before I composed myself.

"Yeah, I don't think there are any more father-daughter fishing trips in our future," I said wryly, staring down at my lap. "I never liked them anyway."

"Didn't you?" Ophelia's eyebrows shot up. "I thought you loved fishing."

It took a moment for me to find the words, to work my way past the initial rush of embarrassment that usually kept me from articulating my feelings aloud.

"I liked the attention," I admitted with a half-shrug. "When I went fishing, Dad gave me attention."

"What about that mud run thing you and Mom always did together?" Ophelia pressed. "Did you enjoy that?"

"No. I like running. I don't like mud."

"Huh, here was me thinking I was swapped at birth because I didn't have the same hobbies as everyone else and it turns out you never liked any of that shit either," Ophelia teased, poking my leg through the blanket.

"I didn't mean to make you feel that way." I let out a shuddering breath, willing down the torrent of emotions threatening to overwhelm me before I continued. "And it's not good enough to say sorry now, though for what it's worth, I *am* sorry."

My head was swimming, and I could feel a fine sheen of sweat covering every inch of my skin. As much as I loved Ophelia, and as much as this conversation was overdue, I needed to get rid of her before I passed out.

"Dad *yelled* at me tonight. Yelled at me and insulted me, and all I could think was 'he's never done that before', but that's not true. He'd never done that to *me* before."

"You're already forgiven, Astrid," Ophelia said gently, squeezing my leg.

"You've always been too forgiving," I pointed out affectionately. "Don't you have some important queen stuff to be doing?"

"Yes, actually. It's my coronation in a few days and there are a million things to do and everyone seems to have an urgent question I need to answer. Can I stay here and nap instead?"

"Only if you want your husband to lose his mind and break the 'no Shades in Elverston House' rule."

She groaned dramatically, failing to suppress her smile. "You're right, we don't want that. Take care of yourself, okay? I'll come back and visit. I'm sure it goes without saying, but we're putting a halt on supply runs for the time being. We'll be fine with what we have, and your safety is more important to me than *stuff*."

I swallowed thickly, hating the idea of inconveniencing the others. There were things they needed—I hadn't even brought back the stuff from my apartment as planned. My parents had probably set it all on fire out of spite.

"Just focus on the coronation, baby sister. I'll be fine."

I'm fine. I'm always fine.

God, I was tired.

So tired.

No matter how much I slept—and I'd slept more this week than I had in years—I woke up just as exhausted as when I'd fallen asleep. Plus, every time I got close to actual rest, my brain was like 'hey, do you want a really weird dream? Here you go!' Meera had even asked me about it once when she'd come in to check on me and found me tossing and turning in my sheets, but I'd brushed her off.

I'd take the fact that I'd been dreaming about bright orange eyes and the sensation of being cradled to my grave. They hadn't even been *sexual* dreams, just... intimate and strange.

And unrelated to the Captain.

I wriggled up the bed, sitting back against the pillows and swiping away the constant sheen of sweat on my forehead. For once, I was grateful for the constant cold at Elverston House.

The supplies were laid out on the scratched wooden nightstand next to the bed, so I was guessing Meera had somewhere else to be today. I didn't begrudge her that—she'd been at my side most of the time I'd been awake, though I wasn't entirely sure how often that had been. Surely it couldn't have been more than a couple of days?

The blood loss was kicking my ass.

Carefully, I unwrapped the sticky bandage, exposing the stitches on my hand. Ophelia's lady-in-waiting, or whatever she was called, had sent over a jar of what Meera and I had been calling honey. It was the color of concrete, with a faint sparkle to it, and was produced by buzzing insects. It certainly felt and tasted like honey, and Affra had claimed it was smeared on healing wounds to keep them clean, so we were hoping for the best.

Or rather, *Meera* was hoping for the best because she was maintaining the positivity for both of us.

She and I both knew that I would never regain the full use of my left hand, though. There were no hospitals here, no surgeons. Frankly, I was calling it a win that I hadn't died of sepsis.

I dunked a strip of cloth in the basin of clean water next to me, using it to gently clean the sticky honey off my skin so I could reapply it fresh. Usually, I could hear *something* from downstairs—Tallulah's laughter, or Verity's impressively loud speaking voice, or Meera's gentle humming—but it was weirdly quiet today. The rasp of the wet rag against my skin and the gentle splash as I dunked it back in the bowl seemed oddly loud.

Where *was* everyone?

I finished cleaning around the wound, patting it dry and looking at the pile of clean bandages in resignation. Being cared for wasn't really something I'd ever pined after, but these past few days had made me wonder what it would be like to have someone *want* to nurse me back to health.

Mom had, once upon a time. When we were *really* little, and our worth hadn't been decided by how good our aim was yet. She'd always made chicken casserole with cream of mushroom soup when I was sick, and spaghetti pie when Ophelia was ill. We'd drag our bedding downstairs, get comfortable on the couch, watch cartoons and infomercials, and Mom took care of everything else.

Dad had been nicer in those days too. Was this the way it had always been destined to go? Was this what Hunter ambition did to people? I barely recognized the couple that had been standing in my living room the other night from the parents who'd taken me and Ophelia to the state fair and let us go on the carnival rides until we were sick.

There were footsteps in the corridor, and I twisted on the bed to face the door, wishing I didn't feel so weak and helpless while I was deep in the heart of enemy territory.

"Astrid?" someone called, rapping their knuckles on the door of my room. "It's just me, Tallulah."

"I want to sleep," I grumbled, as though I hadn't been feeling slightly lonely and abandoned here with my stack of clean bandages and the mystery meat jerky I hadn't touched yet.

"I know." Tallulah pushed the door open with a creak, and I glared at her through narrowed eyes.

God, why was I like this? I didn't even know. She'd been nothing but nice to me, and they'd all covered for me to my sister.

Tallulah was unfazed, pushing into my room with a bright smile on her face.

From what I'd heard—mostly via Verity's boombox-like speaking voice—Tallulah was already popular with Shades, and I'd noticed she always had a circle of admirers at dinner. She was certainly a burst of color in this world—while her hair was black and glossy, everything else about her was bright and vibrant. Bold, red lipstick, naturally pink cheeks, and always wearing vintage patterned dresses. Apparently, she made a lot of them herself.

"Verity and I have taken turns trying to wake you all day—Meera thinks you should rest—and apparently I'm the only one brave enough to risk your wrath by physically dragging you out of this room if I have to."

I had no recollection of anyone trying to wake me.

"This is why Meera is my favorite. If I was armed and at full strength, you'd be fearing for your life right now."

Bright red lips twitched in amusement. "I have no doubt you can do plenty of damage just as you are, busted hand and all. You missed your sister's coronation."

"What?!" I barked, throwing off the itchy gray blanket of doom and rolling out of bed. "When?! Why didn't anyone tell me?!"

"We tried!" Tallulah threw her hands up in exasperation. "You're mean as shit when someone tries to wake you up. It's still going on, plenty of time to make an appearance."

I grabbed my nicest clothes—black jeans and a long-sleeved black top that I'd occasionally worn to the gym in the before times—ignoring the sting in my hand as I pulled them on.

"The feast hasn't started yet. There's a short break to give everyone time to make it over from that decrepit chapel thing to the feast hall. Relax, Astrid."

I whirled around to give her my best you-can't-be-serious face.

"I doubt anyone even noticed you weren't at the ceremony! It was packed, there was no telling who was who," she said, holding up her hands defensively. There were only five ex-Hunters in the entire realm and one of them was the queen, I was pretty sure someone noticed. "Just slip in for the feast and smile, your sister will never know you missed the actual crowning part."

"Like a real crown?"

I quickly ran my fingers through my hair and shoved my feet into my sneakers. In my rush, I grabbed the back of my shoe with my bad hand, stumbling forward at the sudden rush of pain that threatened to knock me out completely.

This fucking *hand*. How was I meant to function like this? I needed to get back out there. To train, to figure out how to compensate for my injured limb on the battlefield. I was *ambidextrous*, for fuck's sake.

Or I had been, once upon a time. Despite the flare of agony, I tried to flex my fingers slightly, testing them. They moved a little, but not much. Not enough to properly *grip* something.

Tallulah's heels clipped on the stone floor as she approached, holding her hands up in surrender before kneeling on the ground in front of me.

"Don't," she said mildly when I opened my mouth to protest. With deft fingers, she helped me into my sneakers, quickly lacing them up. Who knew I'd ever be jealous of the ability to easily *tie shoelaces?* It was like being in kindergarten all over again. "God knows you're not going to ask for help, the least you can do is not complain about it."

Tallulah stood, giving me a bright smile that quickly morphed into a frown.

"Shouldn't your hand be bandaged?"

Almost certainly. "It'll be fine. How do I look?"

"Like you just woke up. Want some makeup?"

I snorted, leading Tallulah out of my room. "That will only make me look more guilty."

Fortunately, with the celebratory mood that the Shades were in, it was quite easy to slip into the crowd headed for the feast hall. Everyone still made time amongst their celebrating to look at me as though I'd peed in their cereal, but I was sort of getting used to that.

They all hated me, and there was a very good chance that I'd killed their family members, so I couldn't exactly blame them.

"They'll get used to you," Tallulah murmured.

"No they won't." I shot her a wry smile, slipping away as we caught up to the other ex-Hunters. They wanted to get to know the Shades, wanted the kind of relationship Ophelia and Allerick had, and they weren't going to find that with me hanging around, reminding the Shades of all the reasons they had to hate Hunters.

I didn't bother taking a seat, taking up my regular position with my back to the wall near the front so I could observe the room and keep a protective eye on my sister.

The lightheadedness hadn't gone away, and I hoped the wall would keep me upright. I couldn't shake the constant worry that I was one misstep away from being dead when I was surrounded by Shades.

It didn't take long for the happy couple to emerge, Ophelia draped in a dress of shadows—apparently a rite of passage of some kind here. While I was deeply concerned at how secure a dress made out of shadows could possibly be, there was no question that Ophelia was weirdly cut out to be the Queen of Shades.

It was a little hard to reconcile—the goofy, gap-toothed kid who'd once eaten a mouthful of clay on a dare was now this elegant, regal, incredibly respected figure of authority. I leaned back against the wall with my arms crossed, observing Ophelia as she made bedroom eyes at her husband while they took their seats at the top table.

The Shades cheered, stamping their feet on the ground in excitement. I was competitive by nature, and sometimes struggled to feel happy for others, which was a failing I'd been actively working on, but I felt nothing but pure joy for Ophelia. If anyone deserved the love and adoration of an entire realm, it was her. She'd been on her own for so long, and unlike me, Ophelia didn't thrive in those conditions.

"Too good to eat with everyone else? I see your fellow Hunters have managed to make themselves at home here."

There weren't many people—Shade or human—who could take me by surprise, but Captain Soren seemed to make it his mission to. Where had he even come from?

"They don't like being called Hunters," I said flatly, staring up at the high table and ignoring the looming Shade to my left—quite a feat, given just how *enormous* he was.

Apparently, I wasn't going to get a thank you for saving his life. He despised me, so it wasn't exactly surprising, but I felt a weird twist of disappointment in my gut anyway.

He hummed. "But you're fine with the title?"

"*We* don't like being called that," I amended quickly, knowing the damage was done. I supposed it didn't matter—in the grand scheme of Things Soren Was Holding Against Me, this slip-up was pretty minor. "Don't you have somewhere else to be? Somewhere less in my personal space?"

"No, I don't think so. My job is to protect the royal family, to protect the court, and I can't see a bigger threat here than you."

"I saved your *life*, you asshat," I hissed, my hand throbbing as though it was enraged too.

"You did, for reasons I'm not sure either of us understand, and I'm indebted to you. That doesn't mean you're safe to the rest of us."

There was no 'thank you' in that, I noticed. I meant to tell him as much, twisting to face Soren and finding him closer than I expected. A *lot* closer. My gaze caught for a moment on sharp, inhuman features—the angular shape of his face, and the perfect smoothness of his skin. When he'd carried me back through the portal, his touch had been exclusively over my clothes, and I couldn't help but wonder what his body felt like.

Not in a *sexy* way. Of course not. That would be obscene.

Just in a curious way. Like a scientist, wanting to research a new specimen.

Totally clinical. Nothing weird about it.

I wasn't *into* Shades the way the other ex-Hunters were into Shades. While I could admit they were strangely beautiful here, in their solid form in their own realm, my head had never been filled with elaborate monster-fucking fantasies the way my sister's had, or many of the others who'd moved here by the sounds of it. Sure, Soren had this domineering presence about him, a cool kind of confidence that would make any being of any gender attractive to me, but that didn't mean I wanted to jump his bones.

He was so gruff and stoic, and of course, he *hated* me. The sex would probably be...

Mindblowing.

No. Nope. Not that.

I was not going to let the intrusive thoughts win this battle. Hate sex with a shadow monster would definitely not be *fucking amazing.*

No, definitely not. The blood loss was making me stupid.

That dream had done weird things to my brain, and I wished I could wipe it from my memory completely.

Soren leaned in, his nose almost brushing against my cheek. *Is he... sniffing me?* The movement was so quick, I couldn't be sure. My nails bit into my palms as I clenched my good hand at my sides, forcing myself not to physically shove him out of my personal space.

The last thing I needed was everyone thinking I'd attacked the Captain of the Guard in the middle of dinner. I wouldn't live to see the next course.

"Interesting," Damen said mildly as he passed, startling us apart.

Soren cursed quietly under his breath, shooting me a glare as though *I'd* been the one to ambush *him* while he'd been standing around, minding his own business. He stomped off after Damen, heading for his usual guard post with a view of the dais, and I just *barely* resisted the urge to make an obscene gesture at his back.

Asshole.

I took a deep, steadying breath as I pressed myself back against the wall, doing my best to pretend that entire interaction hadn't happened. Ophelia was definitely trying to get me to make eye contact so she could communicate some secret message with her eyeballs, but I wasn't biting. Both because I didn't know if I'd like what she had to say, and because I was worried she'd see too much.

Both in my vaguely curious hate-sex thoughts, and with the injury I was trying valiantly to downplay.

"Does no one else find it off-putting to eat their dinner in the company of a murderer?" one male Shade asked loudly, drawing the attention of his entire table to him before it switched to me. "I can all but see the blood of our brothers and sisters dripping from her hands as she stands there with that look of disdain on her face. It makes it very difficult to enjoy my meal."

There were some muttered sounds of agreement, accompanied by some looks that felt as though they'd burn me into an early grave.

I kept my eyes trained on the high table, ignoring the running commentary. It was nothing I hadn't heard before.

"It's a pity her sire failed to kill her; then again, the *Hunters* only excel with weak and defenseless targets."

My ears were ringing so loudly, I could barely hear the laughter of the nearby Shades. *That's* what he'd told them? That my father had been aiming for *me* with that blade? That I was so appallingly awful that even my own dad wanted me dead?

That stupid, lying asshole.

He obviously hadn't fed Ophelia that story—she'd known that I'd saved his life. So, what? He was comfortable trashing me to his fellow Shades but didn't want to lie to his monarchs? Or maybe he was just ashamed that he'd be *dead* if it wasn't for me.

The pain in my hand was crippling, shooting all the way up my arm, but I was fueled by spite on the best of days and this was decidedly *not* the best of days.

"What's your name?" I asked, only raising my voice a little but immediately sending the surrounding Shades into silence. "You. Yeah, you, with the grating voice and all the opinions. What's your name?"

"His name is Adrastos!" one of the other Shades called out, sounding borderline gleeful that his buddy was in trouble. I supposed Shades weren't so different from humans or Hunters in that respect.

"Adrastos. Well, *Adrastos*," I began, leaning back against the wall as though I was unfazed rather than on the verge of collapse. "You're certainly right that Shades are weak and defenseless in the human realm. You're also faceless, a moving mass of fear with no personality or backstory. In your case, I think that was probably for the better."

He stood suddenly, claws digging into the wooden tabletop, but I wasn't afraid. Not of him—I'd met plenty of *hims* in my time.

"Is there some kind of challenge system here? A duel for dominance?" I hedged, because when in doubt in the shadow realm, pick something that sounded medieval.

"Yes!" a few others shouted, clearly enjoying themselves. Interesting. Between the king and the captain, I'd pegged Shades as stoic and respectful, but I'd never have used two humans as a sample size for all of humanity. The Shades at this table were sort of messy and living for the drama, and it gave me a whole different perspective on them.

"And yet you'd rather run your mouth about me than issue a challenge; why is that? If I only *excel* with weak, defenseless opponents, then surely there's no risk in challenging me. Of course, my *sire* was very much in close contact with that blade and I seem to have come out of that just fine…"

The creaking sound of Adrastos' claws gouging further into the table was music to my ears.

"Well, I'd hate for everyone to think you're all talk, so when you're ready for that challenge, you just let me know, okay? Let me help you out with that reputation issue of yours."

There were some jeers and laughs, the Shades next to Adrastos elbowing him while he attempted to paste a cocky, amused smile on his face despite how rattled he was clearly feeling.

They're all the same, I thought to myself, resignation and relief warring for dominance. Since I was a teenager, I'd been handing asses to Hunters who thought they were bigger and better than I was. This was no different.

I slipped out of the hall through the side exit I'd stationed myself next to, forcing myself to stay upright and look confident until I could get back to the privacy of Elverston House.

Hadn't I always known that my reputation here was beyond repair? That there was nothing I could do to redeem myself in the eyes of the Shades? I thought I'd known that, thought I'd come to terms with that, but if I truly had then I wouldn't be so fucking *disappointed* in the good Captain, would I?

And yet I couldn't bring myself to regret saving his ass either. Maybe I was as dumb as my father thought I was.

SOREN

CHAPTER 5

For days, I'd stayed away.

I'd had to, after getting that tantalizing sniff of Astrid's interest in me, of her *arousal*. It was unfortunately that Damen had almost immediately noticed it too. Worse, he'd caught me leaning in close, clearly interested. It was only luck that everyone had been too entranced by the king and queen to realize just *how* close I'd been standing.

And more luck still that whatever faint inkling of arousal Astrid had been feeling hadn't permeated the rest of the room, and had almost immediately been superseded by her rage.

I had no idea what Adrastos said, but it couldn't have been any worse than what others had said before him—he didn't have the brain power to form a more interesting insult than what another Shade could concoct.

Elverston House loomed large below me. I'd chosen a spot high up on the hill that rose up behind the house. It made the entire structure even colder and darker than it already would have been.

I didn't need to be here.

Yes, Allerick had asked me to keep an eye on the Hunter, but I knew full well that he didn't mean me personally. He had been asking the Captain of the Guard, which meant I could delegate the task to any other member of the Guard. That would be the sensible thing to do.

So why was I here?

And apparently, I wasn't the only one.

"Captain," Verner greeted, inclining his head as he rounded a rocky outcrop.

"Anything to report?" I asked, straightening my shoulders and pretending I'd come here with a purpose in mind. A purpose other than staring at the Hunter.

"Nothing." He glanced down at the house guiltily. One of the ex-Hunters, Meera, sat underneath the withered remains of a tree alone, writing something in a notebook.

"Then why are you here?" I asked wryly, already knowing the answer. I'd instructed the Guard to stop by on their rotations, and check nothing was amiss, but I'd specifically told them *not* to spy. We wanted them to feel comfortable here.

Except for the Hunter, but she was a special case.

"Well, uh, I just…" he floundered for words, which wasn't entirely unusual for the mostly silent Verner, but it was probably the most I'd heard him speak all at once. "She looks sad."

"She always looks sad," I pointed out, not quite seeing why that induced him to stay. Meera didn't look *unhappy* to be here in a way that inspired concern, but she was quiet and morose in comparison to her peers.

"Right," Verner agreed, shifting uncomfortably. "Well, uh, I'll just leave you to it."

"Wait, have you seen the Hunter?" I asked, scanning the grounds. Prior to injuring her hand, Astrid had spent most of her days outside the walls of the house.

"Maybe?" Verner hedged. "I thought I saw a flash of movement and her hair color—she's very quick for a human. But no one has left the garden, I'm sure of that."

I grunted, stalking to the far edge of the cliff to check the back garden. Astrid wasn't just fast, she trained to be discreet. It would be foolish to underestimate her.

Elverston House had been empty for years—originally it was Allerick's mother's residence, but as she got frailer, Allerick insisted on moving Orabelle into the main palace. Once upon a time, the gardens had been quite something, but they'd withered and fallen apart like the house had. Allerick had assigned some Shades to clean up the front garden so the ex-Hunters had somewhere sort of nice to enjoy outside, but the back gardens were a forest of dead trees and thorny vines, not a blossoming flower in sight.

It matched the Hunter's personality. No wonder she'd found her way here.

I watched with an embarrassing degree of fascination as she wiped her forehead with the back of her sleeve, before lowering herself to the ground, doing one-armed press-ups with her injured hand clutched to her chest.

She's training.

She'd found a walled-in courtyard, once a private spot Orabelle had enjoyed, and was using it as her own personal training ground. I swallowed the growl of disapproval that arose in my chest, not wanting to risk even for a second that she'd hear me. Training. She was *training*. Figuring out how to maintain her current Shade-killing level of ability with one hand out of commission, perhaps? It's what I would have done in her position.

Her good arm trembled, and I took a step forward unconsciously, wincing in sympathy when her strength gave out and she landed on the ground with a thud, turning her head in time to save her nose.

Not that I should be sympathetic, but I'd seen many warriors in my time struggle to adapt to an unforeseen injury. I could appreciate that it was a challenge that took perseverance. I could also appreciate that Astrid appeared to have an abundance of perseverance, and whatever else I thought about her, I couldn't deny that the Hunter was a warrior.

On shaking limbs, she pushed herself up, sitting back on her knees. A red bloodstain had soaked through the white bandage around her hand, and she glared down at it in dismay before slowly lifting her head and turning that venomous gaze on me.

Caught.

Except that wasn't the word that came to mind. What came to mind was *ensnared*. She could probably fell her enemies with that devastating look if she wanted to.

I stared back, letting her know I'd seen her see me, that I had nothing to be afraid of. She looked paler than usual, a thin sheen of sweat covering her skin. Was this the result of her injury? How long did humans need to heal?

I felt, rather than heard Allerick's approach, and in the split second it took me to glance at him, Astrid had vanished into the overgrown garden. It was infuriating that her scent, no matter how she was feeling, was so faint. She might hide herself in the depths of the shadow realm, never to be seen again.

"I knew I'd find you here." Allerick sounded smug. "From what I hear, it's the most popular spot for guard duty these days."

"Don't get any ideas. I'm not here to find a mate."

"What an absurd notion that would be," Allerick agreed, infuriatingly amused. "I already know you're here because you're watching Astrid, though I didn't mean for you to take that task quite so literally when I assigned it to you…"

"You should have meant for me to take it literally. Allerick, I know she's your wife's sister and you want to trust her—"

"She did save your life," Allerick cut in, giving me a reproving look that I wasn't used to being on the receiving end of. "She could have let you die and stayed in the human realm, resumed her life there. Instead, she saved you. At a personal cost, I have no doubt, though Astrid has assured Ophelia the injury isn't that severe."

That was a blatant lie, and I couldn't for the life of me work out what Astrid had to gain by telling it. Anyone who saw her hand, realized how long it was taking to heal, knew that it was a serious injury.

"Anyway, the injury threw off my plans, but Astrid attended the coronation, so I assume she's feeling better. Astrid is highly trained, and I want those skills on our side."

"Not this Guard idea again," I groaned. I'd forgotten about it—or rather, hoped that Allerick had forgotten about it—after Astrid's injury.

"Don't look at me like that, Soren. You know she could be a valuable asset."

"Hunters barely learn close combat, they don't need to. She doesn't have the skills required for the Guard."

"And no group ever benefited from having a diverse array of skills," Allerick said drily. "Besides, she caught that blade just fine at close range."

I don't think I imagined the smug grin he shot me.

"Just give Astrid a trial run. See how things go. It could work out better than you think, and she'll benefit from having a sense of purpose here. And you'll benefit from being able to keep a closer eye on her without sacrificing your training time. A win for both of you."

I followed behind him, grumbling under my breath as we made our way down the slope and around the edge of the boundary line, stopping in sight of Meera.

She stood immediately, setting her notebook aside on the bench and doing a strange, sweeping curtsy to Allerick.

"What was that?" I mumbled.

"Some of them do that," Allerick muttered. "I'm not really sure why."

"Can I help with anything, your majesty?" Meera asked politely, standing a respectful distance back with her hands clasped in front of her.

"Would you be so good as to ask Astrid to come out, please?" Allerick asked, in a gentler voice than I'd ever heard him before, evidently worried about frightening the most skittish of the ex-Hunters.

"Of course." Meera turned away, taking a step towards the house before hurriedly spinning to face us again and offering Allerick another one of those curtsies, dropping all the way to the ground. He grimaced slightly as she rose and jogged back to the house.

I snorted.

"Shut up," Allerick grumbled, shifting restlessly. "Ophelia says they're just trying to be respectful."

It didn't take long for Astrid to appear, hand bound in a fresh white bandage that reeked of méli. She must have at least one Shade on her side to have some of that in her possession.

Who would offer to help her? I'd been watching her closely. There were no Shades sniffing around Astrid in order to feed. No, perhaps one of the other ex-Hunters had been given some and shared it with her. While it was all very chaste and polite so far, there had been chaperoned dates been ex-Hunters and Shades interested in courting them.

"Brother," Astrid said, almost smiling at Allerick. I couldn't tell if it was sarcastic or genuine. Probably sarcastic. "Captain," she added with far less affection. "To what do I owe the pleasure?"

Allerick crossed his arms over his chest, angling himself toward me with an expectant look on his face.

Me? He wanted me to bring it up?

Asshole.

I cleared my throat. "The king has raised the idea of you training with the Guard again, now that you are… less injured."

"No need to sound so thrilled, *Captain*."

Was I imagining things, or was she looking at me with more anger than usual today?

"Of course I'm thrilled to hear you will be infiltrating my Guard."

"Soren," Allerick warned.

"However, as you demonstrated your willingness to defend my kind when we were recently attacked—"

"I defended *you*," Astrid interrupted, glaring at me.

"Does the differentiation matter?"

"Only because you're trying to avoid it. I defended *you*, Captain. I saved *you*. You don't get to pretend that happened to someone else."

"I'm not," I gritted out.

"Mmhm, sure. Fine. When does training start?"

I exhaled heavily, trying to find my composure. Why did *this* Hunter have this effect on me? I'd never met anyone who riled me up the way she did.

"Tomorrow. After breakfast. The training grounds are—"

"I know where they are."

My claws dug into my palms. Of course, she already knew where we trained. She'd probably watched us from afar, learning all our moves without us even noticing.

"Until tomorrow then," Allerick said as the silence stretched. I only just managed to cover my surprise—I'd completely forgotten that he was standing there.

Witnessing that entire conversation.

Great.

Astrid inclined her head politely at Allerick, the corner of her lips tipping up slightly. Her expression flattened entirely as she looked at me, holding my gaze as she backed away, vanishing down one of the winding paths hidden by overgrown garden beds.

Allerick blew out a long breath. "You're in danger, my friend."

"I know. Because of *you*, and your directive to train her."

"No. Not because of that. Not at all."

ASTRID

CHAPTER 6

I watched from afar until I was confident the king and the captain were gone, then made my way to the palace gardens where Ophelia often walked during the day with Levana. It was her way of being accessible to us in Elverston House, without leaving Levana standing around at the boundary, waiting for her to finish.

Before I could get to where Ophelia was sitting with her sketchpad, I tugged my sweater sleeves all the way down so only my fingertips poked out.

"Astrid," Levana said, drawing Ophelia's attention to me.

"Big sis! This is a nice surprise."

"Don't stand up. What are you drawing?" I asked, instinctively leaning over to look at her sketchbook before stopping myself at the last minute.

I knew the kinds of things my sister liked to draw, and my retinas would never recover if I saw a depiction of King Allerick in action.

Ophelia laughed, spinning the book around and holding it up for me. "Relax, it's not a dick pic. Dick doodle? Penis portrayal?"

"Phallustration?" I suggested.

Levana ducked her head, shoulders shaking with the effort of holding in her laughter.

"Perfect," Ophelia agreed. "It's not a phallustration—for a change. I'm sketching a design for a shadow dress for the ball so Allerick knows what I want. Have you thought about yours?"

"What ball?" I asked, frowning. I didn't bother addressing the bit about the shadow dress; that was clearly not going to happen. From what I gathered, shadow clothing was a big deal. It wasn't just about designing someone a pretty outfit—it was a sign of trust.

No Shade trusted me, and I didn't trust any of them either, not really. I didn't think Allerick actively wanted me dead, but only because that might make Ophelia sad.

"Orabelle suggested it; apparently, it was quite a thing in previous royal courts but Allerick never bothered with it for some reason."

Levana looked up, giving Ophelia what I was pretty sure was a wry look while my sister grinned.

"Okay, Allerick isn't super interested in the more *frivolous* court events. But this one sounds fun—apparently, some people choose not to say who clothed them in shadows and it's like a sexy guessing game—and a ball is a more relaxed setting for the ex-Hunters and Shades to get to know each other, don't you think?"

I looked at her blankly. "You're asking me?"

"*Yes.*" Ophelia sighed in exasperation. "Of course, I'm asking you. You might find this hard to believe, but I value your opinion."

"That seems inadvisable, at best," I scoffed. "I don't know anything about balls or Hunter/Shade relations."

"Agree to disagree. Anyway, tell me what kind of dress you want and I'll sketch it," Ophelia replied, carefully flipping her sketchbook to a fresh page before looking at me expectantly.

"Where the fuck would I get a shadow dress?" I laughed, shooting her a disbelieving look. "I'd be stark naked within two minutes of walking into the ballroom, best case scenario. Worst case scenario, I get full-blown *Carrie'd*."

"Um, I will go full medieval tyrannical monarch if someone *Carries* my sister," Ophelia shot back, looking affronted.

"I'll clothe you," Levana offered easily, glancing at me before resuming scanning our surroundings.

I blinked at her. "Why?"

Levana shifted uncomfortably. "So you can attend. Fit in. The shadows will only hold if I'm nearby, so you'd probably want to wear some kind of human clothes underneath, just in case I'm called away."

Oh, there was no question I'd be wearing real clothes underneath.

"Clearly, I wouldn't risk my position to humiliate you. Besides, having spent time with you... Well, let's just say that if Shades were able to kill Hunters in our human realm forms, then I'm confident we would have. Of course we would have—the Hunters were an obstacle between us and feeding. We'd have been conditioned to hurt you, the same way you were conditioned to hurt us, and we wouldn't have questioned it. We probably *did* hurt your kind, back when you were known as the Hunted and we knew we could feed from you. This is generations—*centuries*—of conflict and enmity and powerful authority figures guiding our opinions. It's so much more than just... You. Or me, or any of the Hunters or former Hunters or Shades," Levana finished, looking at me, then my sister before straightening her posture into a more guard-like position. If she could have blushed, I would have bet money that she would be.

Ophelia hummed thoughtfully. "You're probably right, but I doubt many others will come to that conclusion. Or not for a while yet, anyway. But I have hope. We're going to stay here and be our awesome selves, and eventually the Shades will come around."

Probably not with Soren going around telling them that I was so awful even my own father had tried to kill me. I almost brought it up with Ophelia, but I didn't want to run to my little sister with my problems, or for her to feel like she had to go out and solve them.

"So. Astrid, will you come to the ball?"

"When is it? I start training with the Guard tomorrow."

"Well, it's not the same time as the Guard's training session, you wish you were that lucky," Ophelia laughed. "It's the night after next."

"And is it important to you that I go?" I asked, already knowing the answer.

"Well, it might make up for you missing my coronation." Ophelia winked.

Shit.

"About that—"

"Don't apologize, it's fine," Ophelia assured me, packing away her drawing supplies and standing up. "I'm pretty sure you're lying to me about the damage that knife did to your hand and that was a rough week for you, but whatever, it's fine. I understand that you're philosophically opposed to asking for help."

I didn't have a good response for that, so I just rolled my eyes.

"What are you doing right now? Do you want to come to the nursery with me?"

I blinked at her. "The nursery?"

"Yeah, where all the little baby Shades hang out." We may have looked fairly similar, but I was confident that starry-eyed expression had never appeared on my face. "It's an official visit—I'm very queenly—but mostly it's an excuse for me to go and see all the babies. They have these itty bitty claws and horns that are just the *cutest* things you've ever seen."

"I think... I think you and I may have different definitions of cuteness. And no, I can't come to the *nursery* with you, Ophelia. No one wants *me* around their children."

Ophelia's face fell, and I felt a sudden rush of affection for her. I was basically toxic waste in this realm, but she didn't see me that way. She still chose to see something of value in me.

When my hand ached and reminded me that I'd never be the fighter I once was, or when I walked through the feast hall with hundreds of angry, hateful glares directed my way, Ophelia's faith in me gave me the push I needed to retain at least a little faith in myself.

Waiting until the others had left the house for breakfast, I took my time getting dressed in bright red workout clothes, rebandaging my hand before adding my black boxing wraps over the top. The added pressure on the wound was uncomfortable, but at least this way, blood wouldn't soak through the bandage if I ripped the stitches again.

Meera might actually kill me if I ripped them again, but there was a lot riding on this training session. I couldn't appear weak.

I'd deal with the consequences later.

Chewing on a piece of jerky from my hoard, I made my way through the gardens, around the palace, and down to the walled-in clearing that the Guards used for training. While I'd poked around the place to get a lay of the land, I hadn't actually ventured inside and *watched* them train like the Captain undoubtedly assumed I had.

There was no ceiling, presumably in order to keep the place filled with light at all times so no one could shadow-sneak their way in, but the stone walls were high, and I'd had no desire to creep in and find myself unable to get out again. It wasn't as though I actually *wanted* to be surrounded by hostile Shades.

I'd just made a series of poor life choices and ended up that way.

"Ah, here she is. Our newest recruit." Selene, the Captain's second-in-command, stood at the entryway, arms crossed as she stared me down, voice dripping with disdain. "You couldn't have picked anything more conspicuous?" she added, glaring at my red outfit like it personally offended her.

"Well, I *could* have worn black, but I didn't see much point pretending to fit in. It's not as though any of you are going to accept me."

Selene harrumphed, gesturing at the short tunnel that led into the training grounds. "Come on then, *Hunter*. Let's get this over with."

That was an interesting choice of words. Selene made this sound more like a one-off, which hadn't been the impression I'd gotten from Allerick. I straightened my shoulders, examining my surroundings carefully. Maybe they were intending to go back to the king with bad news today about how I'd failed some test. Or died. There was no such thing as too careful.

"We're not using silver today because of you," Selene said bluntly. "No weapons in your presence. Instead, we'll be using batons, like children."

I ignored the grumbling complaint. She could be annoyed at me all she liked, it wasn't as though I was the one who'd banned weapons. I wasn't going to apologize for that.

The Captain was on the other side of the training grounds, partnered up with Andrus to spar, but watching me intently as though he'd been aware of my presence from the moment I'd approached the grounds. I stared with unabashed curiosity as he held out his hand, shadows blooming from his palm like a macabre flower, swirling and extending to form a long line of darkness that solidified into a baton.

That's a neat trick.

While I'd been trying to get acquainted with the shadow realm, to make better sense of the situation I'd found myself in, I had to admit that I'd only scratched the surface of what Shades could *do* with their shadows.

The Captain looked at Selene, tipping his chin slightly in a silent command to move closer.

"Let's go," Selene sighed. "You're with me, *Hunter*."

And didn't that just sound ominous.

SOREN

CHAPTER 7

"I hate her," Andrus muttered, glaring at Astrid while he conjured his own baton of shadows. "I hate her, and I resent the king for foisting her on us."

I nodded curtly, knowing I should do more to defend Allerick's position—and I had, with the others—but Andrus was barely keeping it together as it was. His sister had died on a trip to the human world to feed just a few months ago, his grief was too fresh for reasoning and logic. It could have been Astrid's blade that had taken her life, and that's what anyone who'd lost a loved one at the Hunters' hands saw when they looked at her.

I was beginning to think that being mated had made Allerick stupid. If not stupid, then at least supremely reckless.

Astrid's eyes followed me like a hawk as she and Selene moved between sets of sparring partners, and I shot her a warning look, letting her know exactly why I'd summoned them closer. Astrid returned my stare, completely unflinching.

It annoyed me that her boldness was so... arresting. For all that I distrusted Astrid, for all that I hated her for what she'd done to my people, other parts of me hadn't gotten the memo.

The pairs around us began sparring, only the sounds of their exertion filling the arena since the batons didn't make a noise on impact. It was quiet and unsettling compared to the usual crash of silver-on-silver, but none of my Guard would have been comfortable having the Hunter around so many weapons.

I was, perhaps, less nervous than they were in that regard. A hint of white bandage poked out from the black wraps on Astrid's hand, a constant reminder that she'd saved my life, and immediately discarded the weapon even when I hadn't pushed her to do so.

"Captain," she said pleasantly, coming to a stop in front of me. Always with the eyes that wished vengeance on me and the polite, rather monotone voice that gave absolutely nothing away. "Thank you so much for personally inviting me to train with you yesterday. Coming all the way to Elverston House *just* to ask me—you really know how to make a girl feel wanted."

Andrus went stiff as a board next to me.

I was going to kill her.

"I *didn't*—"

"No? Sure seemed like it was you. In fact, I believe you said you were *thrilled* about it." Astrid tilted her head to the side, eyes brimming with challenge.

"I was being sarcastic," I gritted out, aware of Andrus and Selene's increasingly accusatory stares. "As you well know."

"Were you? Cultural differences, I guess. Now I know." She shrugged with one shoulder, all defiant insolence. I wanted to rip it away, to get beneath that obnoxious mask she put on just for me and lay out all the vulnerabilities that hid underneath.

She could hide it all she liked, but I spent enough time watching *Astra* to know it was all an act, purely for my benefit.

"This isn't going to work," I clipped, wrapping a hand around her upper arm and half dragging her away from the others. "We're going to see Allerick. This was a stupid idea, and I'm going to tell him that."

"We're not in the in-between now, you don't have to manhandle me," Astrid hissed, yanking her arm free with more force than necessary, and stumbling into the tunnel wall.

"I'm no *man*, Astra. You'd do well to remember that," I growled before taking a step back, realizing I was towering over her where she was leaning against the wall.

"Believe me, I'm well aware," she snapped, stalking past me. "Come on, *Captain*. Let's go talk to the king. At least if I'm there, you won't be able to just make up whatever bullshit you like about me."

What?

There was a small dark room we used for travel close to the training grounds, and instead of going past it toward the palace, I grabbed Astrid's elbow and tugged her to the door instead.

"More manhandling," she grumbled, trying and failing to shrug me off. I kicked the door open, grabbing the illuminated orb perched outside the stone structure and bringing it into the otherwise pitch-black space, closing it for travel.

Astrid managed to wriggle free the moment we were inside, and I shut the door behind us, setting the orb in the sconce before turning to face her with my arms crossed.

"Explain."

"Explain what? You know, Captain, conversations are a lot easier when one person doesn't speak in one-word sentences."

"Stop antagonizing me."

Astrid smirked. "But you make it so easy."

"Explain what you said back there. What you said about me making things up."

She raised an imperious eyebrow at me, and it was strange to feel looked down on when she only came up to my shoulder. "I'm talking about that asshole Adrastos at dinner gleefully relaying to everyone that my 'sire' had *failed* to kill me. As though it had been intentional. We both know what happened that day—and judging by Allerick's response to our conversation yesterday, *he* knows what happened that day. Why circulate another story? To make me look bad? I hate to break it to you, Captain, but there is *nothing* you can do to make me look any worse than I already do."

"I didn't say that." My claws dug into my biceps as my hands flexed with tension. "I had only intended on relaying the incident to the king, but Tallulah seemed to think your sister would want to know you were hurt, so I told her also. Other than that, I didn't discuss what happened with anyone else. It was none of their concern."

She didn't look particularly convinced, and it irritated me to have my character questioned. "I don't *lie*. I am an honorable Shade, *Astra*, as much as that might shock you."

She scoffed indignantly. "You? Honorable? Oh yes, color me *shocked*." The sarcasm dripped from every word. "It's your entire identity, Captain, I don't need the reminder. But let's not pretend like that sense of honor extends to me, the Shade Murderer."

"If I wasn't treating you with honor, I'd have ripped your heart out with my claws the moment you stepped foot in my realm."

Astrid tilted her head to the side, completely unmoved. There was no hint of fear in her scent, no anger, just that same controlled ambivalence that she always displayed.

Though… Was it a little *sweeter* than usual?

"Well, I guess I'll consider myself lucky then. Maybe, *just* maybe, you don't hate me as much as you think you do, Captain."

I took a step closer, then another, my hands pressing on the wall next to her head, boxing her in. "I hate you plenty, *Hunter*. But I don't need to resort to making up falsehoods and spreading petty rumors. As you say, your reputation does all the hard work for you."

Her cheeks had flushed the most delicious red, chest heaving with indignation, drawing my eyes downwards to the curves I usually tried *so* hard to ignore.

So soft. So fucking *tempting*.

The air turned syrupy, and my mouth watered slightly. My teeth even felt a little longer and sharper, and they weren't the only part of me experiencing sudden growth.

I hated her.

I *hated* her.

And I wanted to fuck her more than I'd ever wanted anything in my life.

Why her? Why did she have to be the one to have this effect on me?

"Careful, Captain. If you keep looking at me like that, we're going to get into trouble."

"Looking at you like what?" I rasped.

"Like you'd make a whole meal out of me, starting between my thighs."

Her scent was like the most mouthwatering cake, and I drew it in as deeply as I could, wanting to embed it in my memory. "Not very creative, Astra. I'd leave what lies between your thighs for dessert."

Sweeter and sweeter. Why did she have to smell like she'd been designed just for me? There was nothing I wanted to taste more.

"If only it was that simple," I murmured, as though my resolve *wasn't* rapidly slipping. As though all the reasons why this was an objectively terrible idea weren't fading away.

"Isn't it though?" Astrid tipped her head back, giving me a view of the long, smooth line of her neck that made my cock grow painfully harder. "It doesn't have to change anything. Doesn't have to *mean* anything. You get to power up off my battery, and I get this out of my system."

"Get what out of your system?"

I moved closer, my front brushing against hers. The fabric of her clothes clung to her skin, enticing me in.

Astrid sucked in a sharp breath, arching up towards me ever so slightly. "This *idea*. This… curiosity."

Her hips brushed mine, a faint tease of a touch. I chased the movement, unable to stop myself. Why was this a bad idea again?

"I know it won't be good," she whispered, defiant gaze trained on me. "I know I've built it up in my head, and the reality will be a disappointment. So hurry up and disappoint me, Captain."

All my inhibitions vanished. I was a Shade, and Astrid was *my* Hunted. I wanted to fuck her and knot her and mark her, fill her with so much cum her belly would be round with it.

It would be many things, but it wouldn't be disappointing.

I wrapped a hand beneath her thigh, hitching it over my hip, opening her up to me.

"You've been imagining me fucking you?" I growled, pinning my worst enemy against the wall with my hips so I could feel the softness of her breasts pressing against me.

"You *haven't* imagined it? Not even once?" Astrid challenged breathily. "I've seen the way you look at me, Captain. As though you're wondering what I look like when I come."

"Wondering?" I scoffed. "I fucking *need* to know what you look like when you come."

A second too late, I realized what I'd said, how *vulnerable* it sounded, but fortunately for me, Astrid hadn't. She was too busy trying to grind her needy cunt on any firm bit of me she could get to.

"Tell me you want this," I demanded.

Astrid let out a husky laugh that made my already hard cock ache more fiercely. "If you want a needy little huntress who's going to drop to her knees and beg for monster dick, you'd better head back to Elverston House and find someone else."

Stubborn wench.

I ran my nose over her collarbone, sucking down lungfuls of her syrupy sweet desire. "I have a needy little huntress right here, and you don't have to be on your knees to beg."

Astrid scoffed, flattening herself against the wall so she had enough space to slip her hand into her stupid human trousers, shoving it unashamedly beneath the fabric to touch herself.

"Just fuck me. That's as close to begging as you'll get. My panties are so goddamn soaked, I don't even need foreplay," she added under her breath, pulling her hand free and glancing discreetly at her glistening fingers, before hiding them behind her back as though she was embarrassed by the evidence of her arousal.

Wait.

Some sense of logic and reason pierced my haze of lust.

Astrid was surprised by her wetness? She wanted me to fuck her against a wall with nowhere comfortable to rest while I knotted her, especially for the first time?

Did sisters not talk about this stuff?

Astrid clearly knew nothing about how sex between our kinds worked.

"Did I scare you off, Captain?" she asked mildly.

"No. But you have put the idea of you begging in my head, and it's a rather intriguing prospect." I shoved her pants down, leaving her black underthings on. Astrid's pupils dilated instantly, her breath coming in shallow pants.

"Never. I will *never* beg you for anything."

Her *panties*, as she'd called them, were soaked, and I pressed my cock against the fabric, lifting her thigh again to rock against her before grabbing her other leg and lifting her so we were more comfortably aligned.

What was I doing again?

Right. *Not* fucking her. That's what I was doing.

Astrid may have been a highly trained assassin, my worst enemy, and despised by my realm, but I still wasn't about to spring my knot on her in a goddamn entry room.

But I'd rather antagonize her than tell her that. It sounded too... caring. I didn't need her reading into it.

"Pity." I rocked back and forth, rubbing her clit through the soft fabric with my cockhead, enjoying the way her pulse fluttered at her neck.

"What are you going to do if I don't? *Not* fuck me?" Astrid taunted. "Don't I smell all irresistibly breedable to you?"

You have no idea.

"You'll get my cock, but only as much as I want to give you until you beg for the rest. You can't have everything you want, *Hunter*. Panties to the side."

Astrid glared at me, her desire warring with her natural instinct to tell me to go fuck myself.

Watching her internal debate may have been the happiest I'd been in weeks.

"Fine, but only because I want to come," Astrid muttered, hooking her fingers in her stupid panties and pulling them to the side, exposing a glistening pussy that did all the begging that Astrid refused to say out loud.

I didn't drop my shadows completely—it felt too personal, too vulnerable—moving them out of the way of my groin before oh so slowly taking my cock in hand. I was closer to the edge than I thought I was, *embarrassingly* close, though I didn't want to read too much into why that was.

Savoring the moment, I guided my cock to Astrid's hot, wet center, almost coming from the feel of her slick running over my skin alone, before moving upwards to rub slow circles over her clit. Astrid tipped her head back, and I forced myself to look down between our bodies rather than at her exposed neck, not wanting to get any ridiculous ideas about biting her.

This was just about fucking. Or almost fucking. And if I generated some extra power for the stores, so much the better, though I wasn't sure if I would without the knot.

"Are you going to make me come or not?" Astrid snapped, apparently growing frustrated with my leisurely pace.

I snorted, adding a little more pressure. "Make yourself come."

Fuck, she was so *silky*. I didn't want to compare her to a female Shade—they were so different, it seemed moot—but I could get addicted to the soft, wet warmth of Astrid's body distressingly easily.

"Put your cock in me already," Astrid hissed, grabbing my shoulders and digging her blunt, harmless nails into my skin, trying in vain to impale herself on my cock.

"Settle," I drawled, if only to see the sparks of rage fly out of her eyes. "You'll get what you need."

My pace was agonizingly slow not just to torture her, but also because I needed to keep myself in check. As I dragged my cock down, notching it at her entrance, it was *my* control that was most at risk, despite her frustration. Goddesses, I wanted to drown in the slick running freely over my dick. *Not knotting Astrid might be the hardest thing I'd ever done.*

She tried and failed to capture a whimper of need in her throat, and I couldn't find it in myself to tease her for it. Not when that sound had wormed its way into my chest, spurring me on, encouraging me to satisfy this beautiful deadly creature in front of me.

Astrid had never been more dangerous to me than she was at that moment.

I pushed the head of my cock into her tight, hot cunt, squeezing my eyes shut and forcing myself not to go any further. I couldn't. Any more than just the tip, and I'd have her stuck on my knot with her pretty ankles up around my shoulders in no time.

"*Soren*," Astrid moaned, making my balls tighten to the point of pain. The only thing that sounded better than those needy little whimpers was the sound of my name on her lips. "Fuck, that feels so good."

I grunted, because words were too hard, pulling free before sliding a few inches into her again. Even that small amount was a tight fit. How would that feel around my knot? *Fuck, don't think about it, you'll come.*

"Too scared to fuck me properly?" Astrid taunted breathily, not knowing what she was asking for.

"You've never been fucked properly if you think it can happen in an entry room where anyone could find us."

She made a noise of discontent but didn't argue, which was *very* unlike Astrid. Maybe she *hadn't* been fucked properly before. Maybe she'd been too busy killing Shades to find herself a partner who knew how to take care of this pussy. That struck me as rather sad.

Her blunt nails dug into my shoulders, and the reminder of how harmless she was in that moment, that *I* was the fearsome predator out of the two of us, spurred me on. My cock was drenched in her slick when I withdrew fully, and hopefulness briefly flashed across Astrid's face that I was going to thrust all the way home this time. Instead, I gripped my burgeoning knot, squeezing it as tight as I could in a weak imitation of her pussy, and focused my full attention on fucking her clit.

Why was this so good?

I'd always prided myself on my stamina, but I was only staving off my orgasm long enough to get Astrid over the edge. Everything was different when it came to her.

"Fuck," Astrid whispered, throwing her head back as her legs tightened around me, her body trembling as she found her release. I pressed my cock tighter against her clit, soaking her in my cum, in my scent. Marking her pussy the way I couldn't mark her neck.

Where had that thought come from?

I didn't *want* to mark her neck.

"That... that is so much cum," Astrid whispered, looking between our bodies with wide eyes. Carefully, I pinched my claws around her panties, dragging them back into place to keep as much of my cum on her skin as possible, knowing I wasn't doing a good job of hiding the self-satisfied look on my face.

"It's a perfectly normal amount. You should really educate yourself on Shade anatomy."

It was beyond ridiculous to be *happy* that the Hunter smelled so unmistakably of me that every Shade in the realm would be able to tell in an instant what we'd been doing. There was no good outcome here—the only Shades who would be happy would be the worst kind, ones who'd use sex as a weapon, and I wasn't like them. I didn't want to *punish* Astrid by fucking her.

I just wanted her, and I'd had a momentary lapse in judgment and allowed myself the indulgence.

No, no one could find out. I had to get her back to Elverston House, back to the ex-Hunters and their dull senses, before any Shades encountered us.

"Nothing about this is normal," Astrid muttered, wriggling free of my grip and dropping to the ground on light feet. "And I don't need to educate myself, it's not like this is going to happen again."

She grabbed the tight pants that I noticed she favored for training, fumbling with them slightly, cheeks flushed red.

Her hand.

My shadow coverings fell back into place, preserving my modesty, as I gently took the fabric from Astrid, turning the material until it was the right way out. Astrid said nothing, staring determinedly at the ground, her delectable scent now tainted with some unidentifiable and far less pleasant emotion.

"Your sister doesn't know how bad the injury is," I stated, holding the garment by the waist and kneeling down so she could step into it. Astrid looked at me as though I'd sprouted an extra head. "Don't read into it," I muttered, suddenly aware of how submissive the position was.

"Right," she agreed, swallowing thickly before lifting one leg, letting me dress her. "No, she doesn't know. She doesn't need to know."

"*I* need to know. That's something crucial for me to be aware of in your training."

"I thought we were on the way to the king to get me kicked out." The fabric snapped around her hips as I released it, standing and taking a step back.

Right.

That was where we'd been headed.

"You reek of me. If we visit the king now, everyone will know what just happened in here," I grumbled.

"Am I bad for your reputation, Captain?" Astrid asked innocently.

"Yes. But I'm worse for yours, so proceed with caution." It was a bluff, one that relied on Astrid believing the worst of Shades, the worst of herself, or both. There was a strange, uncomfortable feeling in my chest that may have been guilt, and I did my best to ignore it.

"I certainly don't want anyone to know," Astrid said, eyes flashing with some unidentifiable emotion. "Though I guess that means you're stuck with me in the Guard for now," she finished, a hint of triumph in her voice.

"I suppose so," I sighed, reaching for the orb to put it back outside. "I'll shadow-walk you to the entry room outside Elverston House. Try to be less irritating at the next training session, hm? It would make both of our lives so much easier."

"No promises, Captain," Astrid replied flatly. "Irritating you is one of the few things in life that brings me joy right now."

That uncomfortable feeling in my chest grew more pronounced. It couldn't be guilt. Astrid had done this to herself, she deserved the misery she experienced in this realm.

Didn't she?

ASTRID
CHAPTER 8

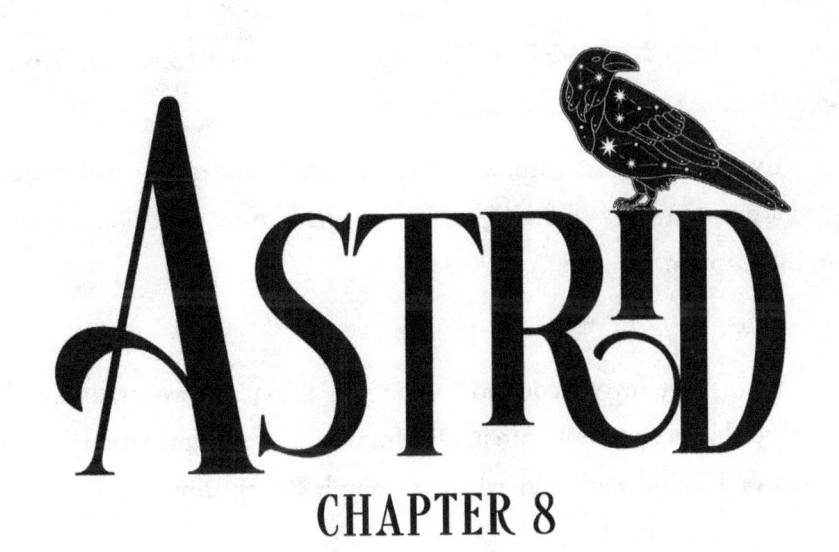

"You'll get my cock, but only as much as I want to give you until you beg for the rest."

Soren spun me away, my breasts pressing against the abrasive stone wall, one hand wrapped around my throat. Claws pricked at the skin below my ear, and another rush of arousal ran down my thighs in response to the hint of pain.

I should hate this.

I was vulnerable. Giving him my back, letting him collar my throat with claws that could rip through my skin like tissue. Viciously sharp teeth pressed down on my shoulder, and while my mind shouted 'danger!' on repeat, my body was not getting the memo.

Everything about Captain Soren was dangerous, but nothing was more dangerous than the way he made me forget myself.

"Beg, Astrid."

Just the sound of my name on his lips had me panting for him, it was fucking embarrassing. And yet...

"Please, Soren. I need you. I fucking need this."

"Such a good little Hunter," he purred in my ear, shoving me harder against the wall as he impaled me on his cock.

I woke up with a gasp, kicking away the blankets that had gotten tangled around my legs while I slept. While I had horny, ridiculous dreams about the Captain.

What the fuck.

It was just my subconscious doing its thing. It was totally fine, I definitely didn't need to read into it. Dreams were a safe escape, a total fantasy zone where I could entertain whatever dumb horny thoughts I wanted without repercussion.

In real life, I'd never beg *anyone* for dick—especially Captain Asshole. I'd never give him my back, or *want* his hand collaring my throat. That would be… absurd.

In dreams though…

I leaned over, opening the nightstand with my good hand. With the absence of electricity, I'd only brought a couple of bullet vibrators and a shit ton of batteries. They weren't my favorite toys, but I wasn't one of those women blessed with fingers that got the job done, so it was better than nothing.

It didn't take much effort for my mind to go back to consequence-free fantasyland. I rolled onto my front with my eyes shut, imagining the weight of Soren's imposing form on my back, the grip around my neck that, in my mind, was somehow safe and dangerous all at once. Dangerous because of what he *could* do, safe because he never would.

Fantasyland.

In my head, he fucked me like he was unleashed. My hips were already rocking, and I slid my hand down my body, flicking the vibrator on and shoving it into my panties, hoping the mattress below muffled the buzzing sound.

I was *soaked*. Something about this realm made my body respond weirdly.

The first hint of vibration against my clit had me biting down on the pillow, just in case. What would Soren do if he was in this bed with me? Hold my head down? Brace his hands on my hips while fucking me into the mattress? Or would he lie over me, teeth pressed against my skin?

Fuck, fuck, fuck. Now I had a biting kink. I was truly losing my mind.

With a quiet groan into my pillow, I found my release, quickly turning off the bullet against my over-sensitized nerves. That was *embarrassingly* fast, even for self-pleasure, where I knew exactly what buttons to press and when.

And now I needed another bath, after practically scrubbing my skin off when Soren had dropped me back at Elverston House.

Stupid fucking Captain and his stupid fucking dream cock.

Stupid fucking dream cock that hadn't even come *close* to how good the real one had felt.

"Astrid?"

I blinked groggily, struggling to wake up. I'd only meant to rest my head after my middle-of-the-night bath, not fall back asleep.

"I'm coming in," Meera announced. "Don't throw anything at me."

"No promises," I replied, just so she didn't think I was going soft on her. She rolled her eyes as she kicked the door shut behind her, a plate piled high with grayscale food in her hands. "What's that?"

"Breakfast. You eat a truly alarming amount of jerky, and I'm putting my foot down."

"I eat vegetables," I replied defensively.

"You eat *pickles*. Do you know how much sodium is in pickles?"

"Nope, and I never want to know." I sat up against the pillows, accepting the plate she handed me. Breakfast in bed? *Don't mind if I do.*

Meera tsked, muttering some hard truths about heart disease that I wasn't ready to hear as she sat at the end of the bed, picking at a loose thread on the blanket.

"Something on your mind?" I asked casually, panicking slightly at the concept of a deep and meaningful conversation. People didn't come to me for this kind of thing, but Meera looked like someone who wanted to *talk*.

She hummed. "A few things."

I shoved a piece of mystery meat in my mouth to avoid responding. There had to be someone here better qualified for this than me. Where was Ophelia? How busy could a queen be, really?

"Astrid, I'm worried about you," Meera said eventually.

Oh god, it's worse than I thought.

"Because of my sodium intake?" I replied, attempting to deflect with humor.

"Yes," Meera said bluntly, staring at me. "And your hand. And your loneliness."

"I'm not lonely. And my hand is…" *Ruined. Unusable. Agonizing.* "Fine. It's fine."

"It's not fine, and we all know it. All of us except Ophelia, because you didn't want us to tell her and we felt it was your story to tell."

There was a hint of censure in her voice. I didn't want the others to lie on my behalf, that wasn't fair on them.

"They're nice, you know. The others." Meera gestured vaguely at the door that led to the corridor where the other bedrooms were. "Tallulah and Verity are good people. They want to spend time with you. We all *want* to spend more time with you."

I didn't even taste what I was eating.

"Why?"

Meera blinked at me. "What do you mean *why*?"

"Why would you want to spend more time with me? I'm not really the kind of person that people seek out for company, and even if I was, being seen with me isn't good for establishing a long, happy future in the Shade realm. I'm basically a walking, talking silver dagger to the heart here."

"Astrid," Meera laughed, a sort of pitying, hysterical sound. "Is that how you think of yourself? That is so…"

"Realistic?"

"*Grim.*" Oh. "If people don't seek out your company, it's only because they're intimidated by you and—sorry to disappoint—but none of us are intimidated anymore."

"Because of my dud hand?"

"Because you're not half as scary as you think you are," Meera corrected, raising an eyebrow at me. "Because you care about things like our reputations and your sister's feelings, and the reason any of us are here, able to be courted by Shades who'd move heaven and earth if it would help them get in our pants is because of you. You thought of the solution, you thought of us, you made it happen. Astrid, I hate to break it to you, but I think you might be... *nice*."

"Take that back," I deadpanned, narrowing my eyes at her.

Meera was already shaking her head. "I can't, I've put it out in the universe now. I accept that you're still clearly in denial, and that's fine, but at least try spending some time with us, okay? Give the others a chance. Give *yourself* a chance."

I shot her a half-hearted glare, shoving another piece of meat in my mouth. Meera stood, looking far too pleased with herself.

"You can start today. Ophelia suggested we all get ready at the palace together for the ball, but Verity knew you'd feel overwhelmed so she's staying here so you two can get ready together and meet us there. Isn't that kind of her? It almost seems like the kind of thing friends do for one another..."

Meera wandered out of my room, humming contentedly to herself and I snorted quietly, finishing my breakfast in silence.

Maybe she was right.

I doubted I had a future in the Guard, whatever Allerick's plans were. I couldn't control my tongue enough around the Captain, it was only a matter of time before he succeeded in kicking me out. What was weird was how little that bothered me, and it wasn't just because they were Shades and they hated me.

Where had my competitive spirit gone?

The old Astrid would have rather died than failed to make the cut for *anything,* but these days I just wanted…

I just wanted…

What *did* I want?

The realization that I had no idea was chilling.

I finished my meal, heading downstairs to the always-empty kitchen to wash up, and restricting myself to one pickle. Tallulah and Meera left by early afternoon, and I vaguely remembered that getting ready for prom all those years ago had been an event itself. Snagging a bottle of spiced wine and two goblets on the way, I headed up to Verity's room at the end of the hall, feeling as though I was walking to the gallows.

The door swung open, and I did a double take, trying to work out what I was looking at. Verity's pink hair was wrapped in strips of white fabric, only her dark roots showing at the top. It sort of looked like she was sporting white tentacles, but whatever, I didn't know shit about fashion.

"Cool hair."

Her lips twitched. "I see you're new to the concept of rag curls. Come in."

Verity's room was almost identical to mine in layout, though it was on the other side of the corridor and her window faced towards the palace. The black trees hid it from view, but I knew it was there just 500 feet or so away, the brooding Captain of the Guard within its walls.

While my room was cold and sterile, Verity's was filled with personality. I'd brought back enough of her stuff on supply runs to know how many clothes she had, and most of them were strewn over every available surface and most of the floor.

"Wine?" I asked, picking my way through the sea of fabric to the dresser and setting the goblets down.

"Please. Are you going to let me do your hair?" I don't think I imagined the amusement in her voice.

"Why do I feel like you're all conspiring against me?" I sighed, uncorking the bottle with my teeth.

"We are. All aboard SS Friendship, first stop: hair braiding. Tallulah is sewing us matching dresses."

"You better be joking."

"Of course I'm joking, she's actually making friendship bracelets. Now, I'm thinking we do like a half-up, half-down thing and then go wild with a bold lip—make those Shade boys drool when they see your mouth."

"That... that's not a thing that happens to me." Interlude with the Captain, aside. And that hadn't been about *attraction*. That was just stress relief or something. A momentary break in sanity for both of us, perhaps.

"It is tonight. Besides, you must have some suitors, right?"

She accepted the goblet I handed her, clinking it against mine before taking a sip.

"Suitors?"

There was a seat she'd already set up in front of the dresser and I let her usher me into it, noticing a small hand mirror on the vanity. It had been so long since I'd seen my reflection, I wasn't even sure I wanted to look.

"Suitors. You know. Shades who are courting you." She perched on the edge of the dresser, goblet dangling from her fingers, and stared at me like this was something I was definitely supposed to know.

"Yeah, I definitely don't have any of those," I told her. "Do you?"

"Um, yeah. More than I know what to do with. I've fooled around a little, you know, see what all the fuss was about and do my part for feeding the power stores of the shadow realm."

"Generous of you," I deadpanned.

"I think so. Usually, I'd say if I have to fuck to save the world, I'll fuck to save the world, but I keep chickening out before it goes that far. Shades are just so possessive, you know? I don't want to give anyone the wrong idea about my commitment levels."

That sounded like a very rational idea that hadn't popped into my head even once when I'd been demanding Soren fuck me. Then again, there was no risk on either of our sides of commitment.

"But still, power is power and every little bit counts, right? I can't believe I spent so long miserable in the human realm when I could have been here, making miracles happen with my pussy." Verity shot me a sly grin that made me *pretty sure* she was messing with me, but not a hundred percent.

Meow.

I nearly jumped out of my skin at the sound, yanking my feet up off the ground as what I'd thought was a black furry item of clothing stood up and stretched, blinking bright yellow eyes at me.

"What the fuck is that?!"

Verity laughed, crouching down to scratch behind the beast's ears. "A cat, obviously."

"Like a human world cat or a shadow world cat?" I honestly couldn't tell. I hadn't seen any animals around the palace, so I had no idea if they were all black and gray with colored eyes like the Shades were, or if this was just a regular black cat.

"Do you think they have shadow realm cats? My boy is from the human realm, I smuggled him in my bag when I came here, but I think he's a little lonely cooped up in my room all the time."

Now that I was looking for the signs, I noticed a litterbox in the corner, as well as a bowl of water and an empty dish on the floor.

And black cat hair on *everything*.

"You forgot to bring your menstrual cup, but you managed to smuggle in a whole *cat*?"

Verity snorted. "The menstrual cup is great, don't get me wrong, but I am far more attached to the cat. There was no way I was coming here without him—his name is Fester, and he is my true love."

"Like... in a hypothetical true love way? Or in a you-need-an-intervention kind of way?"

She tilted her head to the side, considering, and I could have sworn Fester emulated her posture. "I mean, he's the only male in my life who has never let me down, so my love for him is possibly nearing intervention levels."

Fester yowled before strutting away to leap up on the bed, and I wondered how I hadn't noticed the cat sounds before. The stone walls must be thicker than I thought.

"You were engaged, right?" I asked as Verity stood, leaning against the counter again to sip her wine.

"Yes," she groaned. "God, don't remind me. No, it's fine, don't feel bad, I'm just being dramatic. I was engaged to the Hunter-iest Hunter you'll ever meet. *Sebastian*. He had that preppy, polo shirt-model kind of look that I was really into when I was seventeen, had high prospects in the Hunters, seemed to have a genuine interest in giving oral sex. It all seemed very meant-to-be."

I was sort of familiar with Sebastian—we'd been in regional knife-throwing contests together sometimes—but Verity was on a roll and I didn't know how to drop that information in naturally.

"He was very much college material, and the Hunters were totally happy to support him pursuing law school on their dime because lawyers are always handy to have around. Anyway, I am super *not* college material and I liked my retail job, so we decided to do long distance for a bit."

Verity set her goblet down, coming to stand behind me and sliding the tie out of my hair. Trust wasn't something that came naturally to me, and I fought not to spin around out of habit, not liking someone at my back.

"I guess I pursued some interests I shouldn't have while he was away. Or that's how it felt at the time. Now it's... whatever. I'm unpacking it. But my future mother-in-law poked around my apartment, found what she found, and that was it. Bye-bye, fiance. And Hunters, family, lifelong friends, and everyone else. I lost everything except Fester."

She gently combed the front bits of my hair back with her fingers, overlong acrylics scraping softly over my scalp.

"I'm glad you contacted me to come here, Astrid. The shadow realm just feels like... home. You know? Like I'm returning back to where I was always meant to be. Does it feel like that for you?"

"No? Kind of. I guess. I don't know."

I mean, it didn't *not* feel like home. But then again, everyone looked at me as though I'd just kicked their Fester.

Or potentially murdered their loved ones.

It was hard to feel at home somewhere you weren't wanted.

My silence must have dragged on awkwardly long because Verity suddenly rushed to fill it.

"You know, I thought when I came here that I'd be up to my guts in monster nuts, but I think I'm bored with casual. I want something *real*, get what I'm saying? But no one is really getting my motor running. I think my expectations might be too high."

"What are your expectations?" I asked curiously, wincing slightly as she untangled a knot of hair. "Surely, when entering an interspecies relationship, it's better to go in with no expectations at all. A completely open mind."

Fester meowed, and I liked to think he was agreeing with me. Maybe I needed a cat. Meera wouldn't have to worry about me being lonely if I had a cat.

"My mind is too open. Like I said, I've been taking test runs. Too many of these Shades seem to think that just because their dicks blow up like orgasm-giving balloons that they don't need to put in any work. Where's the creativity, my dude? Where's the effort?"

Orgasm-giving... balloons?

That was an objectively weird analogy for a penis. Nothing about Soren's member had felt balloon-like. Nor had it *looked* balloon-like, from what I'd seen.

"You were high up with the Hunters," Verity said before I could question her, leaning over me and peering at me with wide brown eyes. "Were they keeping any secrets?"

"Yes. Thousands. Millions, even."

"Right, right. But were they keeping any secrets about *types* of monsters? Are there others out there? Beings that aren't Shades?"

I frowned, both at the question and the lack of personal space. "No? Not that I know of, at least."

Verity straightened, huffing out a breath of irritation and muttering a string of curse words under her breath, as well as something that sounded suspiciously like 'tentacles'.

"Anyway, whatever. I want to know more about you, mysterious Astrid whom I'm trying to befriend. Tell me everything. Favorite food, hobbies, what you're missing most from the human realm."

"You really don't have to do all this," I replied as she fiddled with my hair, twisting half of it up and pinning it in place. "You're already going out of your way to help me get ready for the ball."

"Don't be so emo, it's not a hardship to make conversation with you, Astrid," Verity laughed, poking me in the shoulder. I twisted my hands together in my lap, to stop myself instinctively slapping her away.

Were other people always so touchy? I wasn't used to it and it was weird.

"Um, okay then. My favorite food is a cheeseburger with extra pickles. My hobbies... I don't know. Working out, I guess? I used to run a lot, and it was okay. Fun. Whatever. I miss music."

"Oh my god, *yes*. Music! I'd do *obscene* things for a basic, battery-operated MP3 player. Like take-a-long-hot-soak-in-holy-water-afterwards kind of obscene."

"Good to... know?"

"Mmhm. Showers, too. The Shades would lock me up for the things I'd do for a shower."

Verity moved around me, giving my face a scrutinizing look.

"We'll go heavy on the lips for drama, but keep it simple otherwise, yeah? You still want to look like you, after all."

"Right," I agreed as though I knew what I was talking about. I'd never really gotten a chance to do normal things like get ready for a girls' night out with friends. Or just *have* girls' nights out in general. I'd been on duty almost every night since I'd graduated high school. "Is that what you're doing?"

"Me?" Verity laughed. "Hell no. I'm going heavy on the lips, the eyes, the cheekbones, and if my hair doesn't defy gravity, I'll consider myself a failure. More is more is my style."

I could see that.

"Maybe I'll get lucky at the ball," Verity sighed. "I've found someone to *cover* me for the night, as they say—clothe me in shadows—but he really doesn't light my fire. Hey, maybe it's your turn, Astrid. Maybe you'll find a Prince Charming at the ball, and dance the night away in his arms. If you get to experience the inflation station firsthand, promise you'll tell me all about it."

"I don't really know what I'm agreeing to, but sure. Okay. I wouldn't want to knock the SS Friendship off course."

SOREN

CHAPTER 9

"I promise you, I have this under control," Selene assured me for the hundredth time, not quite able to mask her impatience. "Enjoy the ball, Captain. You deserve a night off."

"I don't *want* a night off," I retorted, glancing up at Allerick on the dais. He'd insisted that I attend the ball as a guest—something about enjoying my company—and I was still irritated with him for it.

The dining hall looked nice, at least. The smell of cooked meat filled the air, and the orbs had been dimmed, giving the room an air of mystery. The choir in the corner sang songs that were... well, if not upbeat, were at least pleasant to listen to.

"Will you be keeping an eye on Astrid?" Selene asked. "I have Verner on standby to monitor her, but I thought you may prefer to keep that task for yourself, given whatever happened yesterday."

Selene was fishing for information, and I had none to give her. Nothing I wanted to share, nothing that would make her happy to hear.

"Yes. Well, she won't be here. Everyone in the realm despises her."

Selene stared at a spot over my shoulder. "Well, maybe someone needs to tell *her* that."

I turned slowly. *No. Astrid wouldn't really show her face here.*

But there she was.

Standing near the entrance of the hall, as bold as can be.

The crowd parted for me as I crossed the ballroom floor. A hush had fallen over the room the moment Astrid appeared, everyone's eyes trained on her. Reluctantly, I could admit how impressive it was that she hadn't turned and run at the silent wave of hostility directed her way. It wasn't as though she wasn't aware of it. Astrid was many things, but obtuse wasn't one of them.

I'd been so intent on getting to her that it wasn't until I was close that I realized what she was wearing.

"Whose shadows are those?" I growled, stepping into her personal space so I wouldn't be overheard. It wasn't the question I'd *intended* to ask, but it was the one that had come out.

The dress was plain, even modest, compared to what most were wearing tonight. While the shadows clung to her form, they fully covered her chest and arms, trailing loosely from below the knees.

If I'd been thinking clearly, I'd have noticed that there was no lover's touch to the design, no care or thoughtfulness taken with it. Whoever had created it had done the bare minimum, but I wasn't thinking clearly and the bare minimum was enough.

Because even with no thoughtfulness, there was still *trust*. Who was this Shade that Astrid trusted enough to clothe her in front of most of the realm?

"*Who?*" I hissed, flexing my claws at my side.

I was the Captain of the Guard, one of the most powerful Shades in the kingdom, and I had the ear of the king. Most *Shades* were at least a little terrified of me, and yet Astrid was staring at me as though she'd never been less impressed with anyone in her life.

"None of your fucking business, *Captain*."

"Everything about you is my business, Hunter. Whose shadows are those?"

"You don't appear to be on duty tonight," Astrid replied breezily, sidestepping me and heading for the bar. "Surely, you can find a more entertaining way to spend your evening."

Oh, I could definitely think of a more entertaining way to spend my evening. Once I convinced whoever had clothed her to take back their shadows. I followed immediately, hoping I looked like a diligent guard rather than an obsessed Shade.

"Who the fuck does she think she is?" Adrastos said loudly, entertaining a small circle of Shades around him. "The king—"

"Will not take kindly to your criticism," I reminded him in a low voice, pausing at his back, fairly shaking with a potent mix of jealousy and frustration. "Consider your next words carefully."

"Of course, Captain," Adrastos agreed quickly, spinning on his heel and inclining his head respectfully at me. I took a moment to study him, just long enough to make him uncomfortable. To make him *aware*. I couldn't do anything about him disparaging Astrid—every Shade in the realm was probably doing that—but I could absolutely act on him disparaging the king if he was stupid enough to keep at it.

Satisfied that Adrastos would bite his tongue for now, I made my way to the drinks table where Astrid was sipping disinterestedly on a goblet of wine, surveying the room with practiced nonchalance. She wasn't fooling me—I knew that she was taking in every detail, assessing every risk, noting every exit. It should be another reason to distrust her, and yet I found her competency, her thoroughness, infuriatingly attractive.

They were attractive traits on a *normal* day, let alone when she was wearing red lipstick, her hair down and soft around her shoulders.

I strengthened the shadows covering my groin, just in case.

"You again?" Astrid said flatly, not bothering to look at me. "At this point, it's just sad. You should really consider getting some friends."

I was so stunned, it took me a moment to reply. "I have friends. *You* don't have friends."

She cut me a look out of the corner of her eye, the odd human gesture, the way her eyeballs moved around her head, still hard to get used to. "Wow, that's definitely the worst thing anyone has said to me since I moved here. How will I ever recover from such a devastating emotional blow?" she deadpanned, flicking her attention back to the rest of the room.

The dismissiveness was galling. No one dismissed me. I was the *Captain* of the fucking *Guard*.

I'd had her writhing on just the *tip* of my cock yesterday, left her outside Elverston House with my cum soaking through her pants. And now she was going to just turn away as though that had never happened? As though I was just anyone?

"Who clothed you?" I growled, hoping no one was eavesdropping because even to my own ears, I sounded feral.

"Maybe you have no friends because your conversation starters are so boring and repetitive."

"I want a name."

Astrid's lips twitched. "That's unfortunate."

Difficult woman. Fine. I could be difficult too.

I stepped in closer, reaching behind her for the jug of wine on the table, my chin almost brushing her shoulder in the process. "As I recall, you're far more chatty when you want to come. I could have you screaming the answer if I wanted to."

The oh-so-tempting sweetness of Astrid's arousal permeated the air, faint and yet incredibly fucking potent. There were horny ex-Hunters here tonight, dancing and flirting and making the entire place smell like every Shade's favorite meal, but nothing was as tempting to me as just the mere *hint* of Astrid's desire.

It's just the temptation of the forbidden, that's all.

The fact that she actively *fought* her arousal was an added layer of temptation. Astrid made me work for the sweet scent of her slick. For any hint of emotion whatsoever.

"I suppose I have to give you that one, but I'm in no rush to ask the Shade who so *generously* draped me in this *beautiful* shadow dress to remove it."

My hand tightened around the stem of my goblet. "Then I'll fuck you while you wear it. Better yet, I'll fuck you in front of them. Whose. Shadows. Are. These?"

Astrid turned her head towards me, lips almost brushing my jaw. "You sound like a jealous boyfriend, did you know that? For shame, Captain, salivating over the big, bad Hunter. Have you no self-respect?"

"And where was your self-respect, when your cunt was dripping for me on the floor of the entry room, hm?"

The scent of her desire grew stronger. "Apparently, we're both shameless."

"One of the few things we have in common. Meet me in the garden in five minutes. Where the path splits off towards Elverston House."

I was getting too bold. Only the fact that the entire ballroom smelled like the other former Hunters was providing any kind of cover. Astrid glanced at me uncertainly, chewing on the inside of her lip. If I'd been strategizing, I would have made it seem like her idea. Astrid's desire *for* me warred with her desire to tell me to go fuck myself.

"Fine, but only because this party is boring," she muttered. "Don't keep me waiting."

I watched her back for as long as I could, but Astrid had a remarkable gift for disappearing. She slipped away before she got to the main doors, despite the attention she drew from every Shade she passed.

Nodding greetings as I went, I made my way through the crowd to one of the more discreet side entrances, hoping that whichever Guard was stationed there would be deferent enough to not ask me any questions.

"Soren." *Fuck.* I paused mid-step as Allerick approached, questioning for the first time in my life if it was really *that* important to respect my king.

I did respect him. I just didn't want to *speak* to him. Not when my cock was so hard that I was finding it painful to walk.

"It's good to see you," Allerick said—borderline cheerfully, which was a little unsettling. He clapped me on the shoulder as I turned to face him fully, aiming for a relaxed stance that didn't give away how uncomfortable I was. "I assumed you'd have stationed yourself at one of the exits, regardless of what I said about you having a night off."

"Selene has it under control," I replied tightly, because I owed her that much at least. She was excellent at what she did, and it wasn't fair that my inability to delegate might reflect poorly on her.

"Yes, Selene knows what she's doing," Allerick agreed, surveying the crowd. His gaze drifted back to Ophelia every few seconds, checking that she was safe and happy as she chatted away to Damen. "Did you send Astrid away? You know she was invited here tonight, along with all the other former Hunters."

Fuck.

"No?" That didn't come out as assertively as I'd intended.

Allerick gave me a disapproving look. "I hope not. We're trying to get everyone used to having the Hunters—*former* Hunters—here. Plenty of Shades still have their concerns, and they're completely reasonable ones, but I want to allay them. You're a big part of that, Soren. They look to you, they trust your judgment."

He'd delivered the words casually, but I received them as a condemnation. As though he'd known what I'd done with Astrid yesterday, what I was intending to do again.

"I'm not the one you go to for matters of public opinion. That's more Damen's strong suit."

"Damen has already made his position clear. He's been openly flirting with every ex-Hunter here, with the exception of my wife of course. And her sister," he added after a moment. I couldn't tell if he was staring at me or if my guilt was making me imagine things.

"Well, that's Damen. Flirty."

"Yes. But also looking for happiness." Allerick hesitated. "Your naturally suspicious nature makes you excellent at your job, but you're more than just the Captain, Soren. I know this Meridia situation is stressing you out, but you deserve to find happiness too."

Right. *Right.* My sister who was in the Pit, awaiting sentencing any day now. That probably was what *should* have my attention, but I'd mostly put it out of my mind. I'd *chosen* to put it out of my mind.

I'd tried over and over again to pull Meridia off the path she was on, and she'd ignored me every single time. For my own sanity, I had to let my anger go.

"How was training, by the way? I didn't get a chance to ask you how it went with Astrid."

This was the opening I would have been thrilled with yesterday. The perfect opportunity to tell him that it wasn't going to work, that Astrid was too confrontational, too disrespectful, too polarizing.

But we'd agreed that she was there for now. That I was "stuck" with her for now. It would be dishonorable to go back on my word, and that was the only reason why I didn't jump on the chance he'd inadvertently given me.

"You want her to train with the Guard, so she's training with the Guard. I can't pretend to understand your reasoning, but I trust you know what you're doing."

Mostly. Sort of.

Allerick sighed. "Partly, I'm trying to keep my wife happy, but I would like for Astrid to find her place here. To find her *peace* here. Shades are stubborn, and Astrid has come to be a symbol of everything they hate. In their eyes, Astrid will always be *what* she is. Who she is doesn't matter. I'm not sure it ever will, but I have to try. What if others like her want to come here? See the error of their ways and want to change? Astrid being accepted here, truly accepted, could herald real change for the relationship between Shades and Hunters."

I nodded stiffly, seeing the logic in his argument even if I was struggling to emotionally remove myself from the situation. We were in danger in the human realm, and if we only accepted Hunters here with perfectly clean slates, then we'd probably starve.

"Obviously, it's all easier said than done," Allerick added off-handedly, already wandering away to speak to one of the Councilors waiting patiently nearby. "Contributing to the stores requires a partner."

Like the idea of Astrid finding anyone to fuck her was ludicrous. Like anyone would lower themselves enough to do such a thing.

Astrid was waiting in the garden for me, and my brain helpfully supplied the delicious scent of her need on demand, urging me to seek her out. And why shouldn't I? It was just fucking. It didn't have to mean anything.

But did I want to be that Shade? The one who *lowered* themselves to being with the most hated ex-Hunter in the realm? I didn't go against the grain, I didn't rock the boat. Being Captain of the Guard meant making the *right* call at all times, the sensible decision that benefitted the many, not the few. My reputation had suffered enough by association with my sister, was I really willing to risk another hit?

I slipped out of the ballroom and went back to my room.

ASTRID

CHAPTER 10

"Oh my god, I need an ice bath for my lady bits," Tallulah groaned, slumping awkwardly until she was half-sprawled on the sofa. "We're not ever returning to the human realm, right? Can we make a pact or something? I miss Wi-Fi and I'd sell a kidney for some chicken nuggets and an icy soda, but the *sex*." She sighed, fanning her face dramatically. "I'm not going back to regular sex after—"

I slipped out of the front door before I could hear the rest, swallowing down the bitterness that had arisen in my throat. I'd only been in there for five minutes and all the former Hunters were lounging around in the sitting area this morning, either exchanging stories of flirty dances with courting Shades, or bemoaning the state of the aches and pains they'd gotten in the most intimate of places, and I couldn't take anymore.

Some of us hadn't gotten laid last night. Some of us hadn't even been courted. Some of us had hidden in the chilly garden, horny and alone, shortly followed by *humiliated* and alone.

At least no one had seen me leave. I'd managed to escape back to Elverston House to lick my wounds in private, too annoyed with myself and too embarrassed to even masturbate away the lingering ache between my thighs.

Fucking Soren.

What had I been thinking? He'd never had any intention of following me into that fucking garden. He hadn't wanted me to attend the ball, and he'd found an embarrassingly easy way to make me leave.

I shouldn't have let Ophelia talk me into going in the first place. It wasn't *for* me. It was for the other ex-Hunters—the ones who possessed both Shade catnip pussies *and* unproblematic pasts.

Angry at myself all over again, I stomped through the gardens surrounding Elverston House to the small courtyard I'd taken to working out in. It was a fairly grim place—the paving stones were broken, black weeds sprouting through cracks, and the decorative iron fences twisted and menacing. At least it kept my instincts sharp—one wrong move and I'd be impaled on a broken fence, or succumb to a head injury if I fell.

I picked up the black branch I'd been using to train with, adjusting to the feel of the weight of it in my hand. It looked substantially heavier than the shadow batons the Guards used during training, but it would better prepare me if I ever did have to fight with a sword.

The chances of anyone letting me use one were pretty unlikely, but I liked to be prepared.

I pushed myself until my muscles burned, shooting pains an almost constant presence in my left arm. My entire life, I'd been able to rely on both hands in combat, and I still attempted to brace my weight on my left hand out of habit when I hit the ground.

It was an infuriating weakness.

"Astrid!" Ophelia called, her voice coming from the garden near the front of the house. I doubted she'd find me here—no one else seemed inclined to venture through the spiky vines to get to this place.

"Astrid!" Ophelia yelled, more impatiently this time. I set the branch aside with a quiet laugh, a wave of nostalgia washing over me. Hadn't she yelled at me like that when we were young? Standing at the bottom of the staircase, hollering for me to come down to dinner?

Sometimes I wasn't sure if those memories were real or if I was just making up happy sibling moments to ease my guilty conscience.

I slipped through the tangled vines, snagging my shirt on a thorn in the process, clambering out of the overgrowth at the side of the house. Ophelia was already standing there, looking impressively vicious in a blood-red dress, arms crossed over her chest.

"I don't even want to know," she muttered, glancing at the jungle behind me. "You do know some plants here are poisonous, right?"

I discreetly picked at the tear on my shirt, just above my hip. "I'm careful. What are you doing here?"

"I came to check on everyone after last night, but you'd already slipped out. And you left the ball so early, I didn't even get a chance to speak to you. Didn't you like it? You looked beautiful, I saw you come in."

I must have been starved for affection, because that off-handed compliment made my throat feel strangely tight.

"Thank you. So did you. Sorry, I didn't get a chance to see you. Balls aren't my scene, I guess."

"Maybe you can work the next one?" Ophelia suggested optimistically. "Be one of the guards on the doors. That seems more your speed. You have training soon, right?"

Right. It had been delayed today to give everyone extra time to sleep in after the ball.

And I hadn't intended on going. I never wanted to see Captain Soren's stupid face again, and I didn't care enough about anyone's opinion here to subject myself to the humiliation of showing up there after he'd ghosted me.

"Yes. I'm going to soak first, rest my muscles," I told Ophelia, mostly as an excuse to be alone.

"Oh yes, you should do that. See you at dinner?"

"Of course."

I shot her a tight smile, heading inside and straight downstairs to the hot pool. After stripping off my sweat-soaked clothes and lounging in the almost-scalding water for a while, my resolve hardened.

As much as I wanted to despise everything about him, I didn't actually think the Captain was *cruel* by nature. From everything I'd seen of him, he was fair, but also valued holding the moral high ground.

I didn't think he'd actually feel *good* about ditching me in that garden. In fact—and it was a gamble—I was pretty sure he'd feel super shitty about it, and I wanted him to really marinate in that guilt by getting all up in his face.

So, no. I wasn't going to *skip* training.

I was going to go to training and be as obnoxiously present as possible, like the mature, well-rounded, 26-year-old woman I was. Fuck it.

Dressed in head-to-toe black fitted workout clothes, I slipped out of Elverston House without alerting the others and made my way through the gardens to the training grounds. As always, I felt eyes on me the whole way, but I didn't think they were the Captain's. There was an intensity to *his* gaze that made me feel like I was caught in a predator's trap.

"The Hunter is here," someone called out, the moment I entered the training grounds. Everyone was already sparring, and fewer of them paused to stare at me than last time. Progress.

Soren's gaze snapped to mine from the opposite side of the yard, orange eyes blazing a little brighter. I stared defiantly back at him, refusing to cower. Refusing to let him see any evidence of the humiliation I'd felt last night.

You want a battle of wills, Captain? Bring it on. No one can suppress emotional responses quite like I can.

Selene cleared her throat as our staring contest went on long enough for those around us to notice.

"Hunter. You're with me." The Captain's low, growled command traveled down the length of my spine. He'd always had a nice voice, but after hearing the things he'd said to me in that *nice* voice the other day…

Then again, he'd used that *nice* voice last night too, and look how that had ended up?

Selene wrinkled her nose at me as I passed her, trailing behind Soren to a free spot among the already sparring Shades. He turned to face me, extending his hand in front of him, palm up. I did my best to keep my expression entirely neutral and unimpressed as shadows gathered in the center of Soren's hand, swirling and morphing into a black staff. He tossed it to me without any preamble, and I just managed to snatch it out of the air before I embarrassed myself while he formed a staff of his own.

Soren moved closer, and with how far away the other Shades were standing, it felt like it was just the two of us here.

"Just so you're aware," Captain Soren said casually, sliding his foot back into a combat position while I did the same. "I know your cunt is wet for me right now."

I tightened my grip on the staff, vaguely trying to disintegrate the strange shadow-like material in my fist.

"Just so you're aware, you're full of shit," I replied flatly, hoping that the sounds of the Shades sparring around us would drown out this conversation.

Soren tilted his head to the side. "Well, I suppose your physical reaction *could* have been caused by something—some*one*—else. But your pussy is wet. I know it, everyone here knows it."

How hard would I have to throw this shadow javelin for it to go clean through his chest?

"It's your scent," Soren continued, still infuriatingly smug. "When you—or any of the other former Hunters—are horny, you emit the most mouth-watering smell—"

"Good to know," I clipped, mortification comfortably setting into every cell of my body. I'd been aware on a basic level that Shades had an exceptional sense of smell, and he'd warned me that I smelled like him after he'd all but doused me in cum, but I hadn't realized it was so acute that it could pick up the faintest whiff of arousal.

Why the *fuck* had my sister not mentioned this?

More importantly, how did I *stop* it? Hadn't I given up enough without sacrificing the right to feeling horny in private? Had I been advertising exactly how I was feeling last night in that ballroom?

I'd have been *far* more discreet if I'd known that was a risk.

The guards were standing back but watching Soren and me closely enough for me to know exactly what they were thinking, and *fuck that*. Had Soren gotten me off in spectacular fashion in that entry room? Yes. Did I need anyone to know about that?

Fuck no.

Fuck no on toast. Fuck no with sprinkles on top. This guy—*this fucking guy*—hated me, and everyone knew it. God knows what they'd think of me for dropping my panties for him.

Or worse, for going into the garden with the expectation of dropping my panties for him, and him not showing up.

"Well, I can't help that Selene looks so fucking hot today," I said, meeting Soren's eyes and speaking just loud enough for those close enough to hear me. "Women—sorry, *females*—in power really do it for me, you know?"

His eyes flickered. "Is that so? Enough to let them clothe you?"

"Still stuck on that, are we?" I dropped into a fighting position, tossing the staff in my good hand a couple of times, getting accustomed to the feel of it. Somehow it felt both solid and not, all at once. "As it happens, it *was* a powerful female who clothed me. And unclothed me."

Technically, all that had happened was I'd wandered out of range of Levana, and the shadows had disappeared, revealing the tight slip I'd borrowed from Verity underneath, but whatever. Captain Abandon-A-Ho didn't need to know that.

Judging by the way Soren tightened his jaw, claws flexing slightly around his staff, my taunt had worked. He dropped down, and I copied his posture, raising the staff to shoulder height. While I had no doubt that this conversation wasn't over yet, I'd temporarily gotten the upper hand.

Fighting with a staff didn't come naturally to me—in general, Hunters weren't trained in close combat—but hopefully, the training I'd been doing with the branch would be enough for me to hold my own. Or at least, not entirely embarrass myself.

I struck first, darting forward, my hit meeting Soren's block. There was no satisfying thud of shadow-on-shadow, no vibration in my hand as they made contact, and I was forced to rely on my sense of sight far more than I usually did in training.

For a while, we moved in silence, an unrehearsed dance, one darting forward, the other sliding back. He was going easy on me, moving far slower than I knew he was capable of, and it spurred me on, making me work harder to try to land a hit.

While I still didn't particularly care if the Guard wanted me or not, I could admit that sparring with Soren made me feel more like my old self than I had in a long time.

"About last night," the good Captain began, ruining the silence. He was deliciously guilty, just as I expected. Even with his mostly unreadable face, that much was obvious.

"No."

He stilled for a moment, darting just in time to dodge the swipe of my staff. "No? What do you mean, *no*?"

"I mean exactly that," I grunted in exertion, twisting like a pretzel to avoid his strike. *No. If you make me talk about this, I might stab you and I'm really working on my murderous reputation.*

"I have things I'd like to say." He sounded so genuinely affronted that I wondered how often anyone said 'no' to him.

"Therefore I'm obligated to listen? I can't imagine what it's like having that level of confidence in the importance of my opinions."

Soren growled in frustration, the show of emotion making him sloppy. I didn't hesitate, dropping low and thrusting the staff upwards. At the last moment, he twisted his upper body, my strike glancing off his arm rather than impaling him through the stomach like I'd intended. Not that I thought the shadow batons could do any real damage, but it was the principle of the thing.

Taking advantage of my flash of disappointment, Soren swept my legs out from under me, and I lost my balance, flailing slightly as gravity betrayed me.

So fucking rude, as if I wasn't having a bad enough day.

Before I could crack my skull on the stone ground, I found myself being dragged upwards, Soren's obnoxious face drawing closer. It took me a moment to register that he'd caught me by the front of my top, but as I found my footing and the stretching fabric relaxed, it became *very* clear where his hand was. Even through my nylon workout top and sports bra, I could feel the delicate scrape of his claws against my breasts.

Fuckkkkkkkkkk. That felt way too good, and I was probably broadcasting that fact to every member of the Guard right now.

I shoved him back, panting heavily as I set my best bedroom eyes on a Shade sparring just beyond Soren. Verner, wasn't it? One of the guards stationed at the royal wing of the palace?

It wasn't as though it was a hardship to admire his form. He moved with exquisite grace, like the most violent ballerina, twirling his staff elegantly and efficiently, no movement wasted. Verner didn't get my motor running the way Soren did, but it wasn't a hardship to stare at him and pretend.

"Are you tapping out then?" Soren asked irritably, leaning into my line of sight. His irritation was music to my ears.

"I mean, what am I supposed to do? *Not* admire the finest combat form I've ever seen?" I replied breathily, laying it on a little thick. "Look at that footwork—"

The ground shifted from under me again, but this time I was pitched forward, twisting in midair so my face was hurtling towards the ground. Soren caught me around the waist as though he hadn't been the one to knock me over, his oddly firm lips brushing over the shell of my ear.

"You're a beautiful liar," Soren purred.

"Cheap shot," I snapped, stomping on his instep and twisting out of his grip—his *embrace*—and catching myself on the ground with my bad hand. Pain rocketed up my arm, sharp and uncomfortable, as I ground my teeth to sawdust to stop myself from crying out.

For a moment, everything seemed to seize up, my entire arm jarring as agony paralyzed me in place. No one could know how bad this injury actually was. I'd be handing myself over on a platter if they did.

Soren gazed down at me impassively, both his staff and mine suddenly vanishing.

"The Hunter is unwell," Soren announced while I silently fumed, even if the wave of pain had made me nauseous. "I will return her to the border of Elverston House. Apparently, Hunters don't have the stamina of Shades."

Soren scooped me up, throwing me over his shoulder where my head smacked against his ridiculously solid back, though he was oddly careful not to knock my injured arm. That small act of kindness didn't make me feel any better about the fact that everyone else was laughing at me, patting themselves on the back, and celebrating their physical superiority over the weak little Hunter.

"You are such a stupid, obnoxious asshole," I muttered against Soren's back.

ASTRID

CHAPTER 11

"Put me down," I demanded as we moved away from the others, wriggling to try to get out of his hold.

"I don't think I will. I much prefer you when you're all contained like this. Tied up would be even better."

"You tie me up, I'll cut your dick off."

"You'd only be depriving yourself."

The fucking *audacity*.

"Weird. As I recall, *you* are the one who keeps depriving me. Not that I want it," I added hastily. "I'm not going to lose sleep over the half an inch of dick you graciously gave me access to once before skipping out on me entirely."

Soren hummed, an annoyingly ambivalent sound. How had I ended up in this position? I was meant to be kicking ass at training, showing him just how fine I was on my own while simultaneously crippling him with guilt. Instead, I was thrown over his shoulder like a sack of potatoes, and he definitely wasn't taking me to the border of Elverston House. We were vaguely going in the right direction, but he'd veered west towards the river.

Away from prying eyes.

"Oh, I think you're more than a little upset about both those things," Soren crooned. *Crooned!* He didn't pull out this bullshit, panty-melting voice on anyone else. Asshole. "Lying little liar."

"I'm not lying. I'm not upset." I was both lying and upset. "I have vibrators, I don't need you and your unreliable— Wait, what are you doing?!"

The surface of the river loomed up at me as Soren waded into its gray depths.

"Cooling you off," he replied, almost cheerfully, gripping me tightly so I couldn't escape. Before I could be submerged head first, he flipped me back over his shoulder dropping me into the water on my back. I sucked in a breath at the last moment, scrambling to find the ground beneath me and straightening. The water wasn't *quite* as icy as I thought it would be, and it came to just below my shoulders, moving slowly enough that I didn't feel as though I was going to be dragged away.

I wasn't sure if it was the cold or if the water had some kind of healing properties, but the worst of the pain in my hand ebbed away, leaving behind a dull ache and the constant feeling of weakness in my fingers.

Still.

"Are you trying to kill me?" I spluttered, wiping water out of my eyes and instantly regretting it when I saw how good Soren looked soaking wet. The water lapped at his chest, drawing attention to the smooth, defined muscles. *His shadows had vanished.*

Was this his version of stripping off for a swim? Did the shadows not hold up in water?

Was he naked *everywhere*?

"If I wanted you dead, you'd be dead, Hunter. Like I said, I was cooling you off." He tilted his head to the side, examining me. "It doesn't appear to have worked. Perhaps I should submerge you again."

"No thanks," I replied, instinctively taking a step backward.

He snorted, so much more at ease now we were away from the others. "It's cute you think you could get away from me."

"I can swim."

"I can swim faster."

"I can run."

Soren's eyes flashed. "Don't tempt me."

I huffed a noise of frustration—only one percent sexual—as I waded toward the bank, feeling Soren's eyes on me the whole time. I was going to make him rue the day he was born if these sneakers were ruined, it wasn't like I had shoes to spare.

"Going so soon?" Soren taunted.

"What is this?" I snapped, turning back to face him. The water was only up to my thighs here, and a chill was starting to set in to my upper body, but I planted my good hand firmly on my hip anyway. Crossing my arms over my chest felt too defensive, too much like an admission of vulnerability. "Why are you doing this? Is it an ego thing? We've clearly established that I want to fuck you. I'd be doing this whole realm a favor by fucking you, earning my keep on my back like a good little Hunter. So follow through or don't, Captain. I'm sick of this game."

"There's no game." He sounded sincere, but I didn't trust my own judgment anymore.

"What do you want from me?"

Soren took a slow, deliberate step forward. "Things that I shouldn't, mostly. Not from *you*."

I swallowed thickly. "Because I'm a Hunter?"

"Because you're *the* Hunter."

With one more step, he'd closed the gap between us, his claws plucking at the clinging fabric of my soaked workout top.

"Then you should let me go," I whispered, suddenly struggling to find my voice. "Leave me alone. I'll tell Allerick myself that this whole Guard idea didn't work out, and you can never speak to me again."

Soren hummed. "I should do that, shouldn't I? You're beautiful and deadly—an elegant silver blade pressed right above my heart." The words were resentful and romantic, delivered with enough sweetness to almost disguise the poison. "I should do more than just let you go, *Astra*. I should kill you while I have the chance."

It was always nice to be reminded that I was embarrassing myself over someone who acted like he didn't even know my name. Or worse, *actually* didn't know my name.

He picked up my hand, flipping it over and gripping my wrist. Viciously sharp claws pressed against my veins, just enough to make my heart start pumping a little faster. For a moment, neither of us moved. I wasn't even sure I took a breath, waiting to see if this was the end, wondering if I had a hope in hell of fighting back.

Eventually, Soren lifted his other hand, dragging one claw down my palm, ghosting over the bandage that covered my stitches, tingles following in his wake.

"It's no easy thing, owing a life debt to someone like you."

"Someone like me? You don't know anything about me, Captain," I rasped, heart thundering in my chest. "You've just decided that based on *one* thing, you know *everything*. And you don't owe me shit—I can survive just fine without you owing me a favor."

Soren slowly released my hand before swiping the lower half of my top with his claws, faster than I could even blink. Despite how heavy the sodden fabric was, it tore like tissue paper, parting to reveal a pale sliver of stomach.

"I could have killed you ten times over just in this conversation." Soren smirked, tugging the ripped fabric until I was wearing a makeshift crop top. "Don't give away your one advantage out of pride."

Goosebumps broke out over my exposed belly, only some of them from the cold. "You ruined my top."

"If you want to save your garments, take them off. It's not your clothes I'm interested in ruining."

Don't do it, don't do it, don't do it.

He stood you up last night.

Where's your goddamn self-respect, Astrid?

The sex won't be worth it.

Except my hands didn't seem to be getting the memo, because they were already yanking the remnants of my top over my head. Goddamn it.

"I want you to know that I don't like you," I muttered, tossing the shirt on the bank before climbing up onto the soft ground, Soren following a lot less clumsily. "That this is just stress relief for me. A way to get this weird urge out of my system. And that no one can ever know about this. *No one*. Especially my sister."

Soren shrugged, covering the ground with some kind of shadow blanket and tipping his chin at it in silent instruction to get on the ground. Well, fuck that. I may have to take orders from him as Captain of the Guard, but I sure as hell wasn't going to do it in the bedroom.

Or on a bank next to the river, only semi-hidden by bushes.

That gave me pause. Weren't we a little exposed here? It was unlikely that one of the ex-Hunters would venture down here from Elverston House—generally, they either stayed there or went to the palace—but it wasn't impossible. And we were far enough out from the boundary that Shades could easily wander past—

Suddenly, a wall of shadows went up around us, shrouding us in semi-darkness.

"Consider this the equivalent of your human 'do not disturb' sign," Soren said smugly. "It's not soundproof, so I suggest you stay quiet if you're so set on keeping this a secret."

"We both have a vested interest in keeping this quiet. We already established that," I challenged, trying not to let on how much I was shivering as I kicked off my waterlogged sneakers and peeled off saturated leggings.

Soren stared unabashedly at my clumsy strip show, like I'd shocked him into silence by undressing. I finished dropping my panties, and Soren was on me before I could come up with another snarky comment, half tackling me to the ground, twisting to bear the brunt of the fall before rolling me onto my back.

"You're freezing," he said, sounding surprised, covering my body with his. I spread my legs further apart to accommodate his hips, slightly overwhelmed by just how *big* he was. How commandeering.

I wasn't some shy, retiring maiden. Before I'd lost everything, I'd had a very healthy sex life—men, women, whoever I was attracted to on any given day. None of it had meant anything beyond a pleasurable experience, and I'd always been clear about that.

One thing I'd *never* been was the less dominant partner. It wasn't even that I necessarily *preferred* to be the dominant one, it was just... how it had always been.

"Are you going to catch some kind of illness if you stay out here?" Soren pressed, his voice a low murmur as he ran his claws lightly up and down my side. "Are Hunters too fragile for a quick fuck out in the wilderness?"

"I don't know. Maybe if you ever stop talking and start fucking, we'll find out," I snapped, pressing my feet flat against the ground and lifting my hips, trying to ease the desperate craving between my thighs for friction.

I froze almost instantly, startled by the... *unexpected* feeling of his cock. I thought our brief interlude in the entry room had prepared me, but... no. No, I hadn't expected that kind of *thickness*.

"Getting second thoughts, Astra? You can always change your mind, I won't be offended." Soren leaned down, and for a moment, I thought he was going to kiss me, but instead he shifted to the side, the tips of his fangs scraping my shoulder.

Probably for the best. Fucking was one thing, kissing was another.

"It's *Astrid*. And don't you dare bite me," I hissed, grabbing a horn and yanking his head back. Except I remembered just how good his teeth had felt in my dream, and my scent probably gave away just how much I'd liked it.

Soren groaned, arching into my touch. "Don't worry, I can't imagine anything worse than being bonded to you. Fuck, that feels good. Grab the other one."

I could have fun with this.

With just as little gentleness, I grabbed his other horn, giving his head a rough tug that drew out another deliciously low moan before shoving him down where I wanted him.

Soren inhaled my pussy like he'd die if he didn't, and it made everything in me clench in the most delicious way.

"You're being very subtle," he murmured, voice dripping with arrogance. "What exactly is it you want?"

"Not this again. I'm not going to beg; either lick my pussy or get out of the goddamn way so I can satisfy myself."

He snorted. "I'll take pity on you and your dainty fingers this time."

Vicious claws dug into my delicate inner thighs, pinning me in place. I vaguely worried for the safety of my labia, but Soren was cautious, using his tongue to pry me apart, the rough texture of it rubbing against my clit and making me gasp.

Surely... Surely this level of pleasure was illegal.

I didn't want to admit, not even to myself, how incredibly good Soren's tongue felt. I knew what good head felt like, and this was an entirely different level. The contrast of his roughness and my smoothness, the way everything about him was so *different*, so inhuman, and yet he still seemed to fit me so well... It was all making me question whether this was real, or if I'd fallen asleep in the hot pool and this was all a particularly elaborate dream sequence.

I jolted backward instinctively as Soren dragged his long tongue down, swirling teasingly—dexterously—at my entrance before slowly pushing into my pussy. *Burrowing.* His claws on my thighs tightened to the point of pain to keep me in place, and my pussy clenched in response. I was faintly aware of another gush of slick, but Soren caught it with his tongue, growling his approval.

And strangely, deliciously, it was enough to set me off. The bite of pain, the thick fullness of his tongue, the way I was pinned down beneath Soren's bulk, even the fact that he didn't *like* me. It gave me the rush I'd always enjoyed when I was out hunting, that thrill of danger.

Soren did his best to lick up every drop of slick as though he'd never tasted anything more delicious, and it was a valiant effort, but there was just *so much*.

Was this normal?

I was going to need a gallon of water after this. Maybe some electrolytes.

"Hold your thighs up," Soren commanded, sitting back and swiping his tongue obscenely over his lips, chasing the remnants of my slick on his face. "Don't worry, dainty Astra. I'll be gentle with you."

I kept my feet planted resolutely on the ground, glaring up at him. "I don't need you to go easy on me. I can handle everything you throw my way."

More than that, I *needed* him not to go easy on me. There was no room here for tenderness. This was about fucking the incessant need out of each other, and the more Soren reminded me that he hated me, the better off I'd be.

He fisted his shaft lazily, looking down at me with the most obnoxiously smug expression I'd ever seen. "Hands on your thighs, legs up. Show me what I want to see. Better yet, roll over and present your cunt to me like the good little prey you are."

"You're out of your fucking mind if you think I'm giving you my back," I all but snarled, wrapping my hands behind my knees and pulling my legs up. "Clearly you're talking so much because you can't deliver—"

He filled me in one brutal thrust, knocking the wind from my lungs and the soul from my body.

I needed to say something, to snark at him and put him in his place. He had the upper hand, and I couldn't let that slide.

"Look at you," Soren rasped, annoyingly capable of speech while my tongue seemed to be flailing like a loose sail in my mouth. "You're really rather pretty, when you aren't hissing and snapping like a feral beast."

"I hate you," I shot back, my voice all stupid and breathy because apparently this particular Shade had a magic dick that could fuck that anger right out of me. Almost.

Soren pressed down on my shins, forcing my legs further up to my shoulders. My leg muscles burned, but his cock hit a spot inside me that I didn't know existed, so I wasn't about to move.

"I think there's some parts of me you're quite fond of."

I gasped for breath, pussy clenching around him, idly wondering if they had ball gags in this realm. Soren would look good in a ball gag.

Not that we were doing this again.

Satisfied he'd won that round, Soren began rocking into me with shallow thrusts, maintaining his firm pressure on my legs. Was he even all the way in? I felt full, *so fucking full*, and yet his hips didn't seem to be touching me.

I was going to burn out all of my vibrators remembering this moment.

For the briefest moment, Soren looked down at me with something startingly close to *possessiveness*. Like he was fucking because I was *his*. I wasn't scared of him, but the intensity in his gaze was mildly terrifying.

"Harder," I hissed. "We're never doing this again. Fuck me like you mean it."

Soren flashed his fangs, sending a pulse of desire to my pussy that I didn't want to question. His thrusts grew more forceful, the thin shadow blanket beneath my back not doing much to protect me from the rocks and sticks digging into my skin, but I barely felt them.

"Fuck," I whispered, tightening my grip on the back of my knees. *More, more, more.* It felt so good, and I knew that my impending orgasm was going to drag me to depths I hadn't yet reached, but there was still a *craving*. An itch under my skin, something else I wanted but didn't know how to articulate.

"I can't stop," Soren rasped, finally starting to sound as undone as I felt, except his hips didn't quite press against me with each thrust. "I *can't*."

"Don't stop," I managed to reply, yanking my knees back as far as I could, greedy for him. "I'm on birth control."

There was a flash of an expression on Soren's face that I couldn't quite read, though I struggled to interpret his looks at the best of times.

And then he pushed forward, bearing down on me fully, and somehow his cock felt even *thicker*.

And then thicker still.

Like it was *growing*.

What the fuck?

SOREN

CHAPTER 12

My knot expanded so rapidly, it made my head spin. As though if I didn't quickly trap Astrid's body with my own, she'd vanish from right out under me.

She'd disappear and this one-off, get-it-out-of-our-systems moment, would be over.

I'd never come so hard in my life, and I hoped it soaked into every inch of Astrid's body, forever marking her with my scent. The shadows hiding us flickered as I struggled to keep hold of them, to focus on anything other than Astrid and how good she felt around me.

Dangerous. Wickedly, deliciously, *perfectly* dangerous.

"What the actual fuck?" Astrid whispered, eyes wide as she looked between our bodies, a faintly appalled expression on her face. "What *is* that? What is happening right now?"

"What is what?" I asked mildly, impressed that my voice didn't betray just how lost to desire I was. I'd never knotted anyone before, and the level of pleasure was indescribable. Addictive.

And the *power*. Goddesses. It was like feeding on a hundred humans at their most fearful, all at the same time. I'd never felt so full, so *strong* before.

Astrid placed her palms flat on my chest, attempting to put some space between us which absolutely was not happening while we were locked together. I grunted at the sudden pressure on my knot and Astrid made a noise somewhere between a moan of desire and a squeal of surprise as another orgasm rocked her. A sound that I was confident I would never hear again—Astrid didn't make mistakes twice, and I had no doubt she'd consider letting me hear a noise that adorable a mistake.

"Why is your dick *stuck* inside me?!" she gritted out, cunt convulsing around me as her orgasm rocked her body.

"You really didn't know about the knot? I thought you ex-Hunters would have talked about this kind of thing? Especially, since the ball..."

From what I'd heard, the ball had been on the verge of devolving into a full-blown orgy when Allerick had broken it up and sent everyone to bed. The hall was still saturated in the scent of horny ex-Hunters, and would be for days. Surely, they'd mentioned *something* this morning.

"A *knot*? Oh my god, oh my god, oh my god. This is not happening," Astrid whispered under her breath, attempting to disentangle our bodies again before immediately relaxing into another languid orgasm.

The edge of panic in her voice brought me sharply back to reality. I didn't want to be knotted to a woman who didn't want to be knotted to me, which was unfortunate, because boneless-with-pleasure was the most tolerable Astrid had ever been.

Though perhaps I was lying to myself, not wanting to admit how much I'd enjoyed sparring with her. She was brazenly disrespectful, which was an invigorating change, and she threw everything she had into each movement. She was confident, competent, and competitive. The three Cs that I found more desirable than almost anything else.

"The more you stimulate it, the longer it will go on," I rasped, struggling to think straight while she was draining my balls dry. "Just stay still and it'll go down."

"How long will it take? Sex is one thing, your company is another," she snapped, holding her body frozen in place. "*Orgasm-giving balloons,*" she muttered under her breath to herself, shaking her head.

"I'm not sure, I've never knotted anyone before," I replied, wishing we weren't facing each other. Trying to wish that I'd pulled out, or that we hadn't crossed this line into insanity in the first place, but not quite succeeding. Even though nothing good could come from this, it had been the best sex and most satisfying feed of my life. With Astrid, there was always a fourth C to consider—complications.

She was looking at me like she wanted to ask me *why* I'd never knotted anyone before. Another complication, another question I didn't want to answer.

"I'm going to roll us to our sides," I warned before she could speak. "You'll probably come again."

"The fuck I will," Astrid snarled, her pussy immediately fluttering around me as I shifted us, awkwardly tucking my arms into my side because I was pretty sure she'd slice one off if I suggested she rest her head on my bicep.

I shot her a smug smile as her orgasm rocked through her, and she bared her teeth at me like a tiny little beast.

She was fighting her pleasure, trying not to let on how good it felt, but the way she subconsciously kept exposing her neck to me gave her away. Objectively, neither of us wanted the mating claim, but in the throes of passion…

Was it really the worst idea to claim her for myself? For Astrid to be all mine?

Fuck. I'd thought Astrid was beautiful and addictive, terrible and enticing, before. How innocent I'd been. Astrid was far more of a temptation than I could have ever comprehended.

"You really couldn't have warned me your mutant dick was going to lock us together?" she groused, reminding me that she was also a miserable Shade-hating wretch, no matter how good she felt and how jealous the idea of her with anyone else made me.

"I wouldn't have knotted you if I'd realized it was going to make you uncomfortable. The error is mine for not checking first that you were entirely aware of how it worked." I swallowed thickly, forcing some of my pride down with it. "You test my control, but that's no excuse."

Astrid's cheeks flushed red again, this time not from arousal I didn't think, though her expression was impossible to read.

"Stop that," she muttered eventually. "You already warned me to learn about Shade anatomy the last time we got carried away, and I chose not to listen. I don't like it when you're..."

"Nice?"

"You're not nice," Astrid replied adamantly. "*Civil.* I don't like it when you're civil."

I was pretty sure I was one of the most civil Shades in this entire palace, just not to my enemies.

I have my enemy impaled on my cock.

Shameful. Wasn't it? I *should* be ashamed. The goddesses knew that every other Shade in the kingdom would be ashamed of me if they knew.

Astrid reached between us, eyes wide as she hesitantly patted her bulging belly. Any hint of shame I'd had vanished. "Is that your... What have you *done* to me?"

"Is that my cock?" I asked smugly, pride winning out over my concerns about what the repercussions of this would be. "My cock that you can *see*? Why, yes. Yes it is."

I moved to stroke over her distended abdomen with my claws, but Astrid swatted my hand away before I could make contact.

"This is so fucking weird," she mumbled, not looking at me. But her pussy clenched around me as though she actually found the idea quite appealing.

"I'm just trying to force your stupid knot out," Astrid said hurriedly, cheeks flushing red. "Can I expect any other weird and gross surprises?"

"Weird and gross, hm?"

"Totally weird and gross, and I don't like it at all," she lied.

"No other surprises. There'll be a river of cum. But that's all."

"Oh great. Nothing to worry about then. I never want to be knotted again. *You* are definitely never knotting me again, even if it creates enough power to fuel the whole kingdom," she retorted, all snark and bite until she shifted her hips, the swell of my knot rubbing against her sensitized nerves and setting off another wave of rippling orgasms. "Stop making me come!"

"Stop making yourself come. We both know you're only lashing out because you don't want to admit that my 'mutant dick' is the best cock you've ever had," I growled, leaning in to speak close to her ear. "That my cock has ruined you for any other. That every time your cunt is even a little achy, a little needy, you'll think of me. Of *this*."

I dragged my claws over Astrid's hip, the dip of her waist, the curved underside of her breast. With a shallow thrust, she was clenching around me again while I filled her up, her blunt nails scratching harmlessly at my chest—right over my heart, where she'd undoubtedly embed a solid silver dagger if she had the choice.

"That's it," I whispered roughly, cradling her hip almost reverently, were it not for the slightly too sharp dig of my claws into her lower back. "Remember this. Every single sensation. How fucking *complete* you feel. You'll never feel this way again."

There was a thin sheen of sweat covering Astrid's forehead, her cheeks flushed a brilliant red that this realm hadn't seen in centuries.

Well fucked, drunk on lust, and still perfectly capable of giving me a slow, catlike smile that I felt all the way into my bones.

"Maybe not, Captain. But neither will you."

My gut clenched at the reminder. I couldn't formulate a reply, so instead I stayed where I was, memorizing the silky skin of her hip under my hand, and the syrupy scent of her arousal and mine, combining into something wholly unique and incredibly potent.

Astrid was perfectly still, whether it was because she was trying to get rid of my knot faster or because she was experiencing the same existential crisis I was, I couldn't be sure. For the sake of my ego, I hoped she was struggling with how devastatingly right we felt together too.

The moment my knot softened, I pulled myself free of the temptress who'd been sent directly from the depths to ruin my life, fighting back a groan at the feel of her tight heat around me.

Astrid gasped in horror as a combination of cum and slick flowed free, drenching her inner thighs and the ground beneath her. I tried to keep a straight face, but I couldn't quite suppress my laugh at her wide-eyed expression. Unflappable Hunter, Astrid, shocked by a little bit of fluid.

Well, quite a lot of fluid, I supposed.

But it broke the tension, at least. That chilling, penetrating fear that her words had left me with.

"Neither will you."

That was going to haunt my nightmares.

"Satisfied?" Astrid hissed, glaring at me, a delightful mess.

"I'd be more satisfied if I was pushing back into you," I replied easily, staring unabashedly at the apex of her thighs. Astrid made a strangled noise, attempting to clench her legs together while shuffling back down toward the river at the same time.

I supposed if I was a more chivalrous Shade, I would have scooped her up and carried her.

But I wasn't chivalrous, not to murderers anyway.

I let the shadows I'd created to hide us morph around my body in my usual draped garment instead, standing to watch as Astrid waded into the water.

True to her word, she still refused to give me her back, banding one arm across her chest as she walked backward into the water, not taking her wary eyes off me.

My scent washed away down the river, and I fought against the urge to drag her out and douse her with it again.

Instead, I took a step back. And another. And then a few more, until I was ensconced in the gardens near the palace, safely out of range of the Hunter who'd had me so firmly in her snare.

No longer. This couldn't go on. I'd go to the stores, unload as much power as I could spare, and be grateful that I could contribute while knowing it could never happen again.

"Where are we going?" Damen asked, falling into step beside me, chewing a stick of dried meat.

"*We* aren't going anywhere. It's my day off."

"That's why I'm here. What, you too good to spend time with me now? You're so busy with Astrid these days."

I almost choked on my spit. Had he seen me with her the other day? No, surely not. No one had followed us after the training session, and I'd been careful to avoid her since so we didn't experience a repeat of the most satisfying sexual encounter I'd ever had. Because that would be bad, as I repeatedly reminded myself, even when the reasons why it would be bad seemed elusive.

Damen was just goading me. I should ignore it.

"Some of the Guards were gossiping about her," he continued. "Saying how at one of the training sessions, she was physically responding to all of the Shades, eyeing up Verner and Selene. They were telling me that even though her scent is usually muted compared to the other ex-Hunters that—"

"Stop talking," I muttered, failing to squash my irrational surge of possessiveness that her stupid fake desire for the other Guards had actually fooled them. Astrid wasn't mine to be possessive over, nor did I want her to be.

Why had they not been able to see through her act? It was clear to me that *I* was the only Shade Astrid responded to.

Damen snorted. "Touchy, touchy. Perhaps it's because—as we both know—"

"Did you have a reason for pestering me on my day off?" I sighed. Not that I actually minded—as vexing as Damen liked to be, he was one of my closest friends. He was Allerick's half-brother—slightly younger than both of us—and had followed us around the palace when we were children, toddling on short, unsteady legs. It had become abundantly clear that he would be Allerick's heir from a young age as his power level emerged, but he'd never been given any real responsibility. Perhaps if he had been, he wouldn't be so irritating. Damen needed a job and a hobby.

"It's not like you have anywhere else to be. How many times can you *discreetly* wander past Elverston House before you get bored? You'd have to come find me eventually anyway, for the pleasure of my company."

"You pay far too much attention to my habits."

"Oh, I am definitely not the one paying far too much attention to someone's habits."

I grunted, not wanting to acknowledge the truthfulness in Damen's words. The Shades had all been warned to give the ex-Hunters space and privacy to adjust to life here in this realm, to get to know them on their own terms and not put any pressure on them. Astrid was a unique case, but it didn't justify my borderline obsession with watching her.

If any other Shade had acted the way I had, they'd be thrown in the Pit.

"Actually, I did have a reason for tracking you down. I have a message to pass on," Damen admitted, sounding slightly sheepish. "But I was hoping to put you in a good mood before weighing you down with the bad news."

I stopped in my tracks, turning to face him. "Is Allerick okay?"

"Of course," Damen replied with a laugh. "I know you think no one can guard him as well as you, but Selene is very good at what she does. No, I'm here about your sister."

Ah. The millstone around my neck.

It was easy to enjoy the peaceful lull that I'd been experiencing since Meridia had been thrown in the Pit. For years, she'd been a source of constant humiliation, grasping at increasingly thin straws in an attempt to get Allerick's crown.

"They've finally set a date for her sentencing?" I asked, resigned. Meridia had been unanimously declared guilty. Not that there had been much question—she'd bragged about her misdeeds, all bluster and bravado to the very end. Anything rather than admitting she was wrong.

In spite of everything she'd done, I didn't relish the thought of her sentencing. Our mother would be miserable. I should probably visit her, but Mother was convinced that I could save Meridia, if only I worked a little harder to convince Allerick. As if I would, as if I *wanted* to fight for Meridia when she was a traitor to the realm.

"Tomorrow."

I swallowed thickly, clenching my jaw to hide my shock.

"Don't do that," Damen said quietly. "I'm not going to judge you, Soren. You can be angry. Or sad. Fuck, cheer if you like—I have no idea how you're feeling, you lock down your feelings so tight."

I made a sound of frustration. "What if I want to do all of them at once? Meridia is my sister, and she wasn't always like this. But in recent years... I don't like her. I don't like who she's become."

My feelings of guilt and regret were a tangled mess, and I didn't know where to begin with them. Could I have done more? Could I have prevented Meridia from going down the path she'd chosen if I'd tried harder?

Or was Meridia just inherently evil?

Were some Shades and Hunters just irredeemable? Were their actions too severe to ever earn forgiveness, even if they wanted it?

"Maybe it would help to see her?" Damen suggested, voice free of judgment. "You could visit. Today."

"For what? I don't have any advice to offer her," I replied wryly.

"I don't mean for her benefit. For *yours*. You'll always wonder if you don't."

Because there was a very real chance that Meridia would be put to death.

"Captain—" Verner called, jogging down the corridor towards me.

"It's the Captain's day off," Damen said as Verner approached, an edge of warning in his tone. Damen thought I worked too hard, though his perception was warped by virtue of the fact that he didn't work at all. Damen was full of potential, and I hoped that he'd figure out how to use it one day, both for his own happiness and for the good it would do the realm.

"I know, and I hate to disturb you," Verner replied, sounding apologetic. "But the Hunter, Astrid, was skulking around the portal. We believe she was looking for a way out."

I froze. Was she now?

She'd been avoiding me just as much as I'd been avoiding her, but maybe she was struggling more than I realized after *the incident*.

But she didn't get to just *leave*.

The irritation I was experiencing wasn't rational, and I was vaguely aware that there was a possessive edge to it that I didn't have any right to feel, but feelings didn't always follow logic.

Well, they generally did for *me*, but Astrid defied the rules in every way possible.

I gestured for Verner to lead the way, ignoring Damen's exasperated sigh as he hung back. "Don't do anything rash, Soren," he called after me.

What was he expecting me to do? It wasn't as though I had a prior record of making rash decisions. Not one that he knew about, at least.

Verner led me to a small sitting room, where Andrus stood near the door, keeping guard. His gaze was trained intently on Astrid—who was lounging on a chair, pretending a level of calm that she clearly *wasn't* feeling. She was examining her injured hand with faint disinterest, a jagged, raised scar in the place of the stitches she'd had the last time I'd looked.

"Astra," I said evenly, forcing myself to ignore the urge to gouge Andrus' eyes out for staring at her.

"Still not my name."

"I hear you were trying to escape."

Astrid cut a filthy glare at Verner, and I almost demanded she return her eyes to me. "Well, you were lied to, Captain. I don't know what else to tell you."

A hot flash of anger ran through me. A pertinent reminder of all the reasons why I hated her.

"My Guard don't lie. Nor are they the ones with dubious moral character, so I suggest you save your excuses. They won't do you any good here."

Astrid stood, her ire rising to meet my own. "Well, it seems like you've made up your mind so I guess there's no point explaining myself. Astrid the

Hunter, Astrid the Liar, Astrid Who's Conspiring Against the Shades. You've all made your minds up about me."

I almost said something to counter her words, almost pointed out that no, we hadn't all made our minds up about her otherwise she wouldn't be training with the Guard, wouldn't be walking around free, but I didn't. I *couldn't*. Especially not when Verner hummed quietly in agreement. Maybe if he and Andrus weren't here, I would have, but they looked to me to set the example. It wouldn't be appropriate for me to show Astrid any grace.

Would it?

No, of course not. There was no good reason for her to be anywhere near the portal. I wasn't assuming the worst, I was assuming the logical truth.

"You're with me today, Hunter," I told Astrid. "It isn't exactly what I had in mind for my day off, but apparently you can't be trusted on your own and Selene doesn't need the extra work."

Astrid balled her good hand into a fist at her side, probably silently cursing me in every way she knew how. Her teeth ground together loud enough that we could all hear it, and I could practically see her physically biting back whatever it was she wanted to say.

I could admit that my ego was taking a hit at the overpowering scent of her anger. There wasn't even the faintest tinge of her arousal there, as though the other day hadn't happened. Meanwhile, my body remembered every second of it perfectly, and my cock had been hard as stone since the moment I'd walked into the room. Seeing her lounging obnoxiously on the chair had made me immediately envision bending her over it.

"Where are we going, *Captain*?" Astrid asked, infusing as much disrespect into my title as possible and drawing me back to reality.

"The Pit. Maybe it will give you second thoughts about misbehaving, *Astra*."

ASTRID

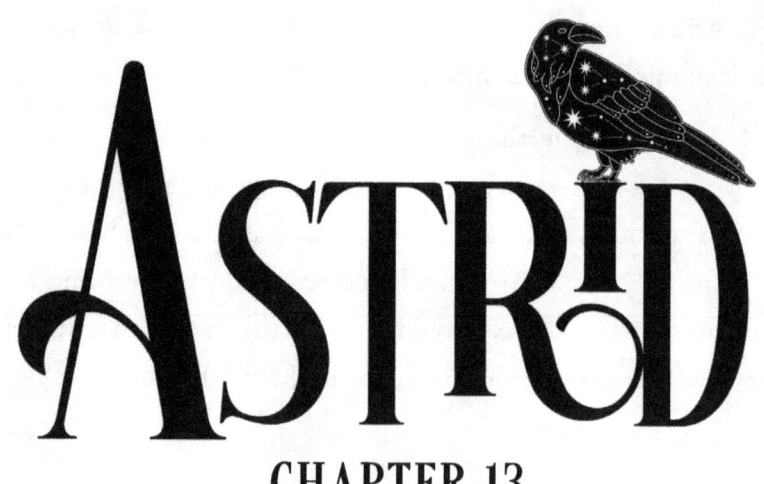

CHAPTER 13

"You're awfully quiet," Soren remarked, tension lining his expression and posture. I cut him an impatient glare, saying nothing.

My silence made Soren uneasy.

Good.

I hadn't spoken a word since he'd imperiously marched me out of the palace, and we'd shadow-traveled to this grim, deserted part of the realm that housed the Shade prison.

It was lit up like an Olympic stadium on opening night, and I struggled to see anything as we approached, my eyes having adjusted to the constant low light of this realm. The entire structure was sunk into the ground, and as we neared the edge, I realized it spiraled down in layers, with silver bars across the front of each cell and not a hint of darkness anywhere that the prisoners could use for shadow travel.

"Maybe it will give you second thoughts about misbehaving."

Was that a threat? Be a good, obedient, shame-filled little ex-Hunter or you'll end up rotting in the pit of blinding light too? God, Soren was such an asshole. And yet...

And yet.

There was always an 'and yet' when it came to Soren—the sex had been mind-blowing, after all. Too bad it had been with *him*.

"Still have nothing to say? I should have brought you to the Pit earlier." He was baiting me, trying to get a reaction, and I wasn't going to give it to him.

I was so goddamn powerless in this realm. I'd gone from having so much control over my life to almost none—I lived where I was told to live, worked where I was told to work, socialized with the very few people who didn't despise me on principle. Even those interactions were limited, mired in secrecy to protect their reputations from being associated with me.

Apparently, I couldn't even walk *near* the portal without being threatened with imprisonment.

If this was the only control I had—over my voice, my reactions—then I wasn't about to give it up for anyone.

"Captain," one of the guards said, inclining her head as she approached.

"Bethia," he replied. "We're here to visit Meridia."

We, I scoffed internally. Though I had to admit, now I knew why Soren had come, I was surprised he'd brought me along. I'd heard all about his traitorous sister from Ophelia, and I suppose I'd assumed that straightlaced by-the-book Soren had nothing to do with her anymore.

"Of course," the guard replied, waving us through a tall gate.

I followed Soren down a sloping stone path, staring at his back and remembering how mad I was at him. I had to hold on to my rage because this was not a good place for me to show any sign of fear, even if the imprisoned Shades pressing themselves against the silver bars, openly staring at me, were slightly intimidating.

Surprisingly, there was no jeering or shouting. Apparently, the fierce scowl on Soren's face was enough to silence anyone.

Under other circumstances, if he wasn't such an asshole, I'd find that level of fierce intimidation intensely sexy.

Too bad it was him.

He turned down a tunnel, brightly lit a sterile shade of silver despite the fact we were underground, and we made our way to the very end, where he unlocked a heavy silver door, holding it open for me.

It was a visiting room, I guessed, though not a very welcoming one. Or maybe it was an interrogation room? There were silver bars down the center, dividing the space in half, and heavy silver doors that led to each area, but nothing else. No seating, no observation window, no other obvious security.

It seemed like a huge security risk, but then again, Soren was Captain of the Guard. Undoubtedly, if anyone else had been visiting, they would have been thoroughly searched, and accompanied here by another guard.

The moment Soren secured the door behind me, the one on the opposite side of the room creaked open, and Soren's sister sauntered in. I leaned back against the far wall with my arms crossed over my chest, observing. At a glance, there were physical similarities between them—mostly in the sharp curve of their horns and the shape of their jaws. But their expressions, the way they held themselves, were so different that they seemed more like strangers than siblings.

And where Soren's eyes were the brilliant orange of molten lava, Meridia's were a deep, demonic red. I'd been one of the most confident Hunters in the Before Time, but even I'd have peed my pants to see Meridia's eyes glowing in the darkness.

"Big brother," Meridia cooed, wrapping her hands around the bars above her head, leaning toward him. Her claws looked as though they'd been cut—blunt and harmless as she drummed them against the metal bars. "Come to say your goodbyes? If you're hoping I'll forgive you now, absolve you of the guilt you're going to carry around for the rest of your life, you're sorely mistaken. I hope you're sick with it. I hope your guilt rots you from the inside out."

Well, she seemed lovely.

"It won't," Soren said flatly. "I warned you more than enough times what the consequences of the path you were following would be to assuage any guilt I may have felt. My conscience is clear."

Meridia switched her attention to me for a moment, before dismissing me with a scoff. "Is this your reward for your obedience to *King* Allerick? A little Hunter pet of your own? This one looks like a cheap imitation of his queen—a little uglier, a little surlier—"

"Enough," Soren clipped. I was grinding my teeth to dust, but Meridia's insults made it easier to maintain my silence if anything. I'd never been good at formulating words when I was truly angry. All of my best retorts came to me hours later, usually when I was alone in the shower. "I came here to see if there was anything redeemable left inside you, but I see there's not. Your bitterness has eaten you alive, Meridia. You're an empty husk of a Shade."

"I am a *movement*," she hissed. "I am a symbol. I am *hope*, for the Shades who don't want to live in King Allerick's soft new world. We are The Resistance. You can sentence me to death, but it doesn't matter. A symbol can't be killed."

"Watch and see," Soren snarled, a rare burst of emotion. "This was a mistake. I don't need closure. I lost my sister a long time ago."

He turned his back on Meridia, stalking back towards the door and quickly unlocking it, wrapping a hand around my upper arm and dragging me out of the room without a word.

If I was speaking to him, if I liked him enough to offer him advice, I'd give Soren a warning. I'd tell him that there was an incredible amount of power in symbols, and it would be foolish not to take steps to mitigate that, but whatever. Fuck him. It wasn't like he was going to listen to me anyway. He'd already demonstrated that.

I'd talk to Ophelia—not as my sister, but as my queen. Tell her just how dangerous a martyr for the cause could be in the long run.

Soren maintained his hold on my arm, frogmarching back up the path to the surface like *I'd* been the one to offend him. Experimentally, I tried to squirm free of his grip, but it only tightened. He was certainly strong enough to hurt me if he wanted to, and I supposed I vaguely appreciated that even in his rage, he was being careful not to.

The guard who'd let us into the Pit unlocked the gate as we approached, bowing her head as we passed. I chanced a glance up at Soren through my eyelashes, wishing his face wasn't so hard to read.

"Still nothing to say?" he gritted out the moment we were out of earshot, alone on the long stretch of path that led from the dark travel point to the Pit. "You don't want to gloat? Revel in the nightmare that is my sister? Maybe it's me. Maybe I just draw the worst kinds of Shades and Hunters into my orbit," he mused.

I twisted, dropping my weight and breaking out of his hold, filled with a rage so potent that it made my limbs shake. How dare he. How fucking *dare* he.

"Your *deranged* sister was conspiring with the Hunters Council for Allerick's throne. The same Council I undermined, walked away from, betrayed, and was exiled by. Whatever—you and everyone else hates me, I'm aware of that—but I refuse to be lumped into the same category of villain as Meridia. We were on opposite sides of the same conflict. You and I were on the *same* side, though you like to forget about that."

"I haven't forgotten," he snapped, not a shred of that usual cool, careful self-control in place. I wasn't feeling so in control myself. We were two spinning tops on a collision course, moving too fast to pull ourselves back now.

Fuck, why was he so attractive, all tense and looming?

"Why aren't you afraid of me? Why is your scent always so unreadable?" he growled, as frustrated as I was.

"Why did you bring me here?" I demanded, ignoring his stupid question, torn between wanting to fuck the stubborn assholishness out of him or fight it out of him.

"So you know where you'll end up the next time you try to escape."

"I *wasn't* trying to escape, you dense prick. I was looking for my sister, who was supposedly in the garden somewhere. I was just *walking*. Sorry for *existing* within the vicinity of the portal. The portal that is *closed* on the human end, if you recall. I'm not a Shade, I can't just walk into a dark patch of the human world and be on my merry way. Do you really think I'm so desperate that I'd choose to walk blindly into the in-between?"

"Maybe you are. Maybe you decided you'd rather run than face the fact that you fucked a Shade and you *liked* it."

I barked out a hollow laugh. "Do you really think your dick game is so good, I'd risk getting lost in the void forever just to get away from it? My god, if there's one thing obnoxious males have, Shade or Hunter, it's the fucking *audacity*."

Muttering furiously under my breath, I stormed back towards the entry room, fueled by righteous outrage. Had I been having a small existential crisis at how good sex with Soren had been? Yes. Was I going to put my life at risk to get away from him because of it?

Fuck. No.

I heard Soren's footsteps behind me, knew he was following uncomfortably close, and too wound up to hide his stomping steps. Good. I was glad he was mad, I was mad too.

I'd been called a lot of names since I'd been here, but being compared to the realm's most notorious traitor when I'd sacrificed *everything* to be here, to help my sister and the former Hunters who'd been left out in the cold, convinced something was wrong with them...

I wasn't Meridia. I didn't deserve that.

Too late, I heard the whistle of the blade. Soren roughly grabbed my shoulders, throwing me sideways as the short dagger embedded itself in the dirt where my foot had been just half a second earlier. I stumbled for a moment, righting myself and bringing my arms up defensively over my chest, eyes searching the barren landscape for the culprit.

The entry room was a flat-roofed stone building, only a few feet wide, and it was the only hiding place around. Sure enough, a Shade who'd been lying on the roof climbed slowly to their feet, dragging a silver sword up with them.

Three more Shades emerged from behind the building as the one who'd tossed the dagger jumped off the roof, prowling towards us.

Soren smoothly stepped in front of me, blocking me from view. Trusting me with his back, though I supposed he knew how goddamn harmless I was right now, completely unarmed.

How could we have gotten so sloppy?

We'd both been too angry, too absorbed in our own issues, to pay attention to our surroundings. It was a stupid mistake that we were both too good to be making.

They were all armed. Soren took a step back towards the Pit, attempting to push me back with him, but the ringleader tutted, pulling another throwing knife out of somewhere and twirling it between his fingers.

"I wouldn't if I were you," he warned. The moment's hesitation cost us, allowing the other three Shades to close ranks around Soren and me. "This doesn't need to be painful, but it can be."

"Death, you mean?" Soren asked, his voice deceptively mild. "You'd be idiotic to try and plan anything else. I have no intention of cooperating with you, Oswyn."

"Yes, death," Oswyn confirmed, sounding suitably contrite about it. "If only you'd listened to your sister, Captain. Followed her lead. It didn't have to be this way."

Despite feeling *painfully* unarmed, I didn't feel any fear because Soren clearly wasn't afraid. He was stubborn and rude, and once we got through this annoying little skirmish, I was going to remind him of all the ways he was an asshole, but he was also quietly badass and these little insects didn't stand a chance.

"You're really willing to throw your lives away over my sister's unhinged ramblings?" Soren shrugged as though it didn't bother him either way. His hand brushed beneath the shadows that covered his thigh, coming away clutching a silver short sword that he must have sheathed under there.

Handy trick.

"Your sister is a *visionary*. The leader we need, we *deserve*. She understands the true, rightful place of Shades. And of *Hunted*." There was a dreamy lilt to his voice that was frankly unsettling. Dragging Meridia into some public sentencing and handing down a death sentence would be moronic, and I was going to tell my brother-in-law as much when I saw him. "The fact that you came here today, as she predicted... It's a sign."

"Ah yes, the Captain visiting his sister the day before her very public sentencing can only be a sign from the universe," I said drily, rolling my eyes. How did I get that dagger on the ground without them noticing? Or did that 'no weapons' rule still apply when my life was at risk? Probably.

"You're an added bonus," the Shade snapped, not that I could see him with Soren blocking me off. "The only thing that will boost our profile more than killing the Captain of the Guard would be killing the murderous Hunter left to roam free at the palace. A walking symbol of King Allerick's poor decisions. In fact, maybe we'll leave you alive. Make it look like *you* killed the Captain. I doubt anyone will contest it."

The tendrils of fear were there—the tremulous, unstable beginnings of the emotion—but I imagined setting a giant fan on them and blasting those reaching coils away. I wouldn't give these idiots the satisfaction of knowing they'd gotten to me, even if they were absolutely right.

I wasn't even entirely sure *Ophelia* would contest that claim.

"If you think that, you don't know the court very well," Soren replied, steady and solid as I slowly turned, pressing my back to his. Four against two, I was unarmed, and the sharp throb in my hand was an unwelcome reminder that not only was I less capable than I once had been, I was also not cut out for close combat.

Soren didn't hesitate, darting forward and impaling Oswyn on his short sword faster than any of them could blink. There was a moment of complete stillness, of complete silence, before Oswyn's body began to *steam*. I'd already turned my head away long enough, and I forced myself to focus on the Shade in front of me, lunging low and tackling them around the legs, knocking them to the ground.

The curved silver blade fell from their hand and I dove on it, ignoring the jarring pain that ran up my arm as I snatched it off the ground, bringing it up over my head just in time to block the blow from another Shade's weapon.

My muscles shook with the effort. Even if both of my hands had been fully functional, this wasn't my usual mode of combat. I didn't have big fuck-off biceps or brute strength on my side.

"I will kill you, *Hunter*." They attacked again, and I half dove, half fell out of the way to avoid the sword. Both of my hands screamed with effort as I swung my blade, trying to use my smaller stature to my advantage to take the Shade out at the kneecaps.

They barely even stumbled, easily sidestepping my swing. Shit. I wasn't cut out for this, I needed the throwing knife and some distance or I was going to get skewered.

The Shade grinned down at me, showcasing a row of merciless teeth. They raised the blade, the silver tip glinting ominously, reflecting the blinding light from the Pit. "I'm going to kill you like you killed so many of my kind, and I'm going to enjoy it. Perhaps I'll mount your head on my wall as a trophy—"

The stream of threats was cut off as Soren attacked, forcing the Shade to block his blow. With each slice of Soren's blade, shadows seemed to rise from their skin like air leaking out of a balloon.

I climbed to my feet, dragging the stolen sword up with me. The Shade I'd disarmed was inching towards me, and Soren's attention drifted his way more than once. It was a distraction he didn't need, and I could do something about it.

The blade grew heavier in my hands, a cold sweat breaking out on the back of my neck. *"Like you killed so many of my kind."*

I had. I'd killed Shades before. I'd been given medals for it. But it wasn't like this. This wasn't a ghost-like apparition, floating through the darkness, seeking out an innocent human to scare out of their wits.

I couldn't spin anything about this as heroism in my head.

This was kill or be killed, and I didn't know if I could do the former. Not anymore. Not like this.

He lunged, and my brain screamed at me to move, to fight, to at least defend myself, but my limbs wouldn't cooperate. I was frozen in place and it didn't matter that I had the guy's blade, because he could shred me to nothingness with his claws.

Before he could connect, Soren was there, ducking down and ramming his blade upwards into the Shade's chest. He released the sword to return his focus to his own opponent, spinning as they attacked.

Soren grunted in pain, a quiet sound that seemed to echo somehow because it was so unlike him to show any sign of weakness.

"Here!" I shouted, tossing Soren the blade I was holding to even up the fight. Guards were *finally* running towards us from the Pit now—we were almost in the clear. Soren snatched the blade out of midair, slicing a deep gash in the Shade's abdomen that had them doubling over in pain.

"I'm not going to kill you," Soren rasped, *definitely* injured, though I couldn't see where. "You are my canary. I'm going to keep you alive, and you are going to *sing*."

SOREN

CHAPTER 14

The guards from the Pit arrived just in time to restrain Godfrey, who was still shouting obscenities as they carted him away. He'd sit in a cell until the king was ready to deal with him, and I hoped Allerick took his sweet time about it.

He'd landed a hit that was frighteningly close to fatal. A second blow *would* have been fatal, and it was only thanks to Astrid throwing me the sword that I avoided it.

I strengthened the cloak of shadows covering my body to cover up the deep gash on my chest.

No one needed to know. I just had to get out of here before the blood started pooling on the ground at my feet. Shadows were already leaking free and only the fact that I was steaming with rage at the attack and losing control over my power anyway was offering me any cover.

It was an unacceptable sign of weakness for me to be injured at all, let alone severely. This so-called "Resistance" were a bunch of untrained, angry Shades whose minds had been poisoned by my sister's bitter ramblings. It should have been impossible for them to get close enough to injure me in the first place.

Humiliating.

"Hunter," I barked, forcing as much impatience into my voice as possible to cover the pain. "You're with me. Let's go."

"Well, fuck you very much, Captain," Astrid muttered, rightfully outraged at the way I was speaking to her.

Astrid had almost died on my watch. It was unacceptable, and I needed to tell her that. To apologize for putting her in real danger—something no training member of the Guard should ever be in, whatever their background.

But I was barely holding myself together.

"Captain, let me escort the Hunter—" one of the lower-level Pit guards began, attempting to grab her arm.

"Don't touch her," I warned, voice shaking with barely controlled fury. Not that the guard had stood a chance, Astrid had already twisted away from his hand, sending him a glare that had him shrinking back on himself. "You don't touch her. No one touches her. She's with me."

My head swam. I needed to get out of here. Bandage myself up, find a way to feed enough to heal without draining the stores completely.

"*She* has a name." Astrid was all bark—I'd seen her hesitation, could smell the faint sour whiff of fear that she was trying to suppress. If snapping at me brought her some level of reassurance, I wasn't going to stop her—it wasn't as though I had room to judge.

I'd hang around and let her snipe at me all she liked if my head wasn't spinning, but if I collapsed here in front of everyone, I'd have to resign to avoid putting Allerick through the discomfort of dismissing me.

Astrid stalked past me, throwing open the door to the dark stone entry room and waiting inside for me to follow. I closed it behind me, reaching for her in the darkness but she was already there, grabbing my wrist, ready for me to guide us back.

As we stepped into the swirling abyss of the in-between, her grip tightened, but I didn't think it was out of fear. No, Astrid was being far more cooperative than she had been when I'd dragged her out here.

"Just a little further, Captain," Astrid murmured.

Each step was agony, and I didn't trust myself to speak. I had to get Astrid home safely. Had to alert Allerick and the Council. Had to *heal*.

We stepped through the portal in front of the palace, and both Andrus and Selene startled, their conversation coming to a sudden halt.

"Captain?" Selene asked, glancing between us. Astrid let go of my wrist as though it had burned her, and I found myself missing her steadying touch. How odd.

"Find the King, report to him that there was an attack on myself and the Hunter next to the entry room at the Pit. It was arranged by the Resistance, loyal to my sister," I instructed, locking my muscles in place so she couldn't see how much I was shaking. "I recognized Oswyn and Godfrey. Relay the message to the Council as well. One survived—he's being detained in the Pit."

"Of course," Selene replied, tipping her chin. "And… you're okay?"

"Fine," I grunted, doing my best to keep my stride steady and even as I headed away from Selene, Astrid falling into step behind me.

My apartment—the apartment that belonged to the Captain of the Guard—was on the lower-level of the palace, only accessible from outside the building, with a small garden courtyard at the front for privacy. I'd walk Astrid back to Elverston House before looping back to my apartment. There were bandages in there, weren't there? Surely, there were. I didn't want to go straight to the stores. In the state I was in, I'd drain them dry.

"Captain," Astrid murmured, a hint of warning in her voice. "Lying to your second-in-command?"

She tsked judgmentally.

"I am *fine*," I replied stubbornly, moving further down the path, away from the portal and the other guards.

"That's my lie, Captain," Astrid said smoothly. "If there's something you need, just ask."

The sharp points of my teeth dug into my gums from how hard I was clenching my jaw. Partly to stop myself from taking her up on her almost-offer, and partly because her throat was looking more inviting than ever.

It wasn't *real*. It wasn't a genuine desire to tie my life, my soul, to hers. It was just a fear response. Astrid had been in danger right in front of my eyes, and claiming her would ease the primal part of my brain that demanded I protect her.

Instinct. It was just instinct.

"You can't possibly be this stubborn," Astrid sighed, planting her feet on the ground and refusing to go any further. Her eyebrows lifted, watching, assessing.

"You should have never been in danger. I'm not feeding from you after that."

"Martyr complex much?"

"Go back to Elverston House," I gritted out, locking my knees as the ground wavered beneath my feet. "*Go*."

Astrid pressed her lips into a tight line, taking one step backward, followed by another, never taking her judgmental eyes off me. The moment she disappeared behind a tree, I stumbled after her, hating having her out of my sight, but my body wasn't cooperating. I grabbed a nearby tree before I could tumble to the ground, the branch crumbling under my punishing grip as I gasped through the wave of pain.

Okay. New plan: Go back to my apartment.

Astrid was tough, she'd be fine on the five-minute walk to Elverston House. I just needed to lie down for a moment, then I'd go back and check on her.

With the last of my strength, I imitated a strong, confident stride around the palace to the side that housed all the apartments. As I made my way into my private courtyard, I'd never been more grateful for the drooping black trees that hid the pathway from view. Determined steps morphed into a slow

limp, breath sawing from my lungs. Every movement pulled at the wound in my chest, and I half expected it to tear me in two completely.

At least no one would disturb me here. Aside from the fact that the apartment was sparse and not particularly welcoming no matter who occupied it, it was well known that I didn't like guests. Didn't *trust* having anyone in my personal quarters. Usually, my privacy here was guaranteed, and yet as I walked through the garden, I couldn't help but feel as though I wasn't quite alone.

I paused for a moment, hoping that the world would stop spinning so fast so that I could focus on my surroundings, but it was no use. Everything was a blur, my stomach churning with nausea from the incessant movement.

I need to lie down.

There was no one there, I was imagining things in my haze of injury. Selene wouldn't ignore my direct order, even if I'd been dying right in front of her eyes, so there was no way she would have followed me. Perhaps Damen would come, once he'd heard. He always treated my no-guests policy as more of a guideline.

At some point, my covering had disappeared, and even sending the small trail of shadows needed to unlock the door was difficult. I barely managed it before stumbling inside, banging my shoulder on the frame and shoving the door closed behind me. It wasn't a large space—an airy room and an attached bathroom—but even crossing from the entryway to the bed on the other side felt like an impossible task.

Surely, the floor was comfortable enough, wasn't it?

I slid down the rough stone wall, lying on my back in front of the door. I felt a trickle of blood run over my torso before hitting the floor with a faint *drip. Better to ruin the floor than the bedding,* I thought wryly. Maybe I could pretend that collapsing here had been the plan all along.

How had that gone so wrong? Meridia had put me in a bad mood, and Astrid had unfairly borne the brunt of it. I'd known even when I was following her back to the entry room that I needed to apologize for comparing her to my sister, and I'd been too lost in my thoughts to focus on my surroundings.

It was a stupid mistake. The kind that I should be years past making.

There was still a sense of uneasiness in the back of my mind that I couldn't quite explain, but trying made my head hurt worse than it already was, so instead I closed my eyes.

This wasn't the end, I told myself stubbornly. The blade had missed my heart, or I'd be dead already. Returned to the shadows from where I'd come.

Any other wound was survivable.

Unless I starve. Healing took power, and I'd given almost every drop of what I'd gained from Astrid to the stores. The injury would draw on whatever reserves I had until it was healed.

I just hoped I had enough.

I woke up hissing in pain as something jostled my body. Some*one*. What happened? Why was I lying on the floor?

Right. The ambush. The injury. The suddenly impossible distance between the door and my bed.

"You're really fucking heavy, Cap. You know that?" Astrid grumbled. I realized with a start that she'd hooked her arms beneath my armpits and was attempting to drag me away from the door. "Aren't you basically made of shadow? Shouldn't you weigh less than this?"

"How did you get in?" I rasped. How did she even know where I lived? "Who told you how to find this place?"

Astrid snorted, infusing an impressive amount of derisiveness and amusement into one short sound. "I'm a *Hunter*, Captain. I didn't need a map or a step-by-step instructional to get here. *I hunted you.* Did you really think I was going to skip off back to Elverston House just because you told me to?"

The words should have been chilling. They should have served as a reminder of everything about Astrid that I despised, all the reasons why I didn't want her in this realm, why she was a danger to all of us. And yet...

If I hadn't been bleeding out on my floor, I might have felt... *aroused*. The idea of her following my trail, skulking through the trees, tracking me... Why was that appealing? I didn't want to be prey. I hated the feeling of helplessness I'd experienced in the human realm whenever I'd caught a glimpse of a Hunter, knowing they had all the power.

Was that the difference? Ultimately, Astrid was fairly powerless here. It made her hunting seem... sexy, rather than terrifying.

"I did expect you to listen to my orders, yes," I managed to reply, wincing as she attempted to drag me across the room again.

"Your orders were stupid, and your stubbornness is going to get you killed." She straightened with a huff, moving to stand over me and giving my body a clinical and entirely unreassuring once over. "You need power to heal, but apparently *asking* for it is a bridge too far, so here I am. I'm going to fuck that injury right out of you."

There was that stirring feeling again. That brush of what would have been lust, if my body wasn't splitting apart at the seams.

"I'd like to think that I'm strong enough to fuck through anything, but a silver blade right next to my heart might be my one exception," I replied, doing my best to sound unaffected. I didn't want Astrid to see me vulnerable, or give her a weakness to exploit. I certainly didn't trust her.

And yet, having her here, her seeing me like this... I knew I would have felt more humiliated if it was someone else—even Damen or Allerick. Perhaps because she didn't look at me with pity. Astrid was a fighter too, she knew what it was to be injured in combat, and she understood better than anyone that I'd hate to see her feel sorry for me.

"Then again, dying between your thighs wouldn't be the worst way to go," I added mildly, because whether I wanted to admit it or not, I needed this. Needed Astrid's lust, needed to be the prey she toyed with for a little while, or I wasn't going to recover.

"Dying between my thighs would be an honor," Astrid deadpanned. "Though, I have to admit, it's rather hard to muster up horniness when you appear to be fading right before my eyes. It's not as though I'm attracted to you for your sparkling personality."

"Liar," I laughed, regretting the movement almost instantly as pain radiated out from my chest.

"Excuse me?"

"You're a liar, *Astra*. You do a good job pretending, but we both know you only perfume for me. Your scent doesn't change around Prince Damen, the only unmated Shade more powerful than me, so it isn't strength that you're attracted to." Astrid's face was turning a rather fetching shade of red, and I decided then and there that it was my favorite color. "There are plenty of attractive Shades among the Guard, but you don't perfume for them. You, my deadly, lying little Hunter, only want *me*."

"In spite of your personality, not because of it," Astrid shot back. "And maybe you're the only Shade I get horny for because you're always following me around like a lost puppy, and I haven't had a chance to meet anyone else."

She could deny it all she wanted, but the more I'd talked, the more her scent sweetened. Maybe Astrid even enjoyed being a little bit mine. I was hazy and vulnerable enough to admit in my own head that *I* liked her being a little bit mine.

"Besides, I'm not so deadly now, am I?" she grumbled, scrambling to maintain some of her usual ire. "Let's not pretend that this injury wasn't one hundred percent preventable. This is a pity fuck since you're injured because I froze and you had to swoop in and save me."

"I'm injured because my sister is a lunatic with a knack for recruiting other lunatics," I replied drily. "And I'm not much interested in your pity, so either fuck me like you mean it, or I'll find another Hunter—"

Before I could even finish the lie, Astrid was shoving her pants and underwear down like they'd personally offended her, moving with that level of speed and efficiency I constantly underestimated.

"Enough. Put that tongue of yours to good use before you die in the doorway. I think you can find a more dramatic way to exit this world than that, Captain." Her knees hit the stone floor with a quiet thud on either side of me, and I almost groaned when she clamped my face between her thighs. Maybe it was the blood loss, but it was perhaps the sexiest thing I'd ever experienced.

"Is that a command?" I rasped, licking a slow line up her inner thigh, stopping just short of where she wanted me. "You might want to rephrase that. I'm the Captain of the Guard, Astra. I only take orders from the king."

Astrid bowed her body over me, peering down at me with wide, guileless eyes. I didn't believe that contrite, innocent expression for a moment. I didn't *want* to. I'd never met anyone with an inner fire quite like hers, and I'd hate to see it go out. Just that hint of silent indifference from her at the Pit had cut me to my core.

"Lick. My. Pussy. *Captain.*"

I stared up at her, refusing to break eye contact as my tongue snaked out of my mouth again, teasing at the inner crease of her thighs, her mons, everywhere but where she wanted me. Despite how ragged I felt, the remaining blood in my body made its way south because Astrid was a temptation I could never quite resist.

She stripped off her top and bra, tossing them to the side before slowly running her fingers down the exposed skin of her stomach, distracting me.

"Do you need a map, Captain?" she asked sweetly, using two fingers to part herself for me, showing me the delicious cunt that I was struggling to resist. "A helping hand, perhaps? I won't judge, you're clearly having an off day."

I moved to lick her thigh again, just so she knew who was really in charge here, but she caught my tongue in her fist, squeezing lightly and shooting me a triumphant and entirely devilish smile.

That fucking *smile*. By the goddesses, it was addictive.

"*Here*, Captain," she instructed, rolling her hips and dragging the tip of my tongue over her clit. Just the smallest *hint* of her taste had me groaning, desperate for more, craving her slick more than I'd ever craved anything. "This is where I want you."

Astrid was truly a menace to society.

I grunted in acknowledgment, but she didn't release me right away, gripping my tongue in place and dragging it over her clit in slow, deliberate strokes. *Using* me with absolutely no shame.

It shouldn't have made my cock harder. It should have made me angry. Who did she think she was? Astrid was a *Hunter*. An *assassin*.

And yet when she finally released my tongue, I continued doing exactly what she asked, stimulating her clit relentlessly, flicking it with the pointed tip before switching to rubbing the sensitive nerves with the rough middle part of my tongue. Because she was *my* Astrid, *my* Hunter, *my* assassin, and I wasn't going to miss this opportunity to remind her just how *mine* she was.

Astrid hummed in satisfaction, grabbing my horns with both hands and further angling herself over my face. It was a good thing I could survive without air, since between the press of her cunt and the slick she was producing, I wasn't getting any.

"Aren't you a good boy, Captain?" Astrid purred, unashamedly trying to irritate me. "You take orders so well. Now go ahead and make me come, so I can save your life with my pussy."

I growled in annoyance at the realization that I was going to owe my enemy a *second* life debt after just repaying the first one, and though I hadn't intended for it to, the vibration against her clit pushed Astrid over the edge. Her hands squeezed my horns almost to the point of pain, and despite how weak I was, my cock was hard enough to break stone.

How did she do this? What kind of cursed Hunter magic was this? When she was riding me like this, wielding her sexuality with such perfect confidence, I'd throw away everything I'd ever worked for to keep her.

Astrid rocked her hips a few more times, riding out the last waves of her orgasm before releasing my horns and lifting herself up on her knees. The cool air hit my slick-soaked skin, and I ran my tongue over my lips, not wanting any of it to go to waste.

Astrid's eyes darkened as she watched me, elegantly rocking back on her heels to stand without using her hands and shuffling backward until she was positioned over my hips. Compared to a Shade, she was small and appeared fragile, but I knew from watching her, from *touching* her, that almost every inch of Astrid was hard muscle. Both on the inside and on the outside, she was stronger than she looked.

"You're so cooperative like this, maybe I shouldn't heal you."

I almost smiled. "Let's not pretend one measly orgasm is enough for your needy cunt. Sit," I instructed. "Fuck."

"I'm giving the orders today, Captain," Astrid replied, bracing her palm in the center of my chest, just an inch away from my wound, and rubbing her clit over my painfully hard cock. "And you know what? I think I don't want to *sit* and *fuck* just yet. I think I want to play while I've got you here, pinned beneath my thighs."

I was going to die from sexual frustration, rather than injury, at this rate.

I reached up to cup the back of her head, tangling my fingers in her bright hair and running my claws over her scalp as I dragged her closer to me. For all her tough talk, Astrid didn't protest when I guided her ear closer to my mouth.

"You can play on my knot."

Showing her that I wasn't quite the wilting flower she thought I was, I held Astrid's head in place, notching my cock at her entrance and thrusting shallowly. It was agony in the most literal sense of the word—my chest burned at the movement—but I was greedy for her. Every second of pain was worth it.

With my other hand, I grabbed her ass, claws digging into her flesh the way I knew she liked. There had to be a bite of pain, a sting that grounded her. That reminded her that she hated me, otherwise she'd turn that hate inwards on herself.

"I hate that you feel this good," Astrid whispered, blunt nails clawing at my chest in frustration, close to but always careful to avoid my wound. "*Why* do you feel this good? Like you're..."

"Like I'm what?"

There was a strange, rumbling sensation building in my chest, and I realized right before the sound escaped that it was a *purr*. I swallowed it down as best I could, terrified of what it meant that it had happened in the first place.

I all but shoved her upright so she was sitting astride, trying to put some space between us to clear my head, and keeping her neck safely away from my rapidly elongating teeth.

"Like nothing," Astrid snapped, glaring down at me as she struggled to find her balance without using her injured hand. "Never mind. Come on, knot up so I can leave."

"I thought you weren't going to let me knot you again," I retorted, spine arching off the ground at the hot, silky feel of her cunt squeezing around me. She shifted her weight, fingers splayed over my stomach, and carefully used her other hand between her legs, rubbing her clit with each roll of her hips. My wound was already knitting itself back together more efficiently as power trickled through my blood.

"This is a special occasion," Astrid gasped. She fluttered around me, her eyes taking on that telltale glaze that meant she was about to come.

Fine by me. Next time I'll come on your skin and rub it in so good, you'll never lose my scent.

With a gasp of pleasure I'd be hearing in my dreams, Astrid came, bearing down until my knot was securely in place, expanding rapidly to lock us together. I came so hard, my head felt faint, and I clung on to her a little tighter, needing Astrid to anchor me while my mind found its way back to this plane of existence.

A strangled, choking sound escaped me as I forced back another wayward purr. It was an intimate sound made between content, trusting lovers. I'd only ever heard rumors of it.

Smears of dark blood crisscrossed Astrid's skin from when I'd dragged her towards me, and she tilted her head to the side, still panting for breath as she swiped her finger through the fluid, examining it curiously.

"Your blood is black."

"It is. Does it repulse you?" I asked, digging my fingers into the flesh of her ass, addicted to the softness of her form compared to the hardness of mine. Her skin was practically petal-thin compared to a Shade's.

"No," Astrid gasped, shifting as my claws pricked her sensitive flesh, setting off another orgasm. "My life would be easier if I were repulsed by you."

I understood that sentiment perfectly.

The power Astrid gave me was potent, a thousand times better than any fear I'd ever tasted. Her lust was my own personal brand of poison. My own *Astra*.

With a shallow thrust of my hips, Astrid fell forward again, and I held her hips in place, grinding her clit against me to draw out her pleasure. Every shuddering orgasm, every clench of her cunt around my knot, was power for me. My wound was calling on most of it, but eventually I had enough to move, and it appeared Astrid was the one who needed to rest now.

Not *just* because of the sex. The attack had frightened her. When she'd frozen in place, sword loose at her side, it was the first time I'd smelled true *fear* on Astrid. The remnants of it lingered now, a slightly sour note to her otherwise mouthwatering desire.

"Wrap your legs around me, I'm standing up," I instructed, moving before she could protest.

It immediately set off another chain of orgasms, and she was in no state to cooperate with my instructions, so I cradled her body to mine as I climbed to my feet. The pleasure around my knot was so forceful, my vision wavered.

Why the *fuck* was my bed so far away? It was unacceptable. The moment I felt better, I was going to move it closer to the door, in case of future emergencies.

Every step set off a fresh chain of orgasms, prolonging my knot and wringing more orgasms and more power out of Astrid. Vaguely, I was worried I was overdoing it. How many orgasms were too many? Could I draw *too* much from Astrid and cause her harm? It wasn't as though anyone had done any real research on this.

As carefully as I could, I laid us on the bed on our sides, Astrid's leg draped over my hip, her belly far more swollen than last time. By the night, the amount of cum I'd filled her with must be bordering on obscene. She didn't seem angry though. Not yet, at least. Not even when I ran my claws over her stomach, pressing down lightly on the tightly stretched skin.

"Having fun?" Astrid asked wryly.

"Very much so."

Goddesses, the peace was *nice*. While I enjoyed our verbal sparring matches—and our physical ones—the gentle quiet while we both marinated in our vulnerabilities was almost as good. Maybe because she was the only one who made me feel this way. Weak and powerful, all at once.

I cleared my throat, mentally preparing myself to say the words I knew I needed to say. Perhaps I wouldn't be dead *yet* without her intervention, but that was the direction I'd been heading in. I owed her my life *again*, as well as the apology I'd been working myself up to give earlier.

"Don't," Astrid whispered, slowly coming down from her high. She'd tipped her head back, stretching her neck and exposing her throat to me. Whether she'd meant to do it or not, it showed an extraordinary level of trust.

One I wasn't sure I'd earned, considering how tempting that unmarked expanse of skin was to me. Did she know how alluring it was? Did it occur to her how much I wanted to mark her?

"Don't what?" I asked, still staring transfixed at the juncture between her neck and her shoulder. That was where I would put my bite, if I was going to bite her. Which I wasn't.

But if I *did*, that's where it would go.

"Thank me. I can see the wheels turning in your head."

"There are no *wheels* in my head."

Astrid snorted. "It's an expression. I can see you *thinking*. You think you should thank me for fucking you back to life."

"That wasn't quite how I was going to phrase it."

"Whatever. Anyway, I don't want your thanks. You could have let them kill me and you didn't. We're even."

I blinked, glad that despite how close our faces were to each other, Astrid wasn't looking at me. We were so exposed like this, connected to each other, unable to escape.

"We're *not* even, not even close," I replied, baffled she would think otherwise. "I already owed you a life debt. Now I owe you another. And I'm not sure I *did* save you."

"I froze." The admission sounded like it was dragged from the depths of her being. The urge to reassure her so potent, I couldn't resist it.

"You would have unfrozen." Astrid glanced up at me through thick, dark lashes, gaze heavy with disbelief. "You would have. Not because you're a fearsome, violent little creature—though you are—but because you know deep down that you are far too good to go out like that."

Astrid's lips twitched, her cheeks glowing a faint shade of red again, and I tried to figure out what had caused it. Usually, that only happened when she was angry or aroused.

"You're right. I'm going out in a blaze of glory, not in some back alley fight next to the prison."

She hugged her arms close to her chest, not quite as relaxed as she tried to portray.

"Shall I insult you?" I asked.

"Excuse me?"

"I don't like when you're all... sad. I want to make you feel not sad."

The corners of Astrid's lips lifted in a soft, almost smile and my heart stuttered in my chest. Goddesses, she was beautiful. Unfairly beautiful. Dangerously beautiful. Astra personified.

"You don't like it when I'm sad?"

"It does terrible things to your scent."

She let out a surprised laugh and I did my best to memorize the sound. Had I ever seen Astrid smile like that? So wide and unabashed, she was like an orb of light all on her own when she smiled. "Sorry for stinking up your room with my feelings."

"Oh, I'm not worried about that. The scent of your slick far overpowers it. My cock is going to ache every time I enter my own apartment for weeks."

"I'm less sorry about that."

I snorted. "I bet you are. Tell me whose shadows you were wearing at the ball."

That bright smile developed a defiant edge. "No, I don't think I will. You're too used to everyone doing exactly what you want, when you want it, Captain. It's good for you to be told to go fuck yourself from time to time."

"I'm the *Captain*. That's precisely why everyone should do exactly what I want, when I want," I scoffed, shaking my head slightly, more amused than anything.

Astrid wasn't quite back to her normal self, but it was an improvement. She just needed one big moment to get her confidence back, and she'd be fine. She'd remember just how lethal she really was and rediscover that quiet cockiness that I shouldn't find so appealing.

Except I shouldn't *want* her to have that moment, should I? I shouldn't, but I did. That was what Astrid did to me, though. Made me want things I shouldn't.

As unwise as it seemed to close my eyes, I was exhausted, and if Astrid wanted to kill me then she'd had plenty of far more opportune moments.

I shut my eyes as the power she'd filled me with healed my injury, and left my life in my Hunter's hands.

ASTRID
CHAPTER 15

He'd fallen asleep.

Under normal circumstances, I might take it as a compliment that I'd worn him out, but Soren had basically been on death's door so it wasn't surprising that he needed a nap.

He'd inadvertently given me the moment of privacy to collect myself that I'd desperately needed. I hadn't really absorbed the fact that we'd gotten into a fight with armed Shades at all, let alone that I'd panicked and frozen mid-combat. As soon as we'd gotten back to the palace and Soren had tried to send me away, I'd been single-mindedly focused on following him, on fixing the injury he was so valiantly trying to hide. An injury that I felt responsible for. Healing Soren had been a compulsion, but not an unpleasant one.

That he'd been so *kind* afterwards was an unexpected bonus. His easy conviction that I would have unfrozen, that I would have fought back, affected me more than I wanted to let on.

Everyone had always *expected* me to make the shot, hit the target, take the risk. To be reliably excellent, no matter what kind of day I was having. But Soren... He hadn't seemed fazed by the fact that I'd screwed up, just confident that I'd have found a way to *un*-screw up when it mattered.

I was reading too much into it.

Having someone look me in the eye and say they were going to kill me had rattled me, I could admit to that, and it was making me grasp onto any sense of comfort I could find. Even ones that didn't really exist.

I took a moment to look around the inner sanctum of the mysterious Captain while I had a chance, trying to glean another missing piece of the puzzle that was Soren. The apartment gave me more questions than answers. It was entirely made of dark gray stone, with high vaulted ceilings that made the one room feel spacious and airy. We were lying on a four-poster bed, draped in heavy black blankets, and directly across from us was a fireplace with a hearth big enough for me to climb into, a heavy black pot mounted on a hook right in front of it.

He had a few leather-bound books on a shelf in the corner, but other than that, the only decor in the room were *weapons*. Glinting, silver weapons, mounted on the walls, on racks, stacked in crates on the floor...

Wow, I was definitely not meant to be here.

Soren's knot deflated and I inched back carefully, cursing silently at the *flood* of liquid that gushed between my thighs, instantly soaking the bed.

How did Ophelia live like this? Did she sleep on a tarp or something? It was absurd.

It wasn't as though I could strip the bed with his giant body passed out on it, so near-death or not, changing the sheets was going to have to be Soren's job. I tiptoed back to the door, trailing slick and cum as I went—how delightful—to grab my clothes and slipped into the medieval bathroom, the only other room in this place.

God, I was like a slug, leaving a trail of slime in my wake.

Embarrassingly, there was a part of me that was quite... *smug* about that. Like I was marking Soren's territory, warning off anyone else who might come here with ideas about getting under the Captain's shadows.

I didn't want to share him, and that was terrifying because I didn't have a choice. We weren't a *thing*. This wasn't supposed to have happened the first time, and somehow we kept finding our way back to each other.

Naked.

He'd really opened up a can of worms by dragging me to the Pit with him. It had shown me a different side of him—not quite a *softer* side—but there was definitely a vulnerable underbelly beneath that steely exterior shell.

They'd probably both hate the comparison, but when he'd been silently standing there while Meridia laid into him, he'd reminded me of Ophelia. Long before our parents found her drawings, they'd sit at the dinner table each night and find ways to criticize her for not being "Hunter-y" enough. Every night, she'd just sit there, saying nothing.

It was a self-preservation instinct, one that had served Ophelia well, but that I hadn't expected to see from a leader and warrior like Soren. Did he have parents who'd tried to slowly squash his spirit for years too? Or did he just know what battles to pick when it came to his sister?

Giving myself a perfunctory clean, I hastily pulled my clothes back on, listening carefully to Soren's steady breathing as I went. He was still fast asleep when I crept out of the bathroom, and I indulged in just one moment of blatant staring. He just looked so *peaceful*, and it was a good look on the usually somber Soren. Not that he didn't suit that whole brooding, stoic thing he had going on. Honestly, it was kind of unfair how attractive he made everything look.

It wasn't just that he looked peaceful that made me want to stay, though.

Soren was still weakened. As much as I'd wanted to fuel him up, and as good as sex with him felt, it was hard to really lose myself in lust when he was hurt. It hadn't been enough, not really.

Maybe I could find a way to sneak back later for a blowjob or something.

Ugh, no. Bad Astrid. This *can't* happen again.

All the monster jizz was going to my head, making me soft.

I paused by the door, a crate of small silver daggers just a few feet away. They were the perfect size for me, and my good hand itched with the need to weigh one in my palm, feel the cool slide of metal against my skin.

And there were so many. He'd never notice if I just took *one*.

But I'd know.

Soren could have stayed awake if he'd wanted to—he was stubborn enough to hold off sleep for *days*, I was sure of it. That he'd closed his eyes was a sign of trust, and I wasn't about to throw it away at the first hurdle.

I darted through the small courtyard outside Soren's apartment, using the plants for cover as I wound my way around the back paths that led to Elverston House. For some reason, the palace grounds were lit up like a Christmas tree, and it was only the fact that all the guards seemed to be busy doing something that my hasty retreat went unnoticed.

Was I supposed to be helping them?

I'd been training with the Guard, but I doubted anyone saw me as a real part of it. Soren had been taking my training more seriously than anyone else, but I doubted he thought I was Guard material after I'd frozen today, despite his reassurances.

Elverston House loomed over me, cold, damp, and unwelcoming, but at least it was private. I had wounds to lick.

I swallowed thickly, grateful that the entrance hall was empty as I slipped through the heavy wooden doors. Much like the garden, the interior of the House was even more brightly lit up than usual. What was going on? There must be someone they *really* didn't want shadow-walking around. I sprinted up the stairs and shut myself in my room, releasing a long breath as I leaned back against the door.

"Hello." I smacked the back of my head against the door in surprise at Ophelia's quiet, curious greeting. She sat cross-legged in the center of my bed, head tilted to the side as she stared at me. "I'm pretty sure that's the first time I've ever got the drop on you and I wasn't even trying to."

"It's been a long day." I rubbed the back of my head as I crossed the room, perching on the edge of the bed. I could have sworn I squelched a little as I sat down, and I hoped she didn't notice. I needed *several* baths. "What are you doing here?"

"Checking on you, obviously. Well that, and everyone is busy so Allerick thought I'd be safest with you, since Selene said you were here."

Ophelia raised an eyebrow at me, all thinly veiled judgment.

"Where's Levana? What's going on?"

"You don't know? I mean, I assumed when you weren't in your room that you were out there searching with the other guards, but now I'm thinking you were doing something *far* more interesting."

I froze, not wanting to lie to my sister, especially since her grin was already looking slightly maniacal. "Ooh la la, if only I had my husband's sense of smell. Do you smell like Shade—"

"We're not having this conversation," I groaned, flopping down on the bed face first.

"Astrid," Ophelia said gently, leaning forward to stroke the top of my head like I was Fester the cat. "I'm sorry. Of course we don't have to talk about it if you don't want to. We can talk about Meridia and you can maintain your big, bad, never-catch-feelings reputation."

I swatted her hand away and rolled onto my back, staring up at her. "What about Meridia?"

"Oh, she escaped."

"She what?!" I sat up, twisting to face Ophelia. *Shit, had anyone told Soren? I had to get back there.* "What happened? How the fuck did she get out of the Pit?"

"I'm not a hundred percent sure," Ophelia admitted sheepishly. "We know that the attack on Soren was a distraction, meant to pull some of the guards away from the Pit which it obviously did. Are you alright? You're taking this worse than I thought you would."

Because the Shade I'm catching feelings for nearly died at the hands of his deranged sister's followers, and now she's on the loose again.

"Selene said you weren't hurt." Ophelia was frowning as she examined me for injuries.

"I'm not. I'm fine."

"Some of the guards from the Pit saw the end of the fight." She fidgeted with the blanket, clearly uncomfortable. "They mentioned you may have, um, well, not lived up to your fearsome reputation."

"So everyone knows I froze? Great," I deadpanned. "I've gone from a murderer to a coward."

"Well, I'm pretty sure no one thinks that…"

"Just tell me," I sighed, noticing the reluctance written all over her face. In some ways, Ophelia and I looked super alike, but our expressions were so different that there was no mistaking us.

"There was some suggestion by the guards that you deliberately hadn't acted. That you were hoping they might overpower the Captain."

"What? No, that's not… *no*."

Hadn't that Shade warned me that this would happen? They'd kill Soren, make it look like it was my fault, and everyone would believe them.

"I know," Ophelia reassured me quickly, those two words doing wonders in easing the knot of tension in my chest. "So does Allerick, and we both defended you from that accusation. But you know what people are like."

"Does the Captain know his sister escaped?" I asked casually, as though I hadn't stalked him through the shadows, then the palace gardens, all the way back to his apartment to jump his bones.

"Damen was on his way to tell him," Ophelia replied, waving away my concern. "Soren is very private about who visits his apartment apparently, so we had to track Damen down to do it."

Whoops.

"Anyway, you have to babysit me now because Allerick is worried I'm at risk and everyone is looking for Meridia, including Levana. Apparently, you're one of the few people Allerick trusts with my safety," Ophelia added brightly. It *was* kind of flattering, if I was being honest with myself. I'd wondered many times why Allerick had suggested I train with the Guard, always coming to a negative conclusion about wanting to keep me under watch, but maybe it was as simple as having some backup to protect his beloved wife and mate? Someone that Ophelia was comfortable having around?

That was a nice idea.

"I know you'd probably prefer to be out there being a badass Guard and being stuck with me is lame, but I brought this weird gray clay-ish stuff with me that makes the best face masks. Maybe we could gather up the others and relax while we wait for news? I get that it's not really your thing," she added hastily, giving me an apologetic look like she was massively inconveniencing me by asking me to take part.

"That sounds really nice."

It didn't, to be honest. I didn't like the sensation of having stuff on my face, and while I didn't mind being around the others one-on-one, I still felt like the odd one out in a group.

But that wasn't going to change unless I made an effort. I had to put myself out there, and if I never found a place for myself that felt totally comfortable… Well, at least I could say that I'd tried.

"Great!" Ophelia beamed at me as she clambered off the bed. "You don't actually have to put on the face mask if you don't want to."

"Even better."

"There she is. The Hunter who can't hunt," Adrastos called, taunting me as he had at dinner every night this week. His little buddies laughed, and I ignored them as I always did, stalking past their section of the table to stand at my usual spot near the side entrance.

"I hear you've been kicked out of the Guard now too?" another asked, leaning back off the bench chair, trying to get my attention.

It was another taunt I'd already heard before. Training had been canceled over the past few days since everyone was out in full force, looking for Meridia. No one had kicked me out.

No one had really spoken to me at all. Including Soren.

I'd contemplated just hiding away in my room, but I knew it would only make things worse in the long run. I'd seen the same thing in the pack-like mentality of the Hunters. Someone would fail to make an easy kill, and those who wore their shame openly and took all the shit they were given tended to move past the incident quicker.

Not that I had first-hand experience.

The only time I'd ever failed to kill a Shade was last week.

The Shades all stood as Allerick and Ophelia made their grand entrance, Damen striding behind them, smiling and greeting everyone. Before Meridia's escape, Soren had usually walked in with them, but he'd been absent, undoubtedly hunting her down.

It was stupid and embarrassing to admit even to myself that I missed him, but I had. Soren made me feel things—and not just in my nether regions. He made me feel angry, and annoyed, and desired, and *seen*.

Soren was one of the few beings in this realm who actually treated me like more than just one thing. The shadow realm felt stifling without him, like I was constantly being shoved into whatever box someone thought I should be in, regardless of who I actually was.

"Still no sign of Meridia," Adrastos was saying loudly. "Hopefully, when they find her, they just kill her this time. The Council announced her sentence in absentia. No need to bother dragging her back to the Pit at this point."

"Yes, but the Captain is the one leading the search and it's his sister," someone muttered, provoking some quiet murmurs of agreement. As though Soren didn't have it in him or something.

He didn't swing his Big Shadow Energy around the way other Shades did, but Soren was a badass and cool under pressure. I'd seen it for myself.

Dinner wound down, and I waited until the Shades were filing out before helping myself to the last pieces of meat on the platters at the center of the table. Ophelia gave me an exasperated look on her way out, and I felt the slightest bit guilty. Originally, I'd taken my meals this way to avoid getting poisoned, but I was possibly being a little overcautious.

I didn't really *want* to sit down and make small talk at dinner, but if it was important to her... Maybe I could try. For my sister.

Once the feast hall was mostly empty, I made my way out to the gardens with the intention of heading directly back to Elverston House, but the quiet murmur of a familiar voice nearby had me veering off-course.

Soren and Selene stood near the portal, speaking quietly, with none of the other guards around. He was usually rigid and alert, holding himself ready for battle, but there was no mistaking the tired slump of his shoulders and the slightly sparser shadows surrounding him. I had no idea how Shade healing worked, but he clearly wasn't at one hundred percent yet.

A sharp pain made my throat feel tight. I hadn't wielded the sword that injured him, and I wasn't about to take on any more guilt than I had to, but he was hurt protecting me. I could have taken out that Shade and a couple of others at the same time if I hadn't frozen up.

Stupid, stupid, stupid.

Neither Soren nor Selene noticed as I approached, and I silently patted myself on the back that I hadn't lost my touch in that regard, at least. As always, I double-checked that I was standing downwind, hoping it would carry away the majority of my scent.

"Captain, let me track Meridia instead," Selene asked, a pleading tone in her voice. "I know you don't like to admit weakness—"

"Don't even finish that sentence," Soren grumbled.

"—but you need rest," Selene plowed on, ignoring him. "You need to feed, and I know you don't want to draw from the stores but it's clear you need to."

"I don't need to visit the stores." He didn't offer any further explanation than that despite Selene's blatant curiosity. I was grateful that he kept to our agreement not to tell anyone, and yet annoyed about it at the same time. A large part of me wanted to march up to Selene and tell her that Soren didn't need the communal power stores because he had me and my magical vagina.

It may have been the dumbest, most illogical thought I'd ever had.

"Besides, we really need you here," Selene continued. "No one can adequately keep an eye on the Hunter except you. As much as I hate to admit it, she's good at evading the other guards when she wants to. Most of the time, I only see her in the feast hall at dinner, standing there as brazen as can be." I was so still, I was barely breathing, hoping desperately that the bush I was hiding behind was covering me. "You already know how I feel about the level of freedom she enjoys. That she stood by and watched as the Resistance attacked you... Well, that just solidifies in my mind that she's still an active threat. She's not on our *side*, Soren. The king is blind to it, but I know you aren't. I know you see the truth."

My head was swimming slightly as I waited for him to respond, and I forced myself to take a breath before I passed out.

Please don't look deeper, Cap. Don't put me in the irredeemable box like everyone else has.

"It's not as though I'll ever *forget* that Astrid is a murderer," Soren replied eventually. "I know her hands aren't clean. I know there's always a risk she'll take advantage of the king's trust and betray all of us."

If I'd taken that sword to the chest for him, it would have hurt less.

It wasn't as though I hadn't heard it all before—I knew exactly what the Shades thought of me, and honestly, I didn't blame them. I'd *never* blamed them, never tried to protest my innocence, never claimed that what I'd done was right. Whatever misguided ideology I'd been raised to believe, the end result was the same. I *was* a murderer, even if I hadn't meant to be. Even if I didn't *want* to be.

I liked to think I was more than just *that*, though, and that even if the majority of Shades couldn't see it, those who mattered to me would. Ophelia saw me as something more. Even Allerick had seen potential in me to be more than who I'd been when I first arrived.

And Soren...

God, I was stupid. So incredibly, embarrassingly stupid.

On silent feet, I slipped away, taking the longer route through the garden so the leafy plants would hide me on my way back to Elverston House.

At the last minute, I veered away, heading for the river. For the spot where we'd been together. I really was a glutton for punishment.

Had I been just a convenient warm body for him? An easy source of power?

Or was it something more malicious than that? Some kind of power play in fucking the most hated ex-Hunter in the realm, in making me needy and desperate for him.

I'm going to be sick.

Had he been laughing at me this whole time? Getting off on my eagerness? *No. No, he's not like that.* He'd even ceded control to me last time and that had to mean something, didn't it?

But did it, really? When he could have overpowered me whenever he wanted? Even bleeding out on his floor, he'd probably still been physically stronger than me.

The humiliation burned its way up my throat, and I half dove, half stumbled into the bushes to empty the contents of my stomach.

I wanted to hate Soren, but I couldn't see past my own self-loathing to find room for it. After all, he'd only told the truth.

Even without a super sensitive Shade nose, I reeked of vomit, and I knew that I was projecting my emotional state with my scent. I needed to get it off. I needed to shock myself back into my usual state of apathy, because I couldn't function with this level of pain.

I moved to the riverbank and with shaking fingers, began unlacing my sneakers.

SOREN

CHAPTER 16

I was so weak, just walking through the garden toward Elverston House felt like climbing a mountain.

I needed my strength, I needed to *feed*, but I didn't want to take anything from the stores when the entire realm was depending on it. I should be *adding* to the stores, should be able to heal myself fully several times over, but I hadn't seen Astrid in days.

That was more my fault than hers. I'd been following Meridia's trail all around the realm, barely stopping to eat or sleep. Perhaps I'd selfishly hoped that Astrid would sneak into my apartment again, even though I hadn't explicitly extended an invitation.

How was Astrid feeling? Was she still giving herself a hard time for freezing during that fight? It bothered me that I didn't know, that I hadn't checked in. Especially because of the stupid, persistent rumors that Astrid's inaction had been intentional. That she was *hoping* I'd be hurt.

Everyone was so wrong about her.

A trickle of unease ran down my spine at the way I'd agreed with Selene. I was no better than they were.

If anything, I was worse. While I hadn't forgotten what Astrid had been, I also knew *who* she was, at least a little. She was stoic, but possessed a deep well of compassion. She was strong and fierce, but could be soft and vulnerable.

She'd trusted her family and her community and believed wholeheartedly that she was doing the right thing, but she'd also questioned the Hunter Council before she'd *had* to. Before Ophelia had been whisked back to the mortal realm, before the Council's nefarious plans for the Shades and the treaty had been revealed, Astrid had known something wasn't right. She'd investigated and drawn her own conclusions, even when they had gone against everything she'd been raised to believe in.

There was more to Astrid than anyone realized, but I didn't know how to communicate that to anyone without giving the intimate nature of our relationship away, and she'd been very clear on keeping that a secret.

I'd agreed to those terms. Why was I now feeling so... *slimy* about it?

There was a splash from my left, and I veered towards the river. The orbs were shining brighter than usual so theoretically, Meridia couldn't shadow walk to the palace grounds, but I was on high alert, just in case.

The orbs illuminated this area enough that it wouldn't be possible to travel through the shadows, but it was still dim here and not inviting in the slightest for a swim.

A flash of red hair beneath the surface was all the encouragement I needed to wade in, sucking in a surprised breath at the chill.

What was Astrid doing here? Were the heated baths below Elverston House not a nice enough spot to bathe?

She surfaced just as I went to reach for her, stumbling out of reach of my claws before I could touch her arms.

"Did I frighten you?" I laughed, holding my hands up. "You're not usually so easy to sneak up on."

It wasn't as though I was at my best either. In my exhaustion, I was clumsier than usual.

"You didn't frighten me." Astrid's voice was always quiet and even, rarely giving anything away, but it was subdued even for her. "What are you doing here?"

I blinked hard, not wanting to let on just how difficult it was to focus. Every part of me was drained, and I selfishly hoped that Astrid would repeat what she'd done immediately after I was injured and take charge. Fuck me senseless and fill me up with power, without making me ask for it. Without making me vulnerable.

I *knew* it was selfish. For the gift Astrid would be giving me, the least I could do was be brave enough to ask for it. Astrid deserved that much.

"Captain, what are you doing here?" she repeated. Right. Question. Answer. That was how this worked.

"Looking for you."

Astrid waded past me, nodding to herself as though that was the answer she'd expected. The moment she was on the riverbank, she began peeling off her soaked top, showcasing all that smooth skin I could never get enough of.

"Well, you found me. I don't need to ask *why* you were looking for me." She pushed down her leggings entirely willingly, without any encouragement from me. So why did I feel like I'd done something wrong?

I fought my way back to the shore, the water providing more resistance than usual in my weakened state.

"Wait," I rasped, softly wrapping a hand around Astrid's wrist. "We don't have to—"

"I know."

I scanned her face, struggling to decipher the emotion I saw there. Or rather, the *lack* of emotion. Astrid was always stoic—unsmiley compared to the other former Hunters—but today was different. There was no flash of defiance in her eyes, none of the tightness in her jaw from the way she always clenched her teeth, constantly on the lookout for threats. If anything, she just looked... tired.

"Go on," she insisted, gesturing vaguely at the space around us. "Put up the shadow tent."

I hesitated for a moment before shrouding us in shadow. "Is this... Do you want this?"

That at least wiped the tired look off her face for a moment. Her features softened for the briefest second, and I could have sworn I felt the burn of her gaze beneath my skin.

"I don't do things I don't want to do. Not even when other people want me to do them," Astrid said, cool mask back in place as she stripped off her panties, leaving her bra on.

There was more to that statement than what lay on the surface, but the sight of all that mouthwatering skin on display could distract me like nothing else.

"On your back," I rasped, hungry for a taste of her cunt. It had been *days*. Too long.

Without breaking eye contact, Astrid lowered herself to the ground, leaning back on her elbows and raising an expectant eyebrow at me.

I blinked, not having expected her to listen. No argument, no huffs of irritation, nothing.

"Did you miss me?" I asked, dropping to my knees and running my hands over the damp skin of her legs. She was so *cold* already. Maybe this wasn't a good idea—

"Yes."

My grip on the back of her legs tightened. "Yes? Yes, you missed me?"

"Yeah, Captain. I did miss you." She sounded miserable about it. "But I'm not really in the mood to talk, and you look like you're about to collapse. Sure you're up for this? Maybe you need to lie back and let me do all the work."

"I'm more than capable of fucking you senseless, no matter how exhausted I am," I growled, climbing over her body. "I'm losing my fucking my mind over you, I have been for days."

Astrid sucked in a quiet breath, the sound somehow too loud and too quiet all at once.

My teeth found their way to her collarbone without conscious thought, scraping softly over the skin without breaking it before working my way down her body. I paused to lavish attention on one breast, then the other, teasing her nipples with my tongue.

She arched up beneath me, hands finding the base of my horns, squeezing them just the way I liked.

I kept moving down her body, nipping at her waist, her hips, before guiding her legs apart, claws digging into her thighs.

"Are you going to feed me, Astra?"

"Do you not always leave well-fed, Captain?" I shifted down, settling myself more comfortably between her thighs. Astrid elegantly, *confidently* draped her legs over my shoulders and my cock grew somehow harder.

I buried my tongue in her cunt, not wanting a single drop of her slick to go to waste. How could I have stayed away from this for days? What was I thinking?

"Captain," Astrid whispered, heels digging into my shoulder blades. "*Harder.*"

I lapped more forcefully at her clit, pressing my mouth against her so she could feel the sting of my teeth against her most sensitive flesh. A hint of danger that she knew I'd never act on.

Her grasp on my horns was almost desperate as she quickly found her release, bucking wildly against my face.

If we had more time, if she wasn't freezing beneath me, I'd drag more orgasms out of her. Have her thighs coated in slick before I impaled her on my knot. We never had enough time—it was always a hurried, secret tryst. I wanted to *enjoy* her, for us to *enjoy* each other.

"That was embarrassingly fast," Astrid panted. "You're far too good at that."

"Needed you to come. Need to knot you," I rasped, struggling to form words. I crawled up her body, rocking the tip of my cock against her clit.

"Wait, I want to try something different," Astrid said suddenly, wriggling beneath me until she had enough space to roll onto her front. "Like this."

Her back.

I'd never seen it before.

More unmarred, silky skin that I wanted to dig my teeth into.

But I'd thought she *didn't* want this? Hated the idea of giving me her back? Maybe her strange mood was a sign of things thawing between us. A sign that she trusted me *more*, not less.

"Of course. Whatever you want," I agreed, sounding reverent even to my own ears.

I braced myself on one arm, gripping the small swell of my knot as I pressed the tip of my cock at her entrance, adjusting to the feeling of this new angle. Astrid's hair had slid to one side, exposing her neck, and I clamped my jaw as tightly together as I could physically manage.

I always wanted to bite her, but the urge was stronger than ever. *Needed to bind her to me. Needed to keep her.*

Astrid lifted her hips, rocking back against me, her silent command clear. And I followed her orders willingly, sliding my cock into her hot, welcoming cunt. Her round, delicious ass pressed against my hips, and I could have sworn I was even deeper inside her from this angle. Between the feel of her pussy and the view of her neck, I wasn't sure I was going to come out of this healed and energized like I'd hoped.

Fucking Astrid from behind might just kill me.

Her harmless, blunt nails scratched at the ground, a breathy moan escaping her as I braced myself on both hands and fucked her like I goddamn meant it.

"Harder," Astrid demanded hoarsely.

"Do you *want* me to fuck you harder? Or is this your way of punishing yourself?"

"Captain," she hissed, rocking her hips back against me to encourage me deeper, her legs trembling with the effort.

I wanted to wrap myself around her, press my mouth to her skin without breaking it, but I restrained myself. I gave her what she wanted, each thrust shoving her knees harder into the dirt because I was helpless to do anything but.

Pushing my luck, I gathered her hair in my hand, my nails scratching lightly at her scalp. Her pussy clenched around me, spine arching as I gave her hair a light tug.

Fuck, she was sexy. This was the Astrid that no one else got to see. Demanding and needy, slick and ready for me, and completely at my mercy. This Astrid was mine. Only mine.

As if she could hear my thoughts, she let out a mewling gasp as her orgasm washed over her, cunt strangling my cock. A small voice in the back of my mind told me to make it last, to draw it out, but I had no idea where it came from. This wasn't the end, it was just the beginning.

With a groan, I found my own release, pressing Astrid down to the ground, draping myself over her back and pushing one of her knees forward to open her deeper to me. My knot swelled even faster than usual, as though my body was rushing to lock us together, to stop her escaping. My teeth felt like they had a mind of their own, and I was engaged in active warfare to keep them safely confined in my mouth where they belonged.

Every cell within me felt restored as we lay together, silent except for our labored breathing. It wasn't just the physical either—being with Astrid soothed a part of my mind that I hated even acknowledging. A part that felt like every facet of my personality had been smothered by my role, and also that I had no right to complain about it because being Captain of the Guard had been the only dream I'd ever had.

Why was it that she had this effect on me? Was it because she had no expectations of me? Astrid didn't care if I was fulfilling the role of Captain perfectly because she didn't respect the role in the first place. Though that didn't feel quite right either. She'd taken every training session seriously, had always shown up and been ready to take orders, despite the hostility she faced.

"This is new," I commented, once I'd caught my breath. My weight was still bearing down on her back, although I tried to keep most of it on my forearms. "I thought you said you wouldn't ever give me your back, hm? You must be warming up to me."

There was a teasing note to my voice, and I thought she might scoff at the very least, or remind me that she hated me, but instead there was an almost deafening level of silence.

The sharp ache in my teeth receded suddenly, far faster than it ever had before. It took me by surprise, and combined with the smell and feel of our coupling, I didn't realize right away that there was a strange note to Astrid's scent.

Shit, was that... fear?

No, fear didn't seem quite right. I'd smelled fear on Ophelia before, it wasn't like this. But this... I'd caught this sour note from the queen before too. What did it *mean*?

My knot seemed to deflate faster than usual, like whatever that scent was signaled my body to back off.

"Astr—" I began, but she was already scrambling upright, slipping past me to slide into the river, washing away the evidence of me between her thighs. I'd tugged her hair free from its usual tie, and she shook it forwards, almost as though she was deliberately hiding her face from view. It looked as though she was rubbing her cheek with the heel of her hand, picking up her pace when I attempted to follow. "Wait, *Astrid*—"

She sucked down a lungful of air before submerging herself completely in the river.

What was she *doing*? The night had only grown colder and darker around us. The river was barely swimmable before, it was infinitely less so now.

She emerged with a gasp, shoving sopping wet hair back from her face.

"Get out of there, you'll freeze to death in that water," I barked, attempting to reach for her. She'd gone so pale that I wondered if she was halfway there already. Humans—Hunter or otherwise—were so fragile.

"I'd save you all a job if I did." She laughed, and there was nothing happy in it. There was an almost *mean* edge to it, which was bizarre because hadn't Astrid always been mean? Why did this sound so different?

With impressive grace considering how much her limbs were shaking, she ducked out of my reach, climbing onto the riverbank and forcing her soaked, weak limbs into uncooperative clothes.

"No one wants you dead." I followed her, pausing a few feet away. Some gut instinct told me to wait, to hold back. That this was prey ready for flight, and that the alternative was *fight*, and I didn't want to fight Astrid.

With a huff of frustration, she yanked her shirt down over her wet skin, the dark material immediately clinging to the contours of her body. Finally dressed, she gave me her full attention, and I almost wished she hadn't.

What was this feeling? These loaded looks between us? We were having an important conversation in a language I didn't fully understand.

"Are you at full strength?" Astrid asked, dismissing what I'd said entirely.

"I am." Was that what this was about? "Thank—"

"Don't *thank* me for fucking you," Astrid interrupted, wrinkling her nose in dismay. "You should have no problem tracking down your deranged sister now, right?"

"No. No, of course not."

"Good. Then you should go and do that. Go be the Captain and do Captain things."

"What was it we said about you giving me orders?" I asked, scrambling to find the levity that our interactions usually had. Astrid's gaze softened slightly, but the levity never came.

"I have one more to give, Captain. This was the last time, okay? We can't do this anymore." She took a deep, unsteady breath. "No more. That's my final order."

"Astr—"

"Please don't argue," she whispered, teeth chattering with cold. She wrapped her arms around her middle, so uncharacteristic of *Astrid*, I didn't know how to respond. "Let me have this one command, okay? And you go out there and be the Captain and track *your* sister down so she doesn't hurt *my* sister."

Astrid took a few steps backward, watching me for a long moment before turning and heading for Elverston House.

Leaving me behind.

ASTRID
CHAPTER 17

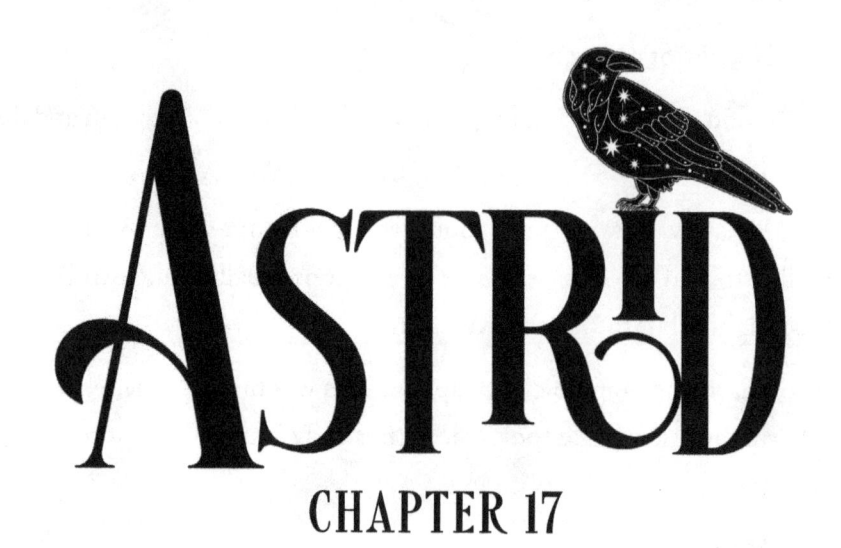

"Knock, knock!"

I tipped my head back against the wall of the window seat with a silent groan as Ophelia carefully let herself into my room, pushing the door open with her hip while carrying a tray of food and two cups of tea.

"Don't you have people for that these days?" I snarked, even though it wasn't her fault that I was in a shitty mood. That I'd been in a shitty mood for the last two days, and probably would be for the foreseeable future.

"Well, aren't you just a barrel of peaches?" Ophelia replied, totally unfazed. "Did you run out of pickles or something? Move your legs. I don't have long—Levana escorted me over and she has other places to be."

With a long-suffering sigh, I folded them beneath me, making room on the window seat for her to set the tray down before sitting down against the other wall.

"Sorry," I muttered, concentrating hard on making both cups of tea just the way we liked it so I didn't have to make eye contact with Ophelia. One of the many ways I'd underestimated my sister over the years was in her ability to read people. "I haven't done my workout yet today, it makes me irritable."

"Or yesterday, from what the girls have told me. In fact, they said you've barely left your room at all."

Traitors.

Ophelia accepted the cup I handed her, raising a questioning eyebrow as she blew the steam away.

"What's going on, Astrid? Are you upset that the Guard didn't ask you to help find Meridia?"

I blinked, not having expected that assumption at all. Then again, both Soren and I had been diligent about keeping our *relationship*—a generous term for it—quiet, so it made sense that Ophelia thought I was nursing a bruised ego rather than a broken heart.

"No. No, of course not. I'm well aware that no one trusts me with anything, and nothing is more sensitive and urgent than recapturing Meridia."

"I trust you." Ophelia frowned, looking personally affronted she seemed to be the only one who felt that way. "I wish the Shades could understand the conditioning we went through. The steady diet of hatred we were fed about them right from infancy."

"It wouldn't help if they did," I replied flatly, focusing on cooling down my cup of tea. "We'd still be the sum of what we *did*. That's why you were so easily accepted here and I never will be. You never *did* anything wrong."

Ophelia was silent for a long moment, and I knew I'd said too much. Been too honest about the things that were bothering me. I didn't want to lean on Ophelia—I was the big sister, and I'd failed her so many times already. She deserved to have family who loved her and put her first in her corner, and our parents sure as shit weren't going to be that, so it was all on me.

"Atti," she sighed eventually.

"Busting out the childhood nickname, this must be serious."

"It is. Shut up and eat a cookie, I have profound queenly wisdom to bestow on you."

I snorted, grabbing an unappetizing-looking gray cookie as instructed and sitting back to listen.

"We're not good at doing this whole sister thing. We never really got a chance to be sisters as adults, and since you've been here, we've both been busy settling in to our new roles. I should have made more time for you, and I'm sorry that I didn't."

"Ophelia—"

"No, let me finish. The other day, when I saw you after the attack, you said you were fine. You very clearly were not fine, and you're not now, and I'm sorry I didn't notice. I get why your guard is always up here, I know that you haven't exactly been welcomed with open arms, but you don't need to have your guard up with me. Let me be your safe space. Know that whatever you say in this room, stays in this room. Please, Astrid, let me *help* you."

"You've already helped me," I mumbled. "You let me live here after I betrayed the Hunters Council and had nowhere else to go."

"Stop that," Ophelia said sharply, taking me by surprise. "You're internalizing the anti-Astrid bullshit. You betrayed the Hunters Council in order to help me and this entire realm. This is your home. This is where you're meant to be."

To my horror, my throat started to tighten, eyes burning with the effort of not crying as the conclusion I'd been drawing in my own head over the past couple of days came tumbling out. "No, Lia. This is *your* home. The Shades will never accept me. No matter what I do, I'll always be a murderer in their eyes, and I don't blame them for feeling that way."

"I disagree," Ophelia replied, shaking her head. "The Shades who've spent time with the other former Hunters, who've learned about how we were raised and the hatred we were taught, are already spreading the word and changing minds among the wider community. That grace and compassion will only grow, and it will extend to you. You saved the Captain's *life*."

"You're an optimist, baby sis. I've always admired that about you." I swallowed past the painful tightness in my throat. "I froze up during that attack because I just... *couldn't*. I looked at that Shade and all I saw were all the times I'd been wrong. All the *innocent*—" I choked on the word, a gasping sob catching in my throat. Ophelia set down her tea before carefully taking mine from my hands and moving the tray onto a side table.

"Come here," she murmured, sitting back on the window seat and opening her arms. And even though I was the older sibling, the warrior, the one who was meant to protect her, I crawled into my baby sister's arms and sobbed into her shoulder while she stroked my hair and encouraged me to let it all out.

I'd frozen up because I couldn't do it, and for the Shades, it was just further confirmation that I had ill intentions, that I'd *wanted* Soren to get hurt. And maybe I could have lived with those wrong assumptions if *he* hadn't thought the worst of me too.

"You're in the middle of doing something really hard, you know. So hard that some people go through life *never* acknowledging their past mistakes, never acknowledging that they did the wrong thing or did it for the wrong reasons. Plenty of those people—including our parents, probably—double down, because it's easier than looking inside themselves and realizing they might not like what they find. Maybe it doesn't feel like it right now, but you're so much braver than you know, Astrid."

I appreciated that she didn't tell me it would be okay. That she didn't try to absolve me of my crimes, because I didn't want nor deserve absolution for them.

"Eventually, the others will see in you what *I* see in you. What Allerick sees in you. What the other ex-Hunters see in you." Ophelia encouraged me to shift until I was leaning back against her, both of us squished up in the window seat, her arms wrapped around my shoulders.

"You know, I was usually the big spoon between us," I joked weakly. "When you were little and used to come and sleep in my bed."

"Did I? I don't remember that," Ophelia replied, sounding surprised.

"You were very little. You used to have nightmares—apparently I never did, so our parents decided to handle it by being total assholes to you about it. You started showing up in my bed in the middle of the night because I was nicer." I smiled wryly at the memory, yanking down my sleeve to wipe away my tears. "I'd comfort you by telling you that you were safe because I'd kill all the monsters before they could get to you. I guess I was a little psychopath, even back then."

"Huh. To me, it sounds like you were a loving, protective big sister, who was comforting me the way you'd been taught how." Ophelia playfully tugged at the end of my hair, the affection causing a pang of longing in my chest. I'd only just gotten her back in my life, and I had to let her go again.

"There's that optimism again. Lia—" My voice cracked and I cleared my throat, taking a deep steadying breath. "Lia, when I said this was your home, that I'd never be accepted here, I meant it. I can't stay."

Ophelia froze before half-shoving me upright so we were facing each other. "Astrid, you can't leave. Think this through—you're not exactly welcome in the human realm."

I twisted awkwardly to look at her, tucking my legs to my chest and wrapping my arms around my knees.

"Well, I wouldn't go back to Denver, that's for sure," I agreed, staring at my feet as I spoke. "But I'm sure there'd be at least one Shade willing to shadow-walk me somewhere else on Earth. I can sneak into a whole new country, give myself a new name, a new identity..."

I blinked hard, trying and failing to get rid of the burning feeling behind my eyes.

"You've given this a lot of thought," Ophelia said softly.

"I'd be naïve not to." And I was done being naïve.

"So, where are you thinking?"

"Australia?" I suggested, vaguely imagining getting a job on the beach and wearing a bikini all day.

"Absolutely not," Ophelia replied, shaking her head. "That's the one country where the shadow monsters are the least scary things around. Even the *sun* is more deadly there."

I snorted. "New Zealand? It's Australia without the poisonous stuff."

"Mm, the UV issue still stands. You'd burn into nothingness like a vampire walking into sunshine on your first day."

"Fine. Ireland? We still have cousins there, don't we? Though I'm guessing they'd lock me up on sight for my traitorous ways," I added drily.

"Definitely nowhere we have relatives," Ophelia agreed.

"Any suggestions?"

"Nowhere." Ophelia looked like a kicked puppy and it broke my already fractured heart just a little more. "I'm trying to be supportive, but I don't *want* you to leave. Neither do the other ex-Hunters, and Allerick would be disappointed to see you go. Levana has grown attached to you, and Damen has always said good things about you and your work ethic. There must be other Shades you've gotten to know through the Guard. What about Soren?"

I nearly choked on my own saliva. "Soren? What about Soren?"

"Oh shit." Ophelia froze, looking at me with wide eyes before bursting out laughing. "You're usually a *much* better liar."

"I know, I know," I groaned, burying my head in my arms. "I'm emotionally fragile right now, and it's playing havoc on my poker face."

"Well?" Ophelia prompted, grabbing my wrists and dragging them away so I couldn't hide. "You obviously have to tell me everything. Does this have anything to do with you suddenly wanting to leave?"

"No. Yes. We generated a little power for the stores."

"Oh, is that what we're calling it these days?" Ophelia laughed. "You guys were just innocently generating power by spending some quality time on his knot?"

I kicked her leg lightly, giving her my most unimpressed look. "Thanks for the heads up on *that*, by the way."

"Hey, you have no one to blame but yourself. You avoided all the informational sessions I held with your fellow ex-Hunters where I explained the ins and outs of knots and bites. This is why we have sex ed, Astrid." I snorted as Ophelia laughed at her own joke.

It was true. I had avoided those sessions, dismissing them as irrelevant to me. And why? Even if they *had* been irrelevant, why did I always opt to be alone instead? There was a strange, almost icky feeling when I reflected on the lack of friendships in my life.

It was incredibly uncomfortable to realize that *I* might be the problem on that front. That I'd never made the effort, and this was the result.

"Well, that explains why Soren looked so energized all of a sudden," Ophelia mused. "Allerick and I had been worried that he was over-extending himself, then we saw him a couple of days ago and he suddenly looked fine. Oh, a couple of days ago." Her expression turned pitying again.

"It was the last time, and yes, I've been licking my wounds here, trying to figure out if there's an uninhabited bit of earth in the human realm that I can move to and live out my hermit dreams in peace."

Ophelia sighed, awkwardly climbing over my legs to get off the window seat. "I don't think you'd enjoy that really, Atti. And there isn't a feasible way back to the human realm now, anyway. The portals are closed, which means someone would have to escort you, and Allerick would never allow it. It's too dangerous right now. Maybe when things calm down..."

I nodded at the brush off, pulling my legs a little closer to my chest. I didn't blame Allerick for not wanting to put any of his kind at risk to make *my* life easier, but I couldn't see the tension between Shades and Hunters calming down any time soon.

"I wish I could stay longer," Ophelia said, giving me a long look. "Unfortunately, everyone seems to think that Allerick and I are the most at risk from Meridia, so I can't get out as much as I'd like to until she's been, um, apprehended."

Neutralized more like.

"You can always visit me at the palace though," she added, raising an eyebrow at me. Oh yes, the palace, full of Shades who despised me, like the chef who looked ready to chuck a carving knife at me every time I'd seen him. My favorite place. "At least come to dinner, Astrid. You can't live off jerky and pickles."

"Meera is such a gossip," I muttered. "Fine, I'll come to dinner."

The king and queen were too busy with the running and security of the realm to find me a way out, and I understood that perfectly.

I'd just have to find one myself.

SOREN

CHAPTER 18

"Mother," I said calmly, emerging from the entry room that led to my family home only to find my matriarch already waiting for me.

My mother was a fearsome Shade, her eyes a darker orange than mine and her horns almost perfectly straight, ready to impale her enemies on. As always, she was draped in onyx and silver jewels—some around her neck and wrists, most dangling from her horns—and had covered herself in a sweeping array of shadows that trailed along the ground behind her.

"How can you do this? To your own *sister*?"

"Said sister is a traitor, to put it mildly. I suggest you consider your next words carefully if you don't want to pay the Pit a long-term visit."

"I am your *mother*."

I stared at her, unmoved, and eventually she began to squirm with discomfort. Shade pregnancies were rare, each one was considered a gift to be revered, but in an ideal world, my mother would have never had children. She *preferred* Meridia because Meridia was ambitious, but realistically, didn't particularly care for either of us.

"There's no need for that. I have no desire to see the king dead."

"But Meridia does?"

Mother stuttered. "I don't know. I haven't seen her."

That was probably true, but she didn't need to *see* Meridia to communicate with her.

"I'm not feeling overly patient, Mother. I suggest you be cooperative and make this entire process easier for both of us."

She sniffed. "And why is that? Is your little Hunter not feeding you well these days?"

"I don't know what you're talking about."

"You took her to the Pit to visit your sister. There's no way you're not fucking her," Mother scoffed. "If it were any of the other former Hunters, I'd congratulate you on securing yourself a power source. But *that* one... It doesn't say much for your integrity, considering how much you've always gone on about how she's a Shade-murdering abomination who doesn't belong in our realm."

"I never once referred to Astrid as an abomination." She was trying to get under my skin, and it was working. I'd always considered myself honorable, always prioritized *acting* honorably.

Until recently. Not because I'd gotten involved with Astrid, not because I'd developed complicated feelings for her that were hard to admit even to myself. But I'd kept her hidden away as though she was a dirty secret instead of a brave, brilliant beacon of hope who I was privileged to know.

"Introspection is hard. Acknowledging you were wrong and working to overcome it is hard. Obviously, you wouldn't know, since you've never attempted either," I replied flatly. "Astrid was wrong about Shades, and she's been eating crow ever since she realized that. And I was wrong about Astrid, and it's time for me to take responsibility for that. To eat some crow of my own, and hope she accepts my apology."

Mother scoffed, unimpressed, but it didn't matter. It wasn't her approval I wanted.

"Now tell me what you know about Meridia so I can leave, and you can save your own skin."

I arrived back at the palace later than expected, heading straight to my apartment to wash up. Mother had sent me on a wild chase to Meridia's father's home in one of the boggiest regions of the realm, and I was coated in mud and without my sister to show for it.

Frustratingly, I had picked up vague traces of Meridia's energy there, though I wasn't as good at identifying the signatures as Allerick was. It meant that I'd both missed catching her *and* I couldn't throw Mother in the Pit for a couple of days for obstruction. The only thing that could make this day worse would be Astrid avoiding me again.

As quickly as I could, I scrubbed myself clean, only filling the bath as much as necessary to wash myself before climbing out and covering myself in my usual shadows. It had been two days since Astrid had walked away from me, told me that this was the end, and I hadn't seen her since.

Was she avoiding me? Absolutely. In a strange way, that gave me hope. She wouldn't bother avoiding me unless I meant something to her. Astrid had walked into a realm of beings who despised her with her head held high, shown up for Guard training knowing she wasn't wanted there and refused to cower. She'd even attended the ball—and I still had to work out whose shadows she'd been wearing that night.

Astrid didn't hide from confrontation. She only hid when she felt vulnerable. She'd done it with the other ex-Hunters in their attempts to befriend her, and now she was doing it with me.

As much as I wanted to go to her, even just to *see* her, her final command had stuck in my head.

"Go out there and be the Captain and track your sister down so she doesn't hurt my sister."

Maybe I did take orders from her after all, because the idea of going to see Astrid with Meridia still on the loose was unbearable. Like I was personally letting her down.

I closed up my apartment, needing to do a round of check-ins with the various guards. I'd be late for dinner, but that was fine. I wasn't intending on eating anyway. After the meal was done, I'd walk Allerick and Ophelia back to their wing of the palace and update them on my lack of progress. It wasn't all bad—Meridia's father was a new lead worth chasing, and he was a sloppy drunk who had none of his daughter's calculated nature. As soon as I'd updated the king, I'd get started on tracking him.

Well, I had one other thing to do first. One very important thing.

"Captain," Verner said as I passed the portal. "Any news?"

"Nothing I can report on until I speak to the king. Anything to report here?" I was already walking away, heading for the palace doors.

"Not much. No unusual activity at any of the entry rooms. Grounds are clear. The murderer is still holed up at Elverston House."

I froze for a moment, turning slowly to face him. It was no different from how any of the other guards had described Astrid, no different than how I'd described her *myself*, but it was time for that to change. *Past* time.

"You were with me when we put down the rebellion at Oroline Rise." It wasn't that long ago, really. A few days after the treaty with the Hunters had been announced. Some Shades—probably fans of my sister—had held a small mountain town hostage in an attempt to get Allerick to change his mind.

"I was." Verner straightened, watching me closely. "It was a difficult fight."

I nodded. Neither Verner nor I were from snowy regions, and the weather had proved to be more of an obstacle than either of us had expected.

"A difficult fight, though we won in the end. But not without some loss of life."

The ringleader had used a small child as a shield, and it took both Verner and me to free the minor and, ultimately, end the Shade's life before he could grab her again.

"How did it feel to make that killing blow?" I asked him quietly.

Verner startled. "It wasn't... I wasn't thinking of it that way. I was thinking of the child, of the town being held hostage by a few aggressive Shades. I was fighting *for* them, not *against* that Shade in particular, not really."

"Right. We picked a side—this side, the king's side—and we fight to defend the cause we believe in. And we hope to the goddesses that we're not wrong. We hope that what we believe to be good and just truly *is* good and just, because it would be catastrophic to be wrong."

Astrid and I had been on opposite sides of a war that had been waged since before either of us was born. She was a soldier, and I'd been holding her to the standards of a general.

"What are you saying?" Verner asked, a slight edge to his voice.

"I'm asking you to consider what it would be like to discover you were wrong. To find out that you'd acted under orders that you trusted were right, then woke up one day and realized *you* were the villain. Would you switch sides? Help who had once been your enemy, at great risk to your personal safety? Take a *knife* to save them?" I shook my head slightly, my chest tight. "I'd like to think I could set aside my pride enough to do that, but I'm not sure I would."

I blew out a shaky breath, noticing that Verner didn't look much steadier than I felt. "Hating Astrid won't bring your sister back. It doesn't bring any of them back. For every Astrid we bring to our side, that's one less Hunter willing to throw a blade at us when we visit the human realm again."

"You care about her." It wasn't an accusation, not quite, but it was close enough to raise my hackles.

Admitting I cared about Astrid could cost me my career, my home at the palace, my place at court. But I'd already panicked once before. I'd let that fear win when I was speaking with Selene and it had weighed on my soul ever since.

"I do. If you want to challenge my suitability as Captain for that, so be it. Astrid is worth it."

ASTRID

CHAPTER 19

I dragged myself down to the basement to burn some of the sadness out of me in the hot pool, before dressing myself in my most discreet black leggings and fitted black top to go to dinner.

My conversation with Ophelia played over and over in my head, interspersed with flashes of moments with Soren—a combination of memories that would be uncomfortable at the best of times, but given the general aura of despair that coated my mind, felt particularly awful.

I didn't like to think of myself as a quitter, but I had to be realistic, both about who I was and how I felt. My presence here just made everyone else uncomfortable. I was a reminder of everything they hated, and why should they be forced to live with that? It wasn't fair to them.

And I wasn't being fair to myself. Not any longer. Not since I'd gone and fallen in love with Captain Soren. Not that I'd ever been in love before, but I was pretty sure that was what the fluttery, giddy, slightly terrifying feeling was.

I couldn't stay here, couldn't work with the Guard, couldn't see him at dinner every night. Just the thought of it was agony. While I'd never stop repenting for my sins, I could do that while finding a way to be a little bit happy at the same time, couldn't I? I'd find a way to anonymously advocate for Shades in the human realm, to seek out Hunters who *wanted* to travel to the shadow realm and help them realize those dreams.

I'd never be able to undo the damage I'd done, but at least in the human realm, I could make some kind of difference. And I wouldn't have to look at Soren every day and remember how he felt like he was made just for me. I wasn't a romantic by nature, but with him... It felt like we were two halves of the same whole. Soul mates, twin flames, whatever the word was.

Just not in this life.

Not for *this* Astrid, who'd done the things I'd done. Soren was the reward I'd have had if I was good. If I was Ophelia, or Tallulah, or Verity, or Meera.

But this version of me hadn't earned him, and couldn't keep him.

I'd seared the image of Soren standing on the riverbank, rivulets of water sliding down his naked body, into my mind forever. He'd been endearingly confused, impatient, and beautiful, and that was how I wanted to remember him. Free from the anger and suspicion he'd so often glared at me with. That was the memory I was going to take with me.

The others were getting ready for dinner in Tallulah's room, and I slipped past on silent feet, letting myself out of Elverston House and winding around the palace towards the training grounds. For once, there were no eyes on me, no Shades attempting to follow my trail. All resources were being spent on Meridia, which meant I could move around in peace.

Huh. If I squinted a little and ignored all the circumstantial evidence, it almost felt as though the Shades trusted me to move around unsupervised.

Selene was sparring alone as I knew she would be this time of day. If she didn't hate me so much, perhaps we could have been friends. We were both creatures of habit.

"What do you want?" she asked, throwing a shadow-dagger at me that dissipated right before it would have made impact with my forehead. "I'm busy, and unlike the Captain, I get no joy out of babysitting you."

I wrinkled my nose. "Neither does he. But wouldn't it be nice if I was out of your way permanently? A whole realm away, even? The Captain would have so much time on his hands for more important things than babysitting duty."

Selene dissipated her baton, straightening and pinning me with a look that I couldn't interpret.

"You want to go back to the human realm."

I wished I had a shadow baton. Something to do with my hands and make me feel a little less small and helpless. "Yes."

Selene tilted her head to the side. "And what did the Captain have to say about that?"

"It's none of his business."

Selene barked a harsh laugh. "Everything about you is his business, *Astra*."

I threw up my hands in exasperation. "Case in point—he doesn't even know my name. While I'm in this realm, yes I'm his problem—thanks to my brother-in-law's edict. But once I'm back in the human realm, I'm not. You know I'm not going back to the Hunters; they'd lock me up on sight. Or worse."

The nerves in my palm prickled, a constant reminder of how dangerous the Hunters were to me these days. Family, friends, former lovers... I could never see any of them again.

Selene's prolonged, silent stare was unsettling, but as difficult as she made it, I stayed quiet. I'd played this game before—I knew she was trying to make the silence uncomfortable enough that I'd speak to fill it, to give away the inner workings of my mind.

That wasn't going to work on me. Only one Shade had the ability to pluck thoughts I didn't want anyone else to know directly out of my brain.

"The Captain doesn't call you 'Astra' because he doesn't know your name," Selene said eventually, sounding less hostile than I'd ever heard her. "Or at least I don't think he does. We've never discussed it, but Captain Soren is very intelligent, with an exceptional memory. He knows your name just fine."

I scoffed, more than ready to argue that he did it on purpose to annoy me, but Selene forged on before I could speak.

"There's a rare flower, black as pitch, that grows in some parts of this realm. It's called an *astrasettia*. Most Shades shorten it to *astra*."

There was a weird little flutter in my chest, and I employed all the skills of denial I possessed to ignore it.

"Let me guess—it's a gross, terrible flower. It smells bad. Ooh, maybe it's a weed that destroys all the beautiful flowers in its path," I said flatly.

"It's poisonous," Selene replied, her tone deceptively casual. "Just the smallest brush of skin against one petal causes the most agonizing pain imaginable, and there is no known cure. For a Shade who is afflicted by *astra*, a silver blade through the heart is a kindness."

I nodded my head, hoping that my expression didn't give away how much that hurt to hear. "Poisonous astra. That tracks. Perfect. What a delightfully thoughtful nickname." I swallowed, trying to get ahold of my rambling. "So glad we had this chat. Are you going to take me back to the human realm then? Clear the shadow realm of the dreaded astra infection?"

Selene glanced down, and I could have sworn she was trying not to laugh. "No, I'm not. You might be willing to risk the Captain's wrath, but I am not. If I returned you to the human realm, he'd never forgive me for it."

"He'd probably thank you, but *fine*, whatever," I grumbled, giving up on any pretense of looking cool and unaffected as frustration took hold. I all but stomped back to the palace, assessing my options.

Selene had been my first choice because she'd pretty openly despised me, knew the human realm well enough to transport me to a specific location without getting lost, and was honorable enough not to drop me at the bottom of an active volcano for the fun of it.

Now it was time for the backup option.

More reckless than Selene, filled with far more hatred, but also infinitely stupider.

It was a risk worth taking.

It was early enough that the feast hall was empty save for the Shades who were setting up for dinner, all of whom gave me a wide berth as I threw myself down on the bench seat where Adrastos always sat, waiting for him to show up early as he always did. I'd known plenty of Hunters like him in my life, I knew how they operated.

Adrastos was desperate for power, for approval. He had just enough social cachet to run in court circles, but not enough that he could coast by on reputation alone. From what I'd determined, he wasn't powerful, wasn't a fighter, wasn't naturally good at anything in particular, so he'd set his sights on becoming a *personality*.

Well, I could help him with that.

If there was one thing I could promise, it was notoriety.

Just as the palace staff finished, leaving the feast hall mostly empty before the courtiers trickled in for dinner, Adrastos showed up, all swagger and bluster until he saw me in his spot.

His eyes narrowed on me, body tense with anger as he stalked down the long lines of tables. I could admit that I'd half expected him to turn around and bolt rather than talk to me alone—he seemed like the type to lose all the bravado without an audience. Maybe Adrastos was less of a coward than I'd assumed.

"What do you want?" he demanded, standing a healthy distance away from me with his arms crossed defensively over his chest.

"A ride home."

He blinked at me, opening his mouth before closing it again.

"I want to return to the human realm," I elaborated, enunciating my words in an only slightly patronizing way. Whatever. This guy had been a dick to me from day one, and I couldn't muster up any kind of politeness when it came to him.

"Why are you telling me?"

"Because I want you to take me there."

Adrastos' teeth ground together so loudly, I could hear them as I watched him weigh up the pros and cons in his head in real-time.

Pro: Get rid of the Hunter I've always hated.

Con: Possibly upset the king and queen.

Pro: I'd be the Shade who got rid of the Hunter, this might make me less of a weaselly loser in the eyes of my peers.

Con: If the king is mad at me, this might make me more of a weaselly loser in the eyes of my peers.

I sighed loudly, tapping my foot on the stone floor. "I thought Shades respected strength?" A few more Shades were filtering into the hall now, and I made a show of standing up and raising my voice a notch. "I should have known you'd be too much of a coward to act on everything you've been saying. Never mind, I'm sure there are other Shades who actually have the guts to follow through—"

"Shut up," Adrastos hissed, glancing back at the courtiers whose attention was already on us. "Fine. The king will see eventually that I did us all a fucking favor. Meet me at the far edge of the garden after dinner, by the wall of the King's Garden, and don't *tell* anyone."

I hummed in agreement. "Easier to ask for forgiveness than permission. Maybe you're not as dumb as you look. See you later, Drasty."

Ignoring the curious looks from the other Shades, I wandered to my usual spot near the front of the hall, pressing my back against the wall and crossing my arms. The room was filling up quickly, and I was quietly glad that Adrastos hadn't wanted to leave right away so at least I could have a couple more hours with Ophelia, even if it was just watching over her from afar.

She'll be fine. She's well-protected, and stronger than she looks, I reminded myself, digging my nails into my palm. *I'm not betraying her by leaving. The only time she needed me was in the human realm. I could be more useful to her there.*

Everyone stood a moment before my sister and her husband entered, Damen hot on their heels, waving jovially and calling out greetings while the king and queen were entirely engrossed in each other. Strangely, I didn't find the intense love they had for each other quite so nauseating these days.

I was jealous in all honesty, but I'd rather die than tell anyone that. If Soren was the milk to my cookies, then Allerick was undoubtedly all that and more for Ophelia. Except she got to have the fairy-tale ending. She *deserved* the fairy-tale ending.

Ophelia waved to me the moment she sat down, giving me, then the table where some of the other former Hunters were sitting a pointed look. *Go join them. Sit with them. Make friends.*

I shook my head slightly, giving her a half-smile. *I'm fine, don't worry about me. Enjoy your dinner.*

Soren wasn't here yet, and I was grateful for that. Even with the two days of space I'd given myself to refortify, Soren tore down my defenses in a way that I didn't currently have the strength to fight.

Dishes were served, the clatter of eating and talking filling the hall. I stared up at the ceiling as though I was bored of the entire thing while eavesdropping on Adrastos' little circle, curious to see if he would stick to his decree not to say anything when he was such a loudmouth by nature.

"...I've heard that the king has been interviewing replacements for Captain Soren," he told the Shade next to him, delivering his pronouncement before leaning back with the smug self-satisfaction of someone who'd just delivered a particularly salacious piece of gossip.

"It does make sense," the other Shade agreed gravely. "The sense I've gotten from everyone I've spoken to is that Captain Soren is far too skilled, too experienced, to be outsmarted by Meridia. That his failure to find his sister can only be deliberate."

A vein in my temple throbbed. Meridia was wily as hell, as demonstrated by her ability to escape the Pit in the first place, and these assholes were being super disingenuous by pretending otherwise. Secondly, Soren hated his sister and there was no scenario in which he was more loyal to her than he was to the kingdom. Thirdly, I was pretty sure Allerick would rather give up his throne than give up on Soren.

He was a great captain. The best. Adrastos and his ilk didn't appreciate how lucky they were to have him.

There was a flicker of movement in the top corner of the hall, up in the rafters, so faint I wondered if I'd imagined it.

Every inch of the hall was illuminated so that no one could shadow walk into the palace unseen, but the ceiling was definitely *less* illuminated, and the guards' attention was on the doors. I tipped my chin down, glancing upwards through my eyelashes as discreetly as I could so as not to tip-off whoever was up there that I'd seen them.

If only I had eyes like a Shade that didn't *move* so obviously.

I sucked in a breath as I spotted another dark, blurred movement. Oh, there was definitely someone up there, creeping over the rafters, and sticking close to the walls. They had cloaked themselves in shadow, disguising their identity, but it only made their presence more obvious to anyone who bothered to look up.

Which was apparently... just me?

Selene was stationed near the dais in the spot Soren usually kept watch from, having slipped in at some point after her solo training session. I blinked hard in her direction, willing her to look at me, but she contentedly ignored me as usual.

There were other guards stationed at the side doors, but their purpose was to keep uninvited guests *out*, not monitor what happened inside.

Fuck's sake. *Fine.* I'd manage the situation myself. There was a very good chance it would backfire and earn me more enemies, but I was leaving anyway. What was one last blow to my already abysmal reputation?

I strode over to the closest section of table, getting a small amount of enjoyment out of the way these particular Shades flinched at my approach because I'd seen them yukking it up with Adrastos.

"What's on the menu?" I asked, obnoxiously leaning over a female Shade's shoulder to grab a piece of sliced meat with my fingers. "Gray cow? Gray chicken? The variety here is wild, I tell you."

"Savage," one of them muttered as I swanned away, shooting them a sugary sweet smile over my shoulder between bites of the gamey meat. *Gray venison, perhaps?*

The four-inch silver pin I'd stolen from the Shade's hair felt cool against my arm where I'd tucked it up my sleeve, the point digging into my flesh enough to give me some confidence that it could do damage. I should have stolen a knife from Soren's apartment. Even if I could get her attention, Selene would probably rather swallow her daggers than share them with me, so I was going to have to make do.

The shadowy blur moved again, taking care not to attract attention to themselves by rushing. They were undoubtedly heading for the dais where Ophelia, Allerick, and Damen sat, and it was no secret who'd been gunning for the king.

I kept one eye on the almost-certainly-Meridia-shaped shadow, while occasionally trying to make eye contact with Selene, Ophelia, Allerick, or Damen for backup. Oh my god, this place needed cell phones. Or at least walkie talkies. Morse code. *Something.*

I wasn't in a rush to see Soren again, but I did wish he was here right now for backup. He would have noticed me trying to get his attention right away, because he'd have already been watching me—for better or for worse.

As though my thoughts had summoned him, Soren appeared at a side door.

Why'd he have to look so handsome? It was unfair, honestly. His horns gleamed in the orb light, thick shadow tunic thing in place, crisscrossing over shoulders to showcase all the solid, defined muscle underneath. He stood tall and proud, haughty and dignified, and that confidence was more alluring than anything else.

I still didn't think I was a card-carrying monster-fucker in the way Ophelia and Verity were. I was just a Soren-fucker. I didn't care about fancy appendages, I just wanted him. And I couldn't have him.

He gave me a once-over as though he was verifying to see I was whole and healthy, holding up one finger when I did my best to beckon him over with my eyes and pausing to speak to Selene. *Damn it.* The shape above picked up its pace, now with far less finesse. Soren's presence had panicked them, and that was really all the confirmation I needed. Besides, they were getting closer to the dais, and I wasn't taking chances with my sister's life.

A sense of calm and focus descended, just like it always had when I'd gone hunting in the past. I headed purposefully towards the dais as though I was going to speak to Ophelia, keeping a few feet ahead of Meridia.

Now. It has to be now. Before my scent gave away my nerves.

I let the makeshift weapon drop into my good hand, spinning right before I got to the dais and drawing my arm back before letting the silver pin fly.

Time seemed to slow down, both as I watched its trajectory and waited for someone to tackle me to the ground at the very least. There was a muffled shriek as the pin embedded itself somewhere, the shadowy cloak falling away instantly.

The hall was at least two stories high, and Meridia seemed to fall in slow motion, landing on the ground with a horrific thump that would have easily killed a human. There were shocked gasps throughout the room, hushed cries of her name as though Meridia was the boogeyman and not a conniving power-hungry lunatic.

Meridia clambered to her feet with a snarl, raising her arms defensively as Soren rushed her, the silver blade in her hand glinting in the light for a moment as she turned away from me to face her brother before she covered herself and her weapon in shadows again.

There was no hesitation this time. Maybe he'd seen it, maybe he hadn't, but I wasn't taking the risk. That blade wasn't getting anywhere Soren on my watch.

I launched myself onto Meridia's back, arms over her shoulders and legs around her waist, using the element of surprise to grab her wrist. She grunted under my sudden weight, attempting to buck me off, but I held strong. If she hadn't been weak from the fall, I would have never managed to overpower her, but I pressed my advantage, using both hands to twist her wrist, lining up the dagger before plunging it into her chest.

Or attempting to.

It wasn't like assassinating a Shade in the human realm. The silver blade didn't swoosh through shadow, whistling seamlessly through the air. There was no satisfying puff of black smoke, followed by the sense of a job well done.

It sure as hell wasn't *easy*.

The ridged hilt of the dagger had clearly been designed for thicker Shade skin, and it dug into my already throbbing hand as I attempted to push the blade in. I'd broken the skin, but realized with horror that I wasn't strong enough to finish the job. Especially not from this angle, barely clinging onto her back.

My stomach churned at the agonized noise Meridia made. I didn't want her to suffer, I didn't want to prolong her suffering—

Before my mind could spiral any further into a state of panic, a warm, strong hand wrapped around my wrist, claws pricking into my skin.

I met Soren's eyes over Meridia's shoulder, finding only calm determination in his gaze. Gently, my fingers were pried off the hilt, and then with a sickening *crunch*, Soren shoved the blade forward through to the vital organ beyond. Meridia doubled over, and I released her instantly, falling hard onto my tailbone.

The landing was jarring, and I froze in place, getting my bearings as Meridia stumbled forward. Just from those few clumsy steps, it was clear that she was no longer a threat. Those strange, smoky dark shadows that I'd seen coming from members of the Resistance at the Pit were already seeping out of her skin.

No, Meridia wasn't a threat to me or to anyone else. Not anymore.

There was movement in front of me, blocking Meridia from view, and I scrambled backward on all fours, my breath sawing painfully out of my lungs, sweat making my palms slip on the stone floor. Pain rocketed up my arm, but I barely noticed it.

The Shades at the tables were on their feet, pushing forward in a surge to see what was going on, though the more sensible ones were running for the doors. Who knew if Meridia had come alone?

In the back of my mind, I recognized that was a risk. That I should be surveying my surroundings, making sure there was no one else, but my muscles were frozen. I couldn't turn my head to look around, couldn't force myself to my feet even as larger bodies buffeted me from every side.

Claws wrapped around the back of my shirt, hauling me upright before I could be trampled. Words were being said, but I couldn't hear anything over the ringing in my ears.

I'd killed someone. Or very valiantly tried to, at least. Embedded a blade in her body, and attempted to push it into her heart.

I really was a murderer. A Shade killer. The incurable poison Soren referred to me as.

They were labels that had felt pertinent before, but distant at the same time. They didn't feel that way now.

I needed to get out of here. I needed to get to the King's Garden.

I needed to go home.

SOREN

CHAPTER 20

I twisted Meridia's own blade into her chest, the final killing blow, as shadows poured out of her wound, her body rapidly disintegrating into nothingness in front of the entire court. My mother was screaming nearby, Selene holding her back while she hurled insults at the king, but it all felt so far away. Like it was happening to someone else.

How had Meridia gotten in *here*? It was so beyond reckless, so brazen and idiotic, that I was struggling to comprehend it. Was she that desperate to end the king's life?

And was it terrible that I was relieved that it was over?

I only wished I'd been the one to plunge the knife in first, to save Astrid that choice.

"Goodbye, sister," I murmured, watching the light leave her dark red eyes. I released her as shadows billowed, her body unraveling into smoky nothingness.

"Captain! You did it!" someone shouted, standing in front of me, blocking my view as I tried to scan the crowd for my Hunter. My Astra. My beautiful, deadly lover who'd just added another tribulation to her list of sufferings. "Adrastos and I were just saying what a wonderful Captain you are, how suited you are for the role—"

"Where is she?" I murmured, pushing past him into the crowd. She was *just* here. How was she so good at that? Astrid disappeared in light the way Shades disappeared in darkness. A result of all her Hunter training—the training that had just saved Allerick or Ophelia's life, possibly both.

How could I be anything but appreciative for her lethal skills now? They'd saved both her life and the lives of the monarchs I'd served.

"Lucky the Hunter was watching the ceiling," someone said behind me.

"Luckier still that Hunters practice throwing projectiles," another added, but they sounded awed rather than bitter. "Did you see her throw that thing? I think it was a hairpin…"

Their reverence made the tight, uncomfortable feeling in my chest grow worse. I could have done more—should have done more—to improve Astrid's reputation. There was no excuse for *not* doing that. I'd known Astrid was more than what she appeared since…

Since the moment I'd met her. She'd defected from the Hunters and fought for this realm and saved my life *twice*. The very least I could have done was publicize that. Countered the rumors and gossip against her with the truth of her actions.

I'd been planning on pulling her aside tonight. Apologizing for the way I'd treated her. Asking—begging, if necessary—for a chance to court her, the way the other Shades were courting ex-Hunters.

There was still time. I could still ask her. The mood was slightly ruined now, though...

"Where is she?" I asked Selene, my urgency bleeding into my voice. I glanced back to where Ophelia was firmly ensconced in Allerick's arms, searching the crowd as thoroughly as I was. "Ophelia will want to see her."

Selene gave me a withering look. "Give my powers of observation some credit, Captain. I *know*."

"You'd be a poor second-in-command if you hadn't noticed anything," I muttered, only slightly defensively. Mostly because I felt stupid and embarrassed for not publicly claiming Astrid for my own right from the beginning. Stupid and embarrassed and selfish. "I'm going to Elverston House—"

"Wait, there's something you should know. Astrid came to me before dinner, asking me to return her to the human realm."

"What?" I snapped, whirling to face her. "Why would you not tell me immediately? Regardless of the... situation between her and me, I was assigned by the king to watch her. If she wants to go back to the human realm, she should be talking to me."

So I could say no and give her a million reasons to stay.

Selene shifted her weight, unusually fidgety. "I believe she came to me because she thought you'd say no, and felt my hatred of her was strong enough to overrule my good judgment. That I'd go against you to see her gone."

There was that fucking squeezing sensation in my chest again.

"I wouldn't," Selene added hastily. "Even if I did absolutely despise her, and I'm not necessarily sure I do. Not anymore. After speaking to her, seeing her so willing to go back to the human realm and the certain danger that faces her there... Well, perhaps I could have done more to separate who she is from the things she *did* in what was, realistically, an almost entirely different life. I know I view Hunters differently now; it's not a stretch to think perhaps her view of Shades has changed too."

That, I understood.

But Astrid didn't.

She'd been given no assurances, and she'd just killed a Shade in front of everyone. Who knew what was going on in her head? Panic, probably.

There were Shades who'd been more vocal in their dislike than Selene had ever been. Would Astrid ask them to return her to the human realm out of desperation? *Please, no.* Astrid's life wasn't safe in their hands. What if they abandoned her in the in-between? She could be lost there forever if she didn't find her way to an open portal in time.

Why hadn't she talked to me?

Why hadn't *I* talked to *her*?

She'd ended things with me. Had willingly given me her back. Had been quieter and more withdrawn for days.

All the signs had been right in my face and I still hadn't seen this coming.

"I have to go. Take care of things here," I instructed, waving vaguely at the steaming heap of shadows that was my sister's remains. "Tell the king I'll come and see him as soon as possible."

I didn't wait for Selene's confirmation, pushing through the crowd and running for the exit. For once, I wasn't thinking of my duty to Allerick, to the Guard, to the kingdom. I wasn't thinking about anything other than getting to Astrid before she did something drastic.

Something I couldn't save her from.

I nearly knocked Adrastos to the ground in the entry hall as I made my way out of the palace and through the gardens toward Elverston House. It was packed out here too with Shades who were rightly wary of what had just taken place in the feast hall and were waiting outside to ensure it was safe to go back in.

On any other day, I'd be reassuring them. Sweeping the palace for any of Meridia's allies, coordinating the cleanup, and working with the King and the Council to get it all in order.

Selene could handle it.

I skidded to a stop at the boundary, suddenly paralyzed by indecision. It was one thing to hastily throw my duties at my second-in-command, but defying a direct order from the king still gave me pause, and Allerick would almost certainly have concerns about my relationship with Astrid. This was a literal and metaphorical line that, if crossed, changed everything.

Risked everything.

I took the step. She was worth the risk.

"Oh, thank god." I startled as Verity barreled down the front steps of the building toward me. "Come on, Astrid is *packing*. We followed her back after the, you know, to see if she was okay. She is very much not okay."

I strode after Verity, following her into the house and up the main staircase to the second floor. Tallulah and Meera were standing in the doorway of a room partway down the corridor, exchanging concerned looks. Both of them startled when they saw me, taking a step back so I could see Astrid, neatly folding her meager possessions into a small bag on her bed. Her hands shook as she worked, and my heart ached for her.

Silently, I gestured for the others to leave before letting myself into Astrid's room and shutting the door behind me with a quiet click.

"You're not supposed to be here, Captain."

"You're not supposed to leave, Astrid."

She shot me an impatient look, though it didn't carry the conviction it usually held, shoving a sweater in the bag more aggressively than she needed to. "Yes, well, I'm not very good at following rules, am I?"

"I disagree. You've been very careful to follow the rules since you arrived here. I will have nightmares about the moment you disarmed yourself by ripping that blade out of your hand for the rest of my life."

She threw the bag down, turning to face me properly. The look on her face, her scent... It was agonizing.

Perhaps for the first time, Astrid wasn't holding back. She was showing me every raw, vulnerable emotion she was feeling, and the pain of her suffering almost brought me to my knees. That she could bear it, had been bearing it alone and in silence...

I'd always known she was stronger and fiercer than she looked, but I never realized just how much.

"I killed your sister."

"*I* killed my sister."

Astrid's lip trembled, but I didn't dare take a step closer. I wanted to go to her, to wrap her in my arms and give her the comfort she was silently screaming for, but she wasn't ready for that yet.

"I didn't know if you'd seen her blade. I didn't want you to get hurt," Astrid mumbled, dropping her gaze to the floor. All my defenses crumbled away as if they'd never been there.

"I did see it, but I'm not mad at you for acting, only that you were ever in a position where you felt like you had to. I should have protected you from that."

"I don't need your protection. I can look after myself."

"I know that better than anyone, Astrid. You're a real petulant little brat when you're in a bad mood, did you know that?"

Her jaw dropped, eyes finally meeting mine again. "Did you just call me a *brat*?"

"I did," I replied calmly, leaning back against the closed door. "You're a Guard-in-training. As your *Captain*, you should have never been in a position to make a call like that. That's my job."

I risked pushing off the door, slowly walking towards her.

"As my Captain," Astrid repeated, her voice giving nothing away.

"Yes," I agreed, stopping a few inches away from her. "But we both know I'm more to you than that."

Her eyes flashed with irritation as she turned back to the bed, clipping my arm with her shoulder in the process. "I'm nothing to you. I'm *Astra*. I'm poison. Selene told me all about it."

"I somehow doubt that," I said drily.

"Why?"

"Because you wouldn't be so mad if you knew. Then again, Selene isn't the soft, romantic type. I'm not surprised she didn't explain the significance properly."

"Neither are you," Astrid muttered, struggling with the zipper on her bag. I gently plucked it from her fingers, tossing it further up the bed and lightly gripping her shoulders, guiding her to face me.

"Astrasettia is viciously poisonous." Astrid looked down at her feet. "And hauntingly beautiful. So exquisite, it's almost impossible not to be drawn in by it, even knowing what will happen if you touch it. You, my *Astra*, have always been beautiful, tempting, and dangerous to me. Not, as I previously thought, because you're a skilled Hunter but because you're *you*. Because you make me want to be something more than the always dependable Captain of the Guard. You make me *happy*, and now I've had a taste of it, I'm greedy for more."

"Soren," she whispered, my name sounding like a reverent hymn on her lips even as she shook her head. "Don't. Don't make it harder. We both know I don't belong here. I'll never be accepted here, and that was before I... Before I..."

Her shoulders trembled as she blew out a long, steadying breath. Watching her struggle to compose herself was agony. Astrid was strong. Fierce. Indefatigable.

Nothing ruffled her. Except me.

"Saved the king? Because that's what you did."

She shook her head again, walking over to stare out the window towards the palace, putting space between us. "Take me back to the human realm. Somewhere far away from Denver. Consider it payback for the life debt, the healing, everything. Deliver me somewhere I can start over, and we're even."

"No."

"No?" Astrid repeated, reeling back like I'd slapped her. "You'd be free of me—"

"You're not hearing me." I stalked towards her, flattening my palm on the wall beside her head, boxing her in against the window seat. "I was going to find you tonight and *beg* for you to court me, if that's what it took. I'm not sending you away, Astrid Bishop. If you convince another Shade to take you, then I will hunt every corner of the human realm until I find you and drag you back."

"Court... me?"

"Yes, court you. *Publicly*, openly. I want to spend time with you, to walk you to dinner each night, to bring you gifts, to proclaim to the world that you're mine until you're ready to wear my bite." I took a long, steadying breath, not wanting to say the rest, but needing to. Needing to set aside my selfishness because Astrid's happiness was more important. "And if you don't want that, if you don't want me, then of course, I'll respect your decision. I'll do whatever it takes to make you happy in this realm, to find a role that fulfills you whether it's with the Guard or not. I want you to be *happy* here, Astrid. Nothing matters to me more."

Astrid stared up at me with guarded, distrustful eyes, but I couldn't ask for her vulnerability until I'd given her mine first. And maybe I was selfish, but I had to try. If she didn't want me, I'd leave, but I had to at least tell her how I felt first.

"I *love* you, you beautiful, infuriating woman." She sucked in a small, surprised breath. "I love you, and only you. You are lethal, and you are compassionate, and you are *mine*, and the only opinion I care about on that front is yours. If you think I'm going to let you walk away from me, into certain danger—"

I didn't finish my sentence. Astrid cut me off, grabbing my shoulders and firmly pressing her lips against mine.

ASTRID

CHAPTER 21

Soren startled, jerking back and looking down at me with wide eyes. I stepped back so quickly, trying to put some much-needed space between us that I smacked my head against the wall behind me. Fucking *ouch*.

The throbbing pain in my skull definitely paled in comparison to the crushing wave of humiliation though. I'd kissed him and he couldn't have gotten away faster.

He said he *loved* me. How had I read this so wrong?

I was an idiot.

"Astrid!" Soren said in alarm, yanking me back into his arms and cradling the back of my head. "By the goddesses, you need medical attention. I've never seen your face go this color before."

I groaned, pressing my forehead to his chest to hide my face. "I'm not hurt. Can you let me go so I can climb into a hole somewhere and die of embarrassment? That'd be great."

He tightened his grip around me. "What? Why are you embarrassed?"

"Because I tried to *kiss* you and you leaped away like I was giving you a communicable disease. Obviously."

Soren tugged the ends of my hair, encouraging me to tip my head back.

"Do it again," he instructed, voice barely more than a growl.

"Fuck no," I shot back, giving him an irritated look. "I'm not risking—"

His claws scraped against my scalp as he tightened his grip, angling my head to press his lips against mine, cutting me off this time. It was only when he froze in place that I realized he hadn't been rejecting me at all.

He just didn't know *how* to kiss.

All this time, I'd assumed the no-kissing-during-sex was a way of keeping some emotional distance between us, but maybe it wasn't that deep.

Maybe Shades just didn't kiss?

I swiped his lower lip with my tongue, encouraging him to part for me, tentatively exploring his deadly sharp teeth. *That explained the lack of kissing,* I thought wryly.

Soren was a quick study, his tongue snaking out to meet mine. A tongue far longer and thicker and *rougher* than mine. And he was *rough* with it, fucking my mouth the way he fucked my pussy. My throat constricted, the thrill of being so entirely consumed by him that I was struggling to breathe sending a bolt of lust between my thighs.

Slick soaked my panties, and my cunt *ached*. If I thought I'd craved him before, it was nothing after hearing him tell me he loved me.

We broke apart, both breathing heavily. God, he looked so handsome like this—greedy to the point of desperation, and yet with a level of care and affection that no one had ever had for me.

"What?" Soren asked, growing concerned. "What is it? Is it your head injury?"

I huffed a surprised laugh. "I don't have a head injury. I'm just in love with you. Though maybe that *is* a sign my head isn't quite right—"

Soren growled a sound of warning, tinged with amusement, hoisting me up roughly, claws digging through the fabric of my leggings, pricking at the backs of my thighs.

"I was going to court you, I swear I was. I was going to go slowly and do everything right. Send me away now so I can get ahold of myself. Tell me to leave, my Astra."

The *my* really changed the whole tone of that nickname, and I didn't think I'd ever get sick of hearing it.

"And if I don't?" I rasped.

"Then I'll fuck you and knot you and bite you right now. If you don't want an infant, then you best hope your human birth control holds up to the amount of cum I'll fill you with."

Oof. I was decidedly *undecided* about whether I wanted kids or not, but his words had my ovaries paying attention.

"I want you. I want your knot, your bite. I want you to be mine."

Soren threw me down on the bed and tugged at my leggings like they personally offended him. "How do you get these godforsaken things off? If you don't want me tearing your clothes, you're going to have to start removing them faster."

I quickly peeled down the high waistband that his claws had been struggling with, before kicking off my leggings and panties. And then he stilled completely. There was no throwing my legs over his shoulders, no rough pinning me down, no frantic, furtive rushing. None of the things I was used to from our times together.

Instead, he stared.

I was usually pretty confident in my body, but the staring went on long enough to start making me self-conscious. Soren ran his eyes over every inch of me as though he'd never seen me before.

"You're freaking me out," I told him flatly, crossing my legs at the ankles and pressing my thighs together to preserve the memory of my modesty. "You're staring at me like this is the last time you'll ever see me and you have to savor every second of it."

I should know. I spoke from experience.

Soren's gaze snapped up to meet mine. "This is just the beginning, my Astra. I never want to take for granted how fortunate we are to have these moments together. I intend to savor every one, so you'd better get used to the staring."

My muscles relaxed as he gently gripped my knees, pushing my legs apart and kneeling at the end of the bed.

Then he took his hands away, brushing a soft kiss just above my knee.

There was no pressure weighing me down, no pinning me to the mattress. There was just *us*. His body and mine, and the love and the hate and every moment in between that connected us.

It was terrifying.

"Can you take me?" he asked, his voice curling seductively around me. "Look at this slick—yes, I think you can. Later, I'll have you coming on my tongue for hours, but for now... I just need to feel you around me."

"Wait," I gasped, grabbing one of Soren's horns as he crawled over my body, heavy cock rubbing my clit in the best possible way. He stopped instantly, shuddering at the squeeze of my hand around such a sensitive spot. "What are we doing? This isn't what we normally do."

He opened his eyes, staring down at me with so much love, I didn't know what to do with it.

"I don't want to be rough with you right now, Astrid. Let me make love to you."

"I don't know how to do that," I whispered, sliding my hands down his face to grip his shoulders. There was still a part of me that felt I didn't deserve that, that he *should* be rough with me because I was the enemy and I didn't deserve his softness.

Soren hummed, climbing off me and sitting back against the headboard, extending his legs down the mattress. I sat up, tucking my legs beneath me as I watched him silently.

I *wanted* this, but I didn't know how to reach for it.

But Soren did. And I trusted him to guide me through the scary parts.

"Come here."

"You're bossy," I mumbled, mostly as a defense mechanism. I moved up onto my knees, shuffling up the mattress. He reached for me instantly, hauling me onto his lap and encouraging me to straddle his thighs.

"You like that I'm bossy," he replied smoothly, claws digging into my ass cheeks as he dragged my hips forward, grinding my weeping cunt over his thick cock. "You like that I can fuck you senseless, that you can turn that bright, intelligent mind of yours off for a while and just feel."

He rocked my hips, and I grabbed his shoulders again to steady myself, my mind going deliciously hazy around the edges at the sensation.

And then he *purred*, and my vision almost blanked out completely. I didn't even know he could *make* that sound, but I immediately wanted to hear it every second for the rest of my life. It seemed to travel through every nerve in my body, lighting me up like a beacon of contentment from the inside.

"Eyes on me," Soren commanded, not letting me out of his thrall. "I love that I can give you an escape, but sometimes you need to let me love you too."

"That's it?" I rasped. "That's what I need to do? Just let you love me?"

"That's all," Soren agreed. It was harder than it looked. He stared at me like I hung the moon, and every defensive instinct I had screamed to push him away, to not let him get any closer to my squishy, vulnerable center than he already was, but it was far too late for that. Soren had embedded himself so thoroughly in my psyche, I'd never escape him and I didn't want to.

Slick was pouring from me like a fucking waterfall, there was no foreplay needed. I reached between my thighs, pumping his already-soaked shaft in my hand a couple of times before lining him up at my entrance and sinking down, maintaining eye contact.

"That's it, my Astrid. There's nothing to be afraid of here. It's just you and me."

There was everything to be afraid of, but I didn't hide, rising up on my knees before dropping back down again, eyes crossing slightly at the feel of his cock from this perfect angle.

"Kiss me again," Soren commanded. "Teach me."

I cupped his face, letting myself indulge in the pleasure of touching him freely, and angled him where I wanted him. "Like this," I murmured, pressing my lips to his and guiding him where I wanted him. His hands took control of my hips, and I sunk my teeth into his lip as he bounced me on his cock.

Soren growled, claws pricking at my skin. "I'll be doing the biting, my love."

"Well, hurry it up then." I arched my back, showcasing the length of my neck. "Fuck me senseless, put your bite on me, then pet me after and tell me I'm pretty. And keep purring. You have no idea how long I've wanted this. I've *dreamed* about this moment."

"I have some idea," Soren replied, voice laced with humor. "And I know exactly what it's like to dream of you. To dream of biting you. Claiming you. Keeping you."

He grabbed my wrist, pulling it to his face and laving my fingers with his rough black tongue. "Touch your clit for me. You make me want to cut off my claws just so I can stroke that pretty cunt of yours."

"You have a filthy mouth," I murmured, ignoring his instructions and leaning over to open the nightstand.

"What is that—"

The gentle buzz of the vibrator cut him off and I shot him my smuggest grin as I slid the purple bullet down my body, pressing it to my clit.

I was coming within *seconds*. Soren grabbed my arm before I moved my hand away, and even on the lowest setting, I was shoved headfirst into another orgasm, forgetting to muffle my cries of pleasure.

"Oh, this is my new favorite toy," Soren groaned, fucking me roughly through the waves of bliss until I was bearing down on his knot, gasping to catch my breath. I turned the bullet off, throwing it roughly aside and arching my spine as his knot did its thing, expanding and rubbing against every sensitive part of me with greater intensity than any sex toy ever could.

Soren wrapped a hand around the back of my neck, pinning me in place as he shot forwards, embedding his teeth in my throat.

There was no softness, no hesitation. It was the rugged, savage claiming that we both *needed*, and the accompanying avalanche of orgasms were so thoroughly wrecking me that I wasn't sure I'd ever walk again.

How did this feel so *good*?

There was a vague awareness of pain, but the pleasure was so overwhelmingly intense that the prick of Soren's fangs faded into the background. He groaned like he was enjoying this as much as I was, banding an arm around my waist and anchoring me tightly to his body, as if we could get any closer.

My movements felt sort of sluggish as Soren withdrew his teeth, tracing the bite mark with his tongue. My limbs felt heavy, but my head felt light, the kind of feeling I usually only got from too many tequila shots.

But underneath the drunken feeling was *Soren*. Like he was right there in my heart, somehow. Connected to me. *Mine, mine, mine.*

"You have such a beautiful smile," Soren murmured, his claw scraping lightly over my lip. His purr rumbled through me, and I swore I could feel it in my toes.

"I'm not smiling," I slurred, staring into his hypnotic, glowing eyes. So pretty. Like the sun, but *two* suns. And on his *face*.

"You are absolutely smiling," Soren laughed, pinching my cheek before dragging me close for another soft kiss. "Come here, rest your head on me. Let me look after you."

"Okay, but only this one time because your bite made me feel all sleepy. Sleepy and good. And I can *feel* you inside my body, not just in my vagina either, it's so nice. Mmk, I'm just going to… just rest here for a minute."

"Sleep as long as you like, my love. I'll be here."

"We should probably leave your room at some point," Soren murmured, undermining his words by lightly thrusting his hips, the friction of his knot setting me off again. I writhed and panted beneath him, scratching at his chest in both punishment and gratitude.

"No," I rasped, pulling his torso down so he was crushing me just a little bit, in the best way. "I don't want to go out. Everything is perfect right here."

He hummed in agreement, playing idly with my hair where it splayed across the pillow.

"More than perfect, but I think you'll be surprised at how good things are out there too. Besides, you know I'm not meant to be in this building at all."

"Right." I frowned, having not actually given that much thought. "What does that, um, mean? For us?"

Soren smiled softly down at me, sensing my internal panic at even asking a question about the future despite the very permanent step we'd taken in our relationship. "That you're moving in with me, of course. Or we find another home, but I think my apartment is the best solution. The shadow realm is very spread out because we can quickly travel anywhere we need to go. I'm sure you don't want to depend on me to be able to visit your sister, so it would make more sense to stay at the palace."

"And that won't be a problem?" I asked, running my thumb over the sharp planes of his chest. "Me living in the Captain of the Guard's quarters?"

"We might have to get married."

"Married?!" I squeaked.

Soren snorted. "Yes, *married*. A far less permanent development than that mark on your throat."

He leaned down, licking the bite mark again. It must be some territorial instinct, he seemed to be having trouble leaving it alone. Whatever he was doing was working though—somehow, it had already mostly healed, leaving a prominent scar in its place.

I'd gotten a lot of scars over the years, nicks and cuts from playing with daggers, but I *loved* this one.

"I'm not really a big, white wedding kind of person," I rasped, arching into the feeling of his tongue on my neck and triggering another lazy orgasm.

"Mm, me neither. We'll keep it small, private." I grabbed a horn as he tried to get to my throat again, squeezing it hard enough to make him groan, his knot pulsing within me. "Do you want kids?"

"Undecided," I admitted hesitantly. This was probably a conversation we should have had *before* making a lifelong commitment to one another. "What about you?"

"Also undecided," Soren admitted, kissing my cheek while I kept the bite off-limits. "Especially since we don't know what a Shade-Hunter pregnancy looks like, and I don't want to risk you. Not for anything."

Oof, my insides turned to liquid goo, and not just because of the ridiculous amount of cum I was being filled with.

"You'll have to risk me a little bit, from time to time. I still want to facilitate bringing any Hunters here who'd like to live in the shadow realm. And return to doing supply runs, when it's safe to do so."

"Not without me. We'll be able to communicate in the human realm now, through the mating bite."

I wasn't quick enough to hide my giddy smile at how much I liked that idea, and Soren stared at the expression as though he was greedy for it. Like he could never get enough of the dorky grin I'd always been self-conscious about.

"Don't you ever hide that smile from me again," Soren murmured.

"I imagine we both have things about ourselves we've been hiding," I replied softly, love-drunk and chatty. "That we're both going to learn new things about one another if we let our guards down."

"Now that we've let our guards down," Soren corrected, pressing a kiss to my temple. Was it weird to look forward to that? Generally, I didn't like the unknown—it made me feel unsteady—but with Soren, every unknown was just an opportunity. A mystery that I was excited to uncover.

Eventually, his knot softened, and I vowed to move into his apartment as soon as possible because there was no ensuite in my room here and I didn't want to traumatize my roommates by trailing slick through the halls.

Soren grabbed a towel, helping me clean up as best as possible, looking inordinately pleased with himself before rummaging through the bag I'd packed to find me clean clothes.

"You could always just wear my shadows, you know."

"And end up naked when you get called away on urgent Captain business? I think not," I scoffed, clasping my bra. "Let's save the shadow dress for a special occasion."

Finally dressed and semi-presentable, we ventured out of my room, the bag I'd packed swinging from Soren's hand, his other wrapped around my waist.

"Are you sure about this? Shouldn't you, I don't know, *talk* to someone before moving me into your place?"

"I have to go talk to Allerick now anyway, since I didn't hang around after the incident in the feast hall." That was a nice way of putting it. "But I'm going to get you comfortable at my place first, run you a bath. Then I'll go."

"You don't want to bathe too?"

"And wash your scent off?"

I choked on my own saliva. "*Yes*. An emphatic yes. You can't walk around smelling like—"

"Like what?" Verity asked, leaning against the balustrade at the bottom of the staircase with a sly grin on her face. "No need to answer that, we all got an earful last night."

"Good thing I'm moving out," I replied, cringing at myself. I *knew* it was me she was talking about, Soren was all quiet purrs and the odd growl, while I was shrieking my face off after the millionth orgasm.

Some things were beyond my control.

Verity's smile turned soft and romantic, and happiness was way more infectious than I realized because my cheeks were sore from smiling too.

"Good. I'm so happy for you, Astrid. Being mated suits you." Her eyes dropped curiously to the not-quite-healed bite mark on my throat, and my face heated. "You know this means you have to start attending wine-and-gray-cheese night. You can't just leave Ophelia to answer all the, er, logistical questions about mating alone."

"You haven't been attending wine-and-gray-cheese night?" Soren asked, as if his stalking hadn't tipped him off to how antisocial I'd been.

"I didn't know there *was* a wine-and-gray-cheese night," I admitted. "I guess I could make an effort. Or whatever."

"Don't sound so enthusiastic," Verity teased, sparing one last lingering look at the bite. "One day I'm going to find my own Shade to scream down the stone walls with." Soren almost managed to stifle his laugh. *Almost.* "There's got to be a tentacle monster in this realm somewhere."

Soren blinked. "Any Shade can have tentacles if they want."

He sprouted long, winding shadows from his back, twining them around me in a solid shadow tentacle cocoon.

"Oh my god," Verity whispered, looking as though she was witnessing a real-life miracle. "It's possible. It's *real.*"

"This is not my kink on every level," I sighed, cutting Soren a look. I liked having full use of my limbs at all times. He smirked, dispersing the shadows instantly.

"Thank you, Captain Soren," Verity said solemnly, giving him the most respectful look I'd seen her give anyone since she got here. "You've shown me that my dreams are possible, and I'm never going to give up."

"Soren, I think you've created a monster," I laughed under my breath.

SOREN

CHAPTER 22

It took all of my self-control to *walk* through the palace to the royal couple's wing, rather than skip or run or *dance* my way there. There was such an abundance of *joy* in me that I didn't know what to do with it.

I contemplated singing, but Calix rounded the corner, pinning me with his typically welcoming death stare, and I held off.

"Captain Soren," he choked out, taking a step back. "You've been busy."

"I have. Claiming Astrid as my mate." I stared him in the eye, daring him to challenge me. If he said a single negative thing about her, I'd rip his horns out of his skull like I should have been doing all along.

"Well, congratulations are in order, I suppose," he replied gruffly, tilting his head to the side. "Not sure why you're looking at me like that, Captain. I've always liked Astrid, had nothing but nice things to say about her." He burst out laughing before I could rip into him. "I jest. I disliked her as much as the rest of the realm, but now we know better. She didn't hesitate to jump in and save the king's ass yesterday. You've got to admire her courage. Besides, Ophelia tells me I'm not allowed to be mean to her sister."

"Yes, Astrid is amazing. Never refer to the king's ass again," I grumbled, stalking past him and heading up the stairs. Calix chuckled to himself behind me, and it did ease some of the tension in my chest. Not at how people would respond to the news of us being mated—I didn't care what they thought. But I wanted Astrid to find happiness and acceptance here.

Calix was a good measuring post. If he was warming up to her, then there was a good chance the rest of the realm was too.

"Soren!" Damen called, jogging to catch up with me, a smug grin on his face. "It's finally happened, I'm so happy for you. Goddesses, you *reek*."

"I know," I replied cheerfully, knocking on Allerick's door and waiting until he called us in.

Ophelia sat at the vanity, brushing her hair while Allerick stood by, watching as if it was the most fascinating thing he'd ever seen. His nose wrinkled the second I walked in. *I might never bathe again.*

Or if I did, I was going to immediately demand Astrid soak me in her scent so everyone knew who I belonged to.

And vice-versa.

"What?" Ophelia asked, looking between us. "What's going on? Where's Astrid?"

"Bathing. In my apartment. *Our* apartment. Where Astrid lives now." I looked at Allerick, hoping he wasn't going to contradict my assertion.

"Yes!" Ophelia shrieked, jumping to her feet with a clap. "It's happening! Can I go see her? Has she eaten yet? I'll bring her food—she's probably eaten a pickle and called it breakfast."

"I'll go get Astrid; we can meet you for breakfast in the palace," I said quickly, before Ophelia could rush off. "I wanted to come here to discuss the events that took place yesterday, as well as apologize for rushing off when I should have been dealing with the fallout. That being said, I'm not entirely sorry. Astrid has had a difficult time adjusting to life in this realm, and that is in large part because of me. I could have made that adjustment easier, and I didn't, and I'll spend every day of my life making it up to her."

"Cute," Ophelia whispered, linking arms with Allerick and cuddling into his side.

I cleared my throat. "Astrid doesn't need me to do this—she's more than capable of fighting any battle on her own—but she's done a lot of fighting on her own and she's exhausted, so I'm here to take this one. If you have a problem with Astrid killing Meridia, you can take it up with me."

"That's quite the challenging tone to take with your monarch," Allerick said mildly, watching me curiously. I'd always wondered if our friendship stemmed from the fact that I'd never formally challenged him, even when we were young and foolish. If it was my loyalty he valued over who I was.

I supposed I'd find out now. I wasn't about to challenge him for his throne, but I'd fight him to protect my mate.

"It's not a problem for me. It's not going to be a problem for anyone—except, perhaps, your mother."

"She'd be mad no matter what you did, don't worry about her," Damen scoffed.

"I'm inclined to agree," Allerick said. "Astrid has been training with the Guard. As far as I'm concerned, she was acting in her capacity as a guard. And she saved either my life or my wife's, possibly both. I'm glad Astrid is here, and I'd be comfortable with her carrying weapons now. We're in debt to her quick and creative thinking yesterday, stealing that pin."

Ophelia looked between us. "And you love her... right, Soren?"

It was a very un-Shade-like thing to admit to in front of others, but... "Yes. I love her more than anything."

Ophelia blew out a relieved breath. "Phew. Okay, good. The best, actually. Welcome to the family, new brother. You're a lucky Shade—no one will love you more loyally than Astrid."

"I'm beyond lucky," I acknowledged, tipping my chin.

Ophelia shot me a beaming smile. "Let's go get breakfast then!"

Damen and I hung back for the royal couple to walk ahead of us down the corridor, Ophelia practically bouncing on her feet as she went.

"Oh, and Soren?" Allerick said, glancing at me over his shoulder. "Selene handled the fallout just fine yesterday. Not as efficiently as you would have, but she figured it out. You're a mated male now, you can't work every waking hour. Delegate some responsibilities, your guards can handle it."

"You're right. Selene has been wanting to do more."

We split off in the main hallway, and I briefly stopped in at the stores to offload the overabundance of power I'd gained from a night with my mate before making my way to my apartment.

Our apartment.

All Astrid had done was set her bag in the corner, and already it felt more like an actual *home*. It smelled like her, which was nice, though I'd like it more if it smelled like *us*.

Later. We had a family breakfast to go to first.

"Well?" Astrid asked, nervously tugging the sleeves of her red sweater down over her hands until just her fingertips were showing. "Am I going to the Pit?"

"Never," I growled, stalking across the room and picking her up because she smelled too clean from her bath. "No one is upset with you. Shades respect strength, and you showed a lot of it yesterday. Even Calix commented on your bravery. You're going to be fine, Astrid. Better than fine. You're going to be happy here."

"You sound like you're taking it as a personal challenge to ensure I am," she said, quirking her lips in that almost smile that I'd loved the most before I'd seen what her proper smile looked like.

"I'm going to be stepping back a little from Captain duties, delegating more to Selene. So, yes. I will have plenty of time on my hands to ensure your happiness."

Astrid melted slightly against me, only for a moment before she pulled her mask of unaffected calm back into place. I hoped we'd come to a point someday where she no longer felt the need to hide any part of herself from me, but we had our entire lives to get there. Our entire lives for me to prove to her that I was worthy of seeing that vulnerable part of her that she kept hidden.

Astrid wriggled off me before I could carry her outside, giving me a withering look at my noise of protest. She stuck close to my side though as we made our way through the grounds, and I didn't take it for granted.

"Captain!" Selene called, pausing next to the portal as Astrid and I approached. "Astrid," she added, inclining her head politely.

"Selene," my mate replied cautiously.

"You did a good job yesterday," Selene told her, very consciously keeping her body language non-confrontational. A notable difference from the usual way she approached Astrid. "Even if I'd been watching the rafters and seen her, I'd have never made that shot."

"Thank you," Astrid mumbled, surprisingly uncomfortable with accepting compliments.

"Perhaps you could lead a training session on knife throwing?" Selene suggested, glancing at me to make sure she wasn't overstepping. "You have knowledge we could really benefit from in that area."

"That's a great idea," I agreed, nudging Astrid's arm. "Selene, can you coordinate that? The king tells me you handled everything exceptionally well yesterday after I ran out and left you with it. You should have been given more responsibilities before now, and I intend to rectify that going forward."

"Because you're mated now and don't want to work so much?" Selene asked drily.

"Exactly—"

There was a flicker of movement from the portal, and all three of us both jumped into defensive positions. I attempted to stand in front of Astrid, but she ducked under my arm with a scoff, not taking her eyes off the portal.

If a Shade had broken Allerick's decree and ventured to the human realm, I was going to throw them in the Pit first and ask questions later. I needed a fucking break. I just wanted to have breakfast with my mate, was that too much to ask?

But it wasn't a Shade who emerged from the portal.

It was a Hunter.

A young, *male* Hunter, with pale skin covered in ink, chin-length wavy dark hair, dressed in skintight black clothes that looked as though they'd seen better days. There was a heavy-looking leather case on his back, and I reached for my weapon immediately. Was it some kind of firearm? Those were popular in the human realm.

The man stumbled slightly, a glass bottle half-filled with amber dangling loosely from his fingertips.

"Hey," he slurred, focus wavering as he glanced between us. "I heard we're fucking Shades now."

The bottle fell to the ground with a crash, shattered glass scattering everywhere.

"Oh shit, I can clean that up," the man said, dropping to his knees. I winced as he crushed the shards beneath him.

"Austin?" Astrid asked in disbelief.

"You know him?" I wasn't proud of the jealousy in my voice. Astrid rolled her eyes at me, relaxing her defensive stance.

"Sure, he's a Hunter. Tallulah's cousin, actually."

"What is that thing he's carrying on his back?" Selene asked warily, blade in hand, ready to strike.

"A guitar case. Austin is a, um, musician. I guess."

"I *am* a musician," Austin replied, pointing at Astrid, seemingly struggling to make his eyes focus. "I don't appreciate your tone there, missy. Just because I never got a record deal or became famous like everyone said I would doesn't mean I'm not a musician, mmk?"

"Did you just call me *missy*?" Astrid asked in disbelief. "I could murder you in your sleep, you know."

I snorted, giving Selene the most sympathetic look I could muster. "You did want more responsibility."

"Please, no," she replied, horrified. "You're going to make *me* deal with him?"

"Search him for weapons, then take him somewhere secure to sober up. That should buy you some time to figure out what to do with him," I said cheerfully. "I'll mention it to the king, of course. If you need me, ask someone else. My mate needs food."

"You're such an asshole," Astrid laughed as I tugged her away. "Not that he's dangerous or anything—Austin was more interested in following his dreams than being a Hunter, and he was from one of the wealthiest, most powerful families so he kind of got to do whatever he wanted. No daily training sessions or grueling night guard shifts for him."

"What do you think he's doing here then?"

"No idea. Maybe he saw the error of the Hunters' ways. Or maybe his grandfather wanted him to actually step up and do some work and he panicked and ran here to get out of it. If anyone would have access to the key to unlock the portal, it would be his family."

I grunted. "I'll assign extra guards to all portals, just in case."

"Good call," Astrid agreed, her praise filling me with a warmth I didn't know I'd been missing. "God, I wish Selene all the luck in the world dealing with that asshole."

ASTRID

EPILOGUE

Some months later...

"Stop moving," I groaned as yet another orgasm rocked me. It was right on the edge of too much, my muscles starting to cramp uncomfortably around Soren's knot after being so thoroughly wrung out.

"Sorry," Soren murmured, bracing himself over me and running his claws softly through my hair, gently guiding me back down from my high. He was tense—a normal state of being whenever we were due to visit the human realm. We were going less often these days, focusing on ways to make our lives here sustainable rather than relying on constant trips back, but tonight's trip was special. Different.

"You good?" I asked, brushing his cheekbones with my thumbs as I caught my breath.

Soren hummed. "No. I want to tie you to the bed and keep you here forever. I'd stay with you, of course."

I slid a hand down to pat his chest. "You don't want that, really. You'd miss bossing everyone around after the first few days."

"You're my favorite person to boss around. I'd cope."

I snorted, arching up to nip at his jaw with my teeth. Outside of the bedroom, he didn't have much of a chance to boss me around these days. I was nominally a member of the Guard, but I worked alongside Levana to protect Ophelia, and Soren trusted us to make our own calls. While he always accompanied me to the human realm, I was the expert and he deferred to me.

Luckily, I didn't mind the bedroom bossiness, so long as I got to be in charge sometimes too.

"Kiss," Soren demanded, chasing my mouth as I laid my head back down on the pillow. I parted my lips for him instantly, loving the feel of his thick tongue oh-so-reverently fucking my mouth.

It was still early, but we had to get up soon and start our respective days. Allerick was particularly, *obsessively* careful with Ophelia at the moment, I couldn't be late.

"Will I see you before dinner?" I asked, pulling away to catch my breath.

"I don't think so," Soren sighed. "Allerick is traveling around the realm today, which means I'm traveling around the realm today. We're stopping near my family home too, I believe."

"Oh?" I slipped my hands around his back, rubbing his smooth, leathery skin. "That'll be fun."

"The most fun," he scoffed, matching my sarcasm.

We were something of a power couple after Meridia's death and our work to dismantle the toxic Resistance. Soren's mother had quickly changed her tune after we'd gained popularity, and while I'd been open to getting to know her if that was what Soren wanted, he'd been pretty adamant about having nothing to do with her.

She was persistent, I'd give her that. There's no way he *wouldn't* see her today.

"Though I think I'm going to convince Allerick to come back and eat lunch with Ophelia," Soren murmured as his knot softened. I clamped my legs together as he pulled out, and he scooped me into his arms instantly, carrying me off the bed to the bathroom before I could go full snail trail through the apartment. "I can already tell I'll need a little extra *Astra* today."

He wound his way around the two armchairs I'd gotten for in front of the fireplace, and I squeezed my thighs harder as he walked over the rugs we'd purchased to make the stone floor a little warmer and softer on my fragile human feet.

They were expensive. I didn't want to leak on those.

"So needy," I teased, wrapping my arms around his neck and squeezing him tight. My mate, my husband, my love.

"For you? Always."

I hovered next to the wall of the dark Denver alleyway I'd been asked to meet in, checking the knives in my jacket were still secure.

Being in the human realm made me nervous. It was familiar yet *not*. It definitely wasn't home, not anymore.

"I hate this." Soren's voice drifted into my mind, his hands ghosting over my hair and shoulders, comforting me with his closeness. It was comforting for him too—he struggled with the helplessness of his incorporeal form. *"This location is dangerous for both of us."*

"I know. But that message piqued my curiosity. I have a good feeling about her."

"I don't," Soren replied petulantly. *"At least it's dark enough that we can just leave. We could leave now, in fact."*

"No. Be patient."

"I'm going to spank your ass raw when we get home for putting me through this level of stress, my Astra."

I snorted. "Don't threaten me with a good time, Cap."

He was silent for a long moment. Brooding, probably. *"Tell me whose shadows you wore at the ball."*

My lips twitched and I pressed them tightly together so I didn't laugh and draw unwanted attention to myself.

"No."

I was pretty sure he'd worked out by now that it had been Levana who covered me at that ball, but the lack of confirmation never ceased to annoy him.

"You're going to dinner tomorrow wearing my *shadows."*

"We'll see about that. Sh, I can hear something."

Alright, maybe this hadn't been a good idea. Someone—or *something*—was approaching the mouth of the alleyway, but it didn't sound like human footsteps.

"Astrid..." Soren warned, pressing in closer, ready to swoop me back to the in-between at a moment's notice.

"Wait," I hissed, dagger in my good hand, ready to throw.

A golden lab rounded the corner first, wearing a red and black vest with a sturdy-looking handle on the back. A *service* dog. That hadn't been what I expected.

Holding the handle in one hand and a white cane in the other was a petite young woman, straight brown hair blowing around her face until she was in the alleyway proper, sheltered from the wind.

"Hello," she said eventually. Her voice was soft but didn't waver. "My name is Iris."

"Um, hello," I replied, searching my brain for an 'Iris'. She looked to be around the same age as me, perhaps a little younger, and this was my hometown. I knew all the Hunters here.

"Iris *Nash*. We've never met."

"Nash? As in Moriah Nash?" Moriah was one of the top Councilors, the one who'd basically imprisoned Ophelia in the Council building when she returned from the shadow realm.

"My mother."

"Moriah Nash doesn't have a daughter," I mumbled, more to myself than anything. From memory, she had twin boys in middle school.

"Not one that she wants people to know about," Iris replied. "No Hunter wants a *blind* daughter. Especially not a Councilor. It's a big house though. Plenty of places to hide a spare child."

Hide a *child*? That was a level of cruelty that was shocking, even for a Hunter Councilor.

"We can't leave her here." Soren's voice was pure outrage.

"Do you... Do you want to come to the shadow realm?" I asked. "I can't imagine you've heard many good things about it, living in the Nash home."

Iris smiled softly. "Not a single one, but I know my mother. She wouldn't be so furious if there was no cause for concern. There must be something there to entice Hunters such as yourself and Austin—successful, *popular* Hunters—to leave this world behind. I'm all packed," she added, bumping the backpack she was wearing for emphasis. "Though it's mostly kibble for Tilly."

"Right," I replied faintly. None of the other former Hunters I'd brought to the shadow realm had been so calm at the prospect of going. "Then let's go, I guess. No pressure, okay? If you don't like it, let me know and I'll bring you back."

"I'm not coming back," Iris replied confidently, moving towards my voice, Tilly one step ahead of her. "I've been imprisoned my entire life. The shadows are going to set me free."

Bonus Scene

Print Edition Exclusive

SOREN

"This is very untraditional," Allerick remarked, glancing at our surroundings. "You're certain you want to get married here? I know the temple needs some repairs, but it is still the usual location for a Shade wedding. We wouldn't have to fill it to the brim with spectators, it could just be us."

"Brother," Damen laughed, elbowing Allerick. "You can't insult a Shade's choice of wedding location not five minutes before the ceremony is due to start."

"I didn't *insult* it. I merely suggested somewhere more... conventional."

I snorted, leaving the two of them to argue among themselves. Outdoor weddings weren't so much a Shade tradition, but apparently they were fairly common in the human realm. Once I'd heard about it, I'd become slightly fixated on the idea of marrying Astrid outside.

Next to the river.

If King Allerick knew just how much we'd contributed to fertilizing the soil he was standing on, he'd probably be less surprised that we'd chosen this location for our nuptials. It was significant to us.

Allerick and Damen fell silent as the cheerful chatter of our guests reached us. Tallulah, Verity, and Meera were all in attendance, followed closely by Verner, Andrus, Levana, and Selene. The guards had all been warming up to Astrid, letting go of the anger that we'd all been guilty of letting consume us.

Our guests gathered in a semicircle in front of me, Allerick and Damen joining their configuration, leaving me standing in front of the river. Levana and Selene made a space between them, leaving our "aisle" clear, and I clasped my hands in front of myself, impatiently waiting for my bride to appear.

Through the mating bond, I knew she was approaching, making her way over from Elverston House with Ophelia.

I also knew for a fact that Astrid could move quickly when she wanted to, so the only reason she could possibly be walking so slowly was to torment me.

"How is she?" Damen asked Verity. I eavesdropped shamelessly, knowing Verity had been the one to help Astrid get ready. If I'd had my way, Astrid and I would have gotten ready together, and she'd be walking out here covered in my shadows.

She'd wanted to maintain the human tradition of getting ready with her friends and *not* seeing me—barbaric, in my opinion—but she *had* sworn she'd wear my shadows to dinner tonight.

If we made it to dinner tonight.

Shadows swirled in my palms, twisting around my fingers in anticipation.

"Surprisingly nervous," Verity admitted, a smile in her voice. "You know Astrid, she's usually as cool as a cucumber no matter what's going on. It was weird seeing her so fidgety."

"Then it sounds like the Captain is lucky he already locked Astrid down with a mating bite; she's stuck with him now." Damen laughed, dodging the whip of shadows Allerick sent his way.

"She's not nervous to marry Captain Soren," Meera interjected, giving Damen a slightly bemused smile. "She just doesn't like being the center of attention."

No, I knew that feeling well. Astrid and I both tried to move around behind the curtains for the most part, facilitating the safety of the royal couple so they could shine. But we deserved a moment solely of our own in the orb light too. To celebrate our love with those who we cared most about.

Astrid rounded a large tree, finally coming into view, arm in arm with Ophelia.

While I'd still prefer to see my mate and future bride wearing my shadows, the low-cut red dress she had on instead wasn't without its own appeal. It showcased her smooth shoulders, toned arms, and the swell of her breasts, and fell to midthigh, showing off strong legs and her favorite black running shoes.

A rogue purr rumbled out of my chest, and I made no attempt to suppress it, not even when Damen laughed at me. Someday, he'd fall in love and I'd tease him about his embarrassing behavior.

The sisters reached the group in a few steps, pausing for Ophelia to give Astrid a hug and whisper how happy she was for her in her sister's ear, so quietly that even my more sensitive ears barely picked it up.

Ophelia filled in the gap in the semicircle while Astrid made her way to me. We stood facing each other in front of the river, our profiles to the group. My mate stared up at me, and while she was clearly nervous, it didn't overwhelm her always-muted scent.

She smelled happy.

"My Astra," I murmured, lightly gripping her hips and pulling her closer. "You look particularly dangerous today."

"Do I?" She quirked an eyebrow, palms coming to rest on my chest. "I don't see how that's possible. There is nowhere to hide a weapon in this dress."

"Dangerous to me," I clarified. "To my self-control. It would be impolite of me to tear your dress off and have my way with you in front of our guests."

Damen let out a strangled cough, stepping up in his role as our officiant.

I didn't care for any of the priests who usually conducted the marriage ceremonies—they still looked at Astrid with mistrust, and I had no time for them.

"You'd better hurry up, Damen," I muttered, inhaling deeply as Astrid's scent sweetened. "Or I'm going to shroud myself and my mate in shadows and you will all have the pleasure of listening to us—"

Astrid cut me off with a light slap on my chest, giving me a pointed look to stop talking.

"Alright, let's make this quick," Damen laughed. "These lovebirds have places they'd rather be than their own wedding ceremony, apparently. I had this big, romantic speech planned and everything..."

"Do the speech!" Ophelia called, practically bouncing on the spot with excitement. "It's their wedding day, they can wait an extra five minutes to consummate their marriage."

Astrid's cheeks flamed red as she shot her sister her most impressively unimpressed face.

"I'll do the short version," Damen agreed, pausing for a moment for everyone to settle into silence. I gave Astrid's hips a gentle squeeze, needing her eyes back on me, reassuring her that I was right here.

"For the benefit of the ex-Hunters present, I want to start by saying that marriage isn't all that common here," Damen began, sounding far more serious than I was used to hearing him. "Shades who choose to take that step are making a choice to forsake all others, pledging to stand by one another no matter what challenges the goddesses throw at them, or how great the temptation may be from others. It is a sacrifice and a joy, a gift and a commitment. A choice to love one another, come what may."

I stared into Astrid's eyes, obsessively watching her every reaction. Astrid wasn't a romantic by nature, and I wasn't much better. Listening to someone talk about love and relationships at great length was an unusual way for us to spend our time. "But you two are a slightly different story. You already made the choice to commit to one another in a far more permanent way through your mating bite—a way we don't even fully understand, since that knowledge appears to be lost to time. You took the plunge into an almost-complete unknown purely for *love*, a choice not only to commit to one another, but to be brave in how you went about it."

Astrid and I exchanged knowing looks, both trying not to laugh. It sounded a lot more profound and a lot less driven by horniness when he described it that way.

All that being said, it seems rather pointless to even get you to repeat these vows, but I suppose it ties a neat bow on the logistics," Damen said with a laugh, his voice losing some of the seriousness it had carried. Perhaps there'd even been a little *wistfulness*. I'd never felt strongly about finding a mate before Astrid, but Damen had liked the idea ever since Ophelia came into this realm and wrapped Allerick around her little finger.

"Astrid," Damen began. "Do you take Soren to be your husband in a union recognized by both of our kinds?"

She never took her eyes off me, lips curving into that half smile she limited herself to around others. "I do."

I barely managed to squash down my purr of approval. *Barely*.

"Soren, do you take Astrid to be your wife in a union recognized by both of our kinds?"

"I do."

Astrid's smile grew a little wider at the speed in which I answered, though she was still holding herself back in front of an audience. As much as I understood why she did it, I was eager to whisk her back to the privacy of our apartment so I could see that toothy grin I loved so much.

"Well, that's it then," Damen announced. "You are now officially husband and wife, and I imagine we won't see you for days. I'll make sure someone leaves food by the door of your apartment so you don't starve in there."

"Kiss!" Ophelia yelled, the other ex-Hunters joining in until they were chanting.

"It's a human tradition," Astrid explained wryly, looking slightly done with all the chaos of being around the others. "The married couple kisses at the end of the ceremony."

"Well, I wouldn't want to break tradition."

Kissing wasn't at all a Shade practice, and I knew I'd be scandalizing my peers—with the exception of Allerick—but that was surprisingly fine by me. I wasn't Soren, Captain of the Guard, right now. I was Soren, Astrid's husband,

and I was going to kiss my wife.

I immediately ruined her pretty hair by tangling my claws in it, dragging her face to mine and parting her lips with my tongue, needing a taste of her. Astrid went lax for me immediately—not quite as relaxed as she would be if it was just the two of us, but more at peace than she had been a moment ago.

Maybe because Astrid's scent was usually so muted, because she was usually so in control of her physical responses, I couldn't help but feel possessive over the smell of her desire as it grew stronger, permeating the air around us.

I yanked my mouth away with some difficulty, maintaining my hold on her hair.

"We're leaving," I growled. "I've had enough of sharing your attention for today."

"One thing before you go," Allerick began. *Deep breaths. Remember he is your king, and probably strong enough to beat you in combat.*

Maybe.

I was more highly trained than him.

"I've sent staff ahead to Delam Cliffs. They've opened and prepared the cottage for the two of you to use for as long as you'd like. It's stocked with food."

"And human supplies," Ophelia added with a laugh. "I packed you a bag, Atti. You're going to love it there, it's on the coast. The sand is black and the ocean is silver, it's *majestic*."

"Are you sure about this?" Astrid asked, flattening her palms against my chest. I bet she didn't even realize she was doing it—it was very affectionate for her. "It's very generous."

"Of course." Allerick waved away her gratitude. "It's a wedding gift. Take a break, go enjoy each other's company. The realm will survive without the two of you."

ASTRID

"Oh my god," I breathed, leaning further against Soren's side as we stepped out of the entry room and directly onto the edge of a cliff. Not *all* the way at the edge, but close enough to make my adrenaline spike. "This is stunning."

The ocean looked like molten silver, lapping at an onyx shore. The cliff was black rock, at least four-hundred-feet high, and behind us was a picturesque stone cottage with two seats out the front to admire the view from.

"It's nice," Soren agreed, not sounding particularly impressed as he dragged me over to the cottage.

"You're not going to give me five seconds to admire the view?" I laughed, grabbing his shoulders as he gave up making me walk and lifted me off my feet, carrying me the rest of the way.

"Later."

Ooh, I knew that sound. That was the sound of Soren on the knife-edge of desperation. There was a painful erection under those shadows, I'd put money on it.

I didn't see a single thing in the cottage before Soren had me pinned against the door, tearing the seams of my brand-new wedding dress as he parted my thighs to stand between them.

Tallulah could fix the dress.

Probably.

"Hello, wife."

My pussy clenched on nothing, slick soaking through the pointless pretty lace underwear I'd worn for the occasion. *Wife*. I could get used to that.

"Hello, husband."

Soren broke into the deepest, most intense purr I'd ever heard, dropping his shadow covering to rock his hips into me. His head dropped, teeth scraping over the mating mark. "I don't think I can make it to the bed."

I grabbed the base of his horns, squeezing until his legs trembled, and pulled his head to the side so I could speak into his ear. "Oh, you're going to take me to bed."

"Was that an order?" he rasped, claws digging into the flesh of my thighs as he fucked me through my sodden panties. The feeling of the lace on my clit was the sweetest kind of torture, and my face heated at the light *drip* of slick hitting the stone floor beneath me.

Oh my god, I was going to have to fully sanitize this place once we were done with it or I'd never be able to look Allerick and Ophelia in the eye again.

"Yes, Captain—*husband*—that was an order. Take me to bed and fuck my brains out on a nice, soft surface. I want you to knot me so good, I can feel it in my lungs."

Soren made a strangled sound, stumbling away from the door with me wrapped around his waist. I briefly got a glimpse of pale stone walls and gray exposed beams overhead, as well as an assortment of mismatched, well-loved furniture, but then I was on my back on the mattress, seeing nothing but Soren's orange eyes burning bright with desire.

I carefully shimmied the already-ripped dress over my head, trying not to do any more damage to it, while Soren hovered over me, staring transfixed at the white lace panties.

They were very much *not* my usual style, but if I couldn't wear stupidly impractical underwear on my wedding day then when could I?

"Look at these," Soren murmured, running a claw ever so lightly down the center of the damp fabric. I was already so sensitive, so fucking *needy*, that just that faint touch had me arching up into him.

"Are you going to rip them?"

"Fuck, no. These are to be treasured and brought out on every special occasion," he replied reverently, climbing off me. "Take them off, I don't want to risk my claws catching on this delicate fabric."

"Sure," I laughed, pushing them down over my hips before kicking them off, enjoying the slight look of consternation on his face at my less-than-gentle treatment of his new favorite item of clothing. He was on me before I could tease him, all but throwing my legs up toward my shoulders so he could *feast* between my thighs.

"You're really not messing around today," I gasped, writhing to get closer and get away at the same time, the avalanche of sensation bordering on too much. Soren clamped his forearm down over my hips, pinning me in place as he roughly massaged my clit with his tongue. The pressure of his arm keeping me in place settled my restlessness, allowing me to just switch off and *feel*.

Sharp fangs scraped lightly over my clit, a reminder that he could *literally* eat me if he so desired, sending a surge of either lust or adrenaline through my entire body, pushing me over the edge. Soren's hold didn't waver for a second, no matter how much I thrashed my legs, and before I'd ridden out one wave, he'd already buried that thick tongue in my cunt, fucking me into another soul-crushing orgasm.

We should get married more often, I thought hazily. *Totally worth everyone staring at me with heart eyes for this level of untamed sex.*

Soren growled, the sound muffled against my pussy, sending glorious vibrations through my hypersensitive nerves. A not-so-subtle demand for me to come again, to feel me tighten around his tongue before he'd let me have his cock.

He was a bossy bastard and I knew his game, but my body had no problem cooperating. I didn't bother muffling my moans, and Soren wasn't making any attempt to be quiet either, drinking down my slick with an obscene level of enthusiasm.

When Soren finally withdrew, his face shone with it, and there was another low pulse of desire in my abdomen as he slowly licked his face clean. He looked right on the edge of feral, which was exactly how I liked him, and I rolled over onto my hands and knees because sometimes provoking the beast was the best course of action.

"Don't hold back," I commanded breathily, stretching out like a cat and pressing my breasts to the bed, pushing my ass up the way I knew he liked it. Soren made a garbled sound somewhere between an actual spoken word and a growl before grabbing my hips and roughly yanking me backwards on his cock. I gasped at the sudden stretch, gripping the blankets tightly between my fingers as he *moved* me, bouncing me on his dick like a perfect Hunter fuck doll.

And I *loved* it, because it was him. Only with Soren did I get to be this version of myself.

"That fucking *dress*," Soren growled, the tips of his claws pricking my skin. "Those fucking *panties*. Are you trying to torment me, my Astra?"

"Only a little," I gasped. "You're fun when you're a little tormented."

He managed a raspy laugh before the room was filled with the sound of flesh on flesh, of my breathy moans and his almost frantic purrs. *Knot, knot, knot.* I needed it more than I needed air. Needed to feel that final piece of the puzzle connecting us.

With a final growl as Soren found his release, he flattened me to the bed and I quickly shoved my hand beneath my body, rubbing my clit desperately as his knot swelled, rubbing against my sensitive inner walls. There was *nothing* better than stimulating both at the same time, and my soul left my body for a moment as I clenched around his cock, slick drenching the blanket beneath us.

"Fuck," Soren whispered, rocking into me with slow, gentle thrusts, undoubtedly filling me with enough cum to make me look at least six months pregnant. "The things you do to me..." he muttered, bemused and awed all at once.

I understood the feeling.

He wrapped an arm around my shoulders so I could rest my head on the crook of his elbow, sweating from a combination of exertion and his far-higher body temperature.

"The things you do to *me*," I countered, my body straddling the line between overstimulated and ready for more. "Here we are in this new part of the realm I've never seen before, and all I can think of is when I'm next going to get my hands on your knot."

Soren huffed a quiet laugh in my ear. "Mm, maybe I'll make you wait for it."

"You don't have that kind of self-control, Captain. Not when it comes to me."

"No, not when it comes to you, my wife. My love."

"I love you too," I breathed, hiding my smile against his forearm. Then, with the lightest rock of my hips back against him, I was coming again. As far as honeymoons went, I couldn't imagine anything more perfect.

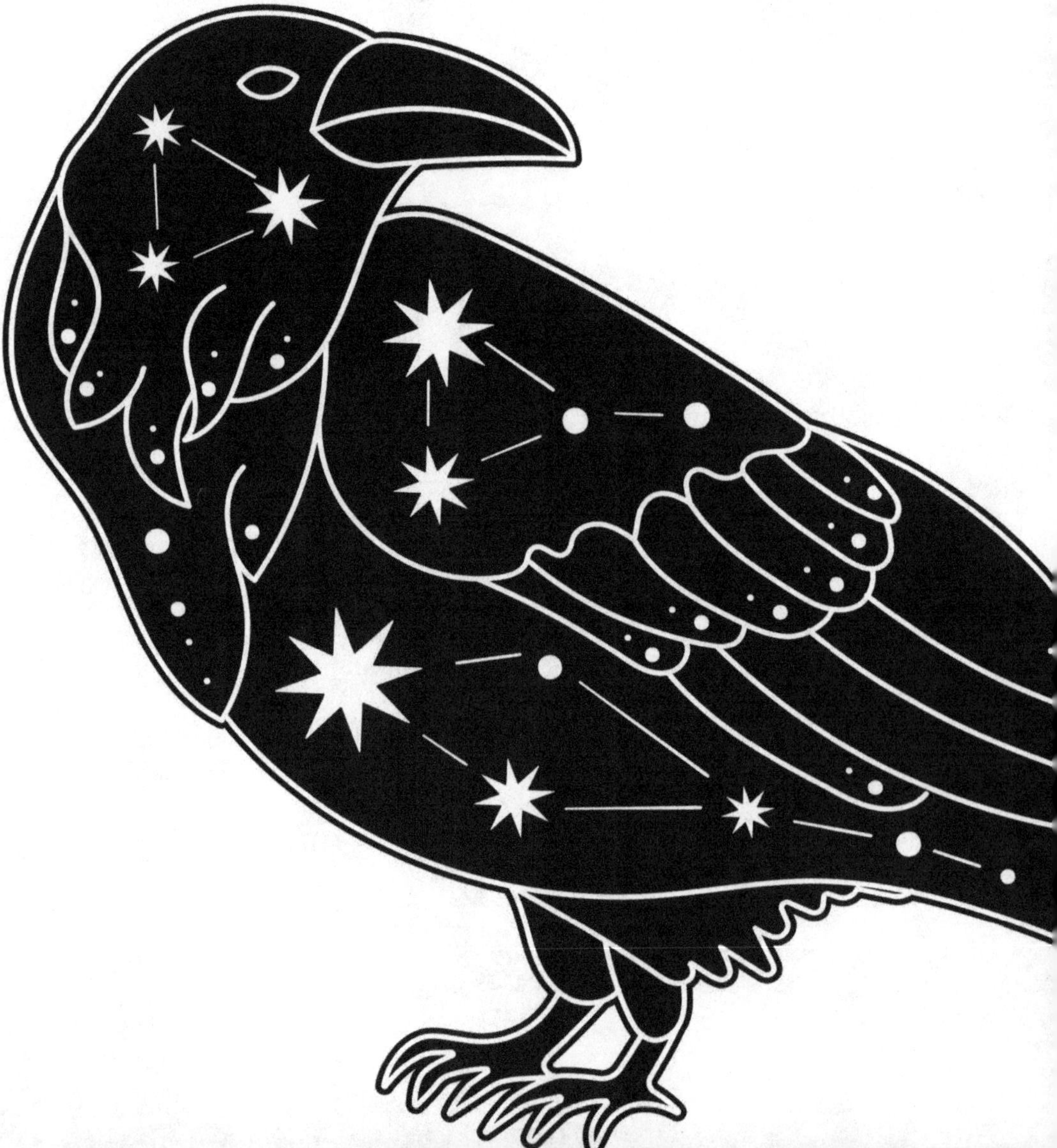

THANK YOU

It's been awhile, hasn't it?

Luxuria came out nearly a year ago, and I can't thank you enough for waiting so patiently for Astrid's book. All of the lovely messages and posts and reviews for Luxuria totally blew me away, and I was so excited to clear some space on my writing schedule to return to this fascinating shadowy world.

There will be seven books in total in this series—one for each sin—and they will take up most of my writing time this year. We've already covered Lust and Pride, next up is Gluttony! Can you guess who? You can preorder Gula now, if you'd like to. The release date will be moved up.

I have to thank my wonderful friends and betas—Lucy, Rachel, Rory and T.S. I couldn't have done it without you guys. My proofreader, Lorie, you are absolutely amazing.

And thank you, dear reader! None of this happens without you, and I appreciate you all so much.

Colette R. xx

P.S. To keep up with the latest news and releases, join my Facebook Reader Group or subscribe to my newsletter.

ABOUT THE AUTHOR

Colette Rhodes is a paranormal romance author from New Zealand. She loves to write about love in all its forms, and adores imperfect heroes and heroines who find perfection in each other. You'll often find her trying to justify her degree by including ancient history and mythological influences in her work.

If she's not writing, then you're almost certain to find her reading—ideally with a cup of tea in hand and a scented candle burning to match the mood.

Keep up with Colette here:
coletterhodes.com
@coletterhodes_author

ALSO BY COLETTE

SHADES OF SIN:
Luxuria

Superbia

Gula

STATE OF GRACE:
Run Riot

Silver Bullet

Wild Game

Dare Not

Saving Grace

THREE BEARS DUET:
Gilded Mess

Golden Chaos

LITTLE RED DUET:
Scarlet Disaster

Seeing Red

KNOTTY BY NATURE:
(RH omegaverse with T.S. Snow)

Allure Part 1

Allure Part 2

EMPATH FOUND:
The Terrible Gift
The Unwanted Challenge
The Reluctant Keeper

DEADLY DRAGONS:
The (Not) Cursed Dragon
The (Not) Satisfied Dragon

STANDALONE:
Dead of Spring (MF - Hades & Persephone retelling)
Blood Nor Money (RH - vampires)
Fire & Gasoline (MF - wolf shifter fated mates)

Colette Rhodes

ROMANCE AUTHOR

www.ingramcontent.com/pod-product-compliance
Lightning Source LLC
Chambersburg PA
CBHW021432070825
30593CB00078B/385